Awake

Awake

Anna Battle

fannypress

fannypress

For more information go to: www.fannypress.com

Cover design by Sabrina Sun

Title Awake
Copyright © 2019 by Anna Battle

ISBN: 978–1–60381–715–8 (Trade Paper)
ISBN: 978–1–60381–716–5 (eBook)

Printed in the United States of America

For Rob, who gave me the reason to write love letters.

Acknowledgments

I am grateful to Janice, Jennifer, Sujata, Barbara, Julienne, Christina, Paula, Bonnie, and Beata, my first readers and constant supporters, my sisters and best friends. And to my brothers, Stephen and Gregory, who demonstrate everyday how to be loving husbands, fathers, sons, and brothers.

I can never thank my parents enough. Dolores and Bill, may his soul rest in peace. Everything I am, I owe to their unconditional love, support and encouragement.

"When a body is separated from the center of its gravity by a relatively empty space, this effort becomes the motion of falling, the essential motion..."

—G.W.F. Hegel, *The Philosophy of Nature*

Chapter 1

Lori had a long drive ahead of her. If she was lucky. Driving the Northeast corridor, the week between Christmas and New Year could be a nightmare, and her sleep-till-noon teenagers weren't cooperating to get them on the road. Insult to injury. Ben, sixteen, and Catherine, thirteen, would plug in, and tune her out, before she hit the entrance ramp to I91.

Was loneliness the worst part of being discarded? After almost twenty years of marriage? She thought about it. Don't be naïve, Lori. It will all be hard. She could count on that, as sure as ill-tempered drivers and holiday traffic. Lori tried again to jam the hardcover novel, a gift from her mother-in-law Eleanor (Lori was pretty sure Eleanor read it before giving it to her) into the eco-reusable tote. Her other gift from Eleanor. Lori had already managed to overstuff the bag.

* * *

It was a Sunday morning. Early that November, when Peter's sucker punch unleashed its wallop. He announced he was leaving Lori, after they'd spent the night before holding hands, chatting with the usual suspects at a colleague's fiftieth birthday party. Lori was sure they comported themselves as a perfectly happy couple. Then Peter was standing at the foot of their bed, hands fumbling in his pants pockets, telling her he'd already rented a house. That knocked the wind right out of her. Lori's speech was barely comprehensible when she called her best friend, from the back porch to hide her retching sobs from the children.

"Peter is... He's... I'm..."

Jeanette tried to sooth her cautiously. "Sweetie, you need to slow down. I can't understand a word you're saying. Has something happened? To Peter? The kids?"

Peter insisted they tell the children that very day. Surely the lowest moment of her life. Lori was so unprepared. Ben thought he was in trouble, that's why they were having a family meeting. Catherine, certain Ben was correct, sat on the edge of the couch eager to tell her friends about the upbraiding the moment she was released. Lori will never forget Ben's face, the way it shifted like a Greek theatre mask from defensiveness to devastation. Catherine remained frozen to the spot, silent tears running down her face.

That same night...how could he? Peter dragged his suitcase to the car, let it bang on each step, over, and over, and over again. She was in Ben's room, encouraging him to get some sleep before school the next morning. Catherine had already sobbed herself unconscious. It was sinking in for Lori that this day—she struggled to hide her own tears from Ben—it might well be her children's defining before and after. Ben was suddenly worried. No one was downstairs to say goodbye to his dad. Lori did that too, so Ben wouldn't have to. Then, she sat on the stairs staring numbly at the shut door.

Peter was so often MIA, physically, emotionally, in all important ways. Still, it occurred to her, like a sudden, painful blow, when bad things happened, she confided in Peter. Peter who could rationalize anything. Peter who was her ally, at least against anyone who threw obstacles in their children's way. Peter, who had just abandoned them.

* * *

Who can know the why of these things? Just months before, they'd had a family portrait taken by a professional photographer. Under a leafy tree, all four wore white shirts or blouses. Lori remembered to put on the gold Tiffany necklace and earrings Peter had given her. He'd stood apart, cranky while they waited for the photographer to set up, trying to keep his clothes free of pollen.

Still, the photos were lovely. Lori had several framed for Peter's office and ordered one to be made into their family Christmas card. The box of 250, paid for and delivered, still sat, like a cruel rebuke, in their front hall closet. Even thinking about it from her in-laws' guest room in Southern New Hampshire caused a vice to tighten around Lori's solar plexus.

Shake it off. Breath deep into the abdomen and hold it there. Lori paused, scanned the room and grabbed up the last of her things. She needed to break away from this house, with its sickening, fun house mirror effect on her memories, and get on the road. The trip had seemed a much better idea back when Lori planned it. They would drive to Peter's parents' home for the holidays, like they did every year. This time without Peter, only Lori and her babies.

She knew it was silly to call them that. Will I ever stop wanting to swaddle and protect them? Ben, with his curly dark hair, had already sprouted a mustache, and the nascent muscles of coming manhood. His straight-line nose and lips were from his father, his father's from Peter's mother Eleanor, but Ben's soft, sleepy eyes were all his own. Catherine suddenly wanted to straighten her wavy, brown curls and experiment with the cat eye make up all the girls were wearing. Lori told her to leave it alone. Catherine was too young—though not a child anymore, her parents' separation had nailed the lid on that coffin. Still, Catherine's eyes needed no enhancement. They were dark, elegant ovals, complimented by shapely eyebrows and full rose bud lips.

Her sweet children… Lori would show them that life hadn't changed despite their parents dropping the D bomb. Lori would be there for her children, dishing out normalcy and stability. Peter's parents would find Lori ever gracious and respectful. Ben and Catherine would even get to do a little skiing during winter break. Totally normal, right?

What the hell was I thinking?

***

Thank god that on the return leg, they were stopping in New York to spend a couple of nights with Emily, her little sister and only sibling. She lived in a town thirty miles or so north of the City. It was where they'd grown up. Emily was the one who stayed. Well, technically, she was the one who came back. After rebellious teen years and dropping out of college; marrying, too young, a ruggedly handsome man who could charm the pants off a car salesman. They'd traveled around the world like glamorous vagabonds. Emily had little choice but to move back near their parents after three babies came in quick succession and it became obvious that ruggedly handsome would never settle into suburban fatherhood.

All the while, Lori plodded through college, then law school. She met Peter soon after starting at a Washington, DC law firm. He was a more senior associate, already well on track for partner, someone her parents could brag about. They were engaged within a year, and their children came at the recommended intervals. A son, two years after the wedding, and only after they scrapped together the down payment on a house in the suburbs. Lori had scored her first nod to partnership before getting pregnant with their daughter.

Funny how things invert and rearrange themselves. Lori jarringly shifted from the life she'd built with such care. While the once insurgent, Emily, was happily ensconced with her second husband, Thomas, in the small bedroom community where they both grew up. Where things seemed never to change. At least Lori could count on Emily for the best part of family love; never judging Lori, even if Emily was the toughest one of the lot.

Chapter 2

Lori was grateful to find her sister waiting at the front door, a full glass of red wine ready for her.

"Oh Sweetie, it was awful, wasn't it?" Emily asked, as she hugged Lori gently to avoid tilting the wine glass, or perhaps fearing that Lori might break.

"Let me take a few gulps and I'll tell you."

Lori's kids, sussing where the conversation was going, gave their aunt a quick hug, then ran straight to Sam's room. He was the remaining child still living at home in Emily and Thomas's blended family.

"That bad?" Thomas chimed in as they moved into the house.

"You've never had the pleasure of meeting my in-laws, Thomas. Everything's said in what's not spoken. The conversations were…, ever so pleasantly, miserable."

Thomas laughed.

"Did they mention Peter?" Emily asked.

"Not once." Lori had sat on a bar stool at the kitchen island.

"Did they at least ask if there was anything they could do to help?"

Lori gave her sister a look to ask, are you crazy?

"I told myself, I'm doing this for Ben and Catherine, and for Peter's parents. They hadn't seen the kids in months." Lori paused, struggling for words. "I guess I wanted something too…, an acknowledgment, that what Peter had done, the awful way he did it… Anyway, I got nothing."

Lori caught Emily and Thomas trading glances. "The worst,"

Lori continued, "I could feel Eleanor starting to circle the wagons. Blood and family, she'll be defending Peter before long."

"What about Ben and Catherine?" Thomas asked. "Did their grandparents talk with them about what's happening?"

"Nope." Lori put down her wine glass, shaking her head. "The kids answered questions about school, removed elbows from tables as commanded, and when I gave them the signal, asked to be excused and sprinted."

"You went skiing, right? Got away during the day?" Emily asked.

"That part was fine except it was freezing, and the slopes were crazy crowded. I couldn't be bothered to put on lip gloss or mascara, what with the cold weather gear. Catherine kindly informed me the second morning that I look much better when I wear makeup."

"You're kidding? You look beautiful," Emily said.

"She was being honest. I look like shit."

"You do not!"

Emily gave Lori another hug, a tight one this time and Lori settled into it, hugging back, letting her head rest on Emily's shoulder. Tears came, for the sudden relief to be home, a place where, and people with whom, she didn't have to pretend.

"Look how skinny you've gotten." Emily pulled away and held Lori's shoulders.

"That's an upside." Lori smiled, then looked down and frowned. "My clothes are hanging off me, and I'm pretty sure I should not be spending money on a new wardrobe."

"You've got to stop worrying. I'm telling you, it will all work out."

That was another thing about family, Lori thought, even their lies can warm your heart.

* * *

They had a relaxing night, their first in weeks. Ben and Catherine acted like zoo animals let out of their cages. They all made plans for the next day, fresh bagels for breakfast, a walk around town, buying special ingredients for dinner the next evening when Lori and Emily's parents would join them. Lori envied the joy Emily and Thomas took in planning memorable meals. It didn't take much, apparently, even a visit from the rejected, deflated sister, to consider it an occasion worth celebrating.

Lori could have mentioned that she had something of her own to do the next day. It wasn't a big deal, that's why she hadn't. She wasn't a total loser, though. Joanne McManus, an old family friend, had emailed to suggest a visit if Lori was around for the holidays.

Normally, Lori wouldn't consider it. It was such a brief visit and Joanne was mostly a Facebook friend now. Still, it was nice that she'd asked. Lori could even bring Emily with her. Back in the day, Emily was good friends with Joanne's daughter, Sarah. When Sarah lived in DC for a while, they hung out a few times. Even their mothers where still friendly. None of that was why Lori was considering the invitation. She might see Brandon, Joanne's son. Sarah's brother. Lori's Brandon.

She hadn't thought about him in forever. Honestly. Just as truthfully, at least once, every day probably, for thirty years now, Lori safeguarded some memory of Brandon. They had a complicated history.

Brandon dated Lori's best friend, Sharon, their senior year of high school. Still, Lori lost her virginity to Brandon. The summer before college when they'd celebrated graduation, their eighteenth birthdays, and becoming adults. Lori hadn't grasped that one summer would become Lori and Brandon's continuing modus operandi. They were best friends. Sometimes lovers. Always creating a triangle. They couldn't stop playing with fire.

Chapter 3

The next morning, as Lori sunk into the plush comfort of the passenger seat of Emily's car, she fell into a daydream—memories really, of those first weeks truly with Brandon. Redolent, involuntary thoughts seemed tossed her way from the very scenery unfolding, as she and Emily drove around town running errands. Lori recalled how she'd been struggling to end things with her first real boyfriend, not Brandon. That was Bobby Dunn.

Lori smiled as she glanced out the window, thinking how funny it was that Emily just recently told Lori that she bumped into Bobby occasionally, with his wife and kids, on these same, familiar roads. He'd taken over his dad's lucrative business, selling building materials or something. Emily made sure to mention that Bobby had gone mostly gray.

Back in the day, Bobby was beyond cute, and carefree, all blue eyes and tousled blond curls. He hung with the popular kids that Lori never believed would include her. It felt a small miracle when she and Bobby got together. She'd watched him play his guitar for months, at a church youth group of all places. Everyone in this town was a vaguely practicing Catholic back then and even the popular kids showed up.

Lori had been drawn to Bobby's unconscious, but sexy-to-a-teenage-romantic, strumming, ever hopeful that he might notice her, maybe even talk to her. Then, for some reason Bobby called and said he wanted to go out. She and guitar boy (her private nickname) seriously fooled around. Lori remembered it, with a flutter in her belly, as she glanced, without seeing, the town's landmarks flit past. Never more than heavy petting. My god, it's like another lifetime…

Times certainly had changed. Not a week went by these days, when Lori didn't get invited to a school meeting, or read an article, or hear from her panicked friends, about the epidemic of teenage sex, hooking up and casual blow jobs. The implication being that every teenage boy was routinely asking girls to send nude pictures from their phone, and every teenage girl was constantly posting sexy, provocative selfies on social media.

Back then, Lori was terrified of pregnancy, or just getting caught. She felt modesty about her body, even shame. She was sure her parents barely touched each other until their wedding night. She inherited from them, church, teachers, from the water they drank, and air they breathed in those ancient days, a vague sense that, for girls at least, it must be bad, if something felt too good. Before guitar boy, the groping, and expectations to go farther, were always something it was her duty to resist, which wasn't very hard, since they never seemed intended for her enjoyment.

What a surprise, was Bobby. He was sweet and attentive and swore he loved her. When he put his fingers those places, it felt, well, wonderful, and she reciprocated, with pleasure, putting her hands those places too. Lori wondered if she convinced her young self, that it was okay to enjoy those delicious temptations, without all the guilt, as long as she held something back. When they weren't making out, though, Lori was bothered, not that she could articulate it. The popular kids had parents who were rich, and though they didn't use the word back then, a boringness clung to them, born of entitlement. She never worried about that with Brandon.

The McManus's had moved from New York City, not Manhattan, one of the boroughs, not a good neighborhood. Joanne was divorced, something almost unheard of in their tiny town. Joanne told her much later why she'd transplanted them, even though it meant leaving her family and support network. She wanted to get her kids away to the suburbs, where it was safer.

She didn't want to rely on Brandon to watch over Sarah. Brandon was too smart for the local schools. She couldn't afford the private ones.

Joanne wanted more for her kids.

Such, was the siren call to parents from time immemorial. The upshot meant Brandon was different from all the boys Lori grew up with. He was a good athlete, that made him popular, but he was self-contained and stoic, worldlier. It's why Sharon had grabbed him.

Lori and Brandon spent senior year feinting and dodging, she thought competing for Sharon's attention. Turned out they were taking the measure of each other, maybe avoiding the elephant in the room. Then, Sharon was gone on a summer internship. Her parents had arranged it to make up for Sharon's lackluster school record, and maybe to get her away from Brandon. Even Lori's parents expressed concern that Sharon was fast, whatever that meant. Lori knew Sharon had no qualms about going all the way. Lori smiled to herself. It's like we had an entirely different language from kids today.

With some regret, Lori had finally disentangled from Bobby. As nice as it felt to have a sweet and loving boyfriend, it was hard to see how they could remain a couple, going to different schools, hundreds of miles apart, with diverging ambitions. Suddenly, she and Brandon were hanging out alone, talking about things she'd never talked about with anyone before. With a gun to her head, she wouldn't be able to say about what. She could recall, exactly, precisely, like she was eighteen again, the breathtaking intensity of her feelings.

Brandon somehow revealed for Lori what she knew and didn't know exactly. How complicated the world, how screwed up people were, and complicit too. That was the danger—and thrill. Lori had smarter things to say when Brandon was listening. It all felt like brilliant, new revelations, when the words came as they gazed, unblinking, into each other's eyes.

It was exhilarating…, and exhausting. Lori couldn't ignore the tight knot of fear. She didn't want to be any less than what

Brandon believed she could be. The more they talked, the more she wanted to trace the outline of his beautiful lips, stare deeply to gauge the blueness of his eyes, ruffle her fingers through his thick, dark hair, not stop there, since she had learned a few things from Bobby. She wasn't sure how to initiate contact, though, and she feared violating the sacred rule. You never cheat with your best friend's boyfriend.

* * *

It was hot, that first time. She still remembered it. There didn't seem so many hot nights back then. No one had air conditioning and Lori and Brandon had escaped from the stifling kitchen of Lori's childhood home to the steps of the front walkway. Lori suddenly got the idea to take Brandon to the woods nearby. She liked to show him places she guessed were different than where he'd grown up, so she grabbed his hand and they bolted, before her parents could ask where they were going.

"Emily talked me into running away." Lori recounted the story to Brandon as they entered the woodsy path, making a face to show him she knew how childish it sounded in hindsight.

"Emily was stubborn and bossy even then, and she'd get furious at our parents. She wanted to scare them. We slunk back home eventually. I don't think they even noticed we were gone." Lori stopped in her tracks.

"Here," she pointed up, "these are the rocks where we hid."

"They're hardly a quarter mile from your house."

"I know. It seemed really far. The woods felt huge and filled with dangers."

Brandon gave her an incredulous look.

"We thought we might get lost, and there were disgusting, mossy ponds with dead trees across that we might fall off. Maybe a serial killer was waiting for somebody to walk by, and..."

"Okay," she said, finally, when Brandon seemed to be laughing at her, "it seemed a lot more dangerous when we were little."

"I believe you."

11

"The rocks were much higher."

"I don't think the rocks have shrunk."

"Ha ha, you know what I mean. They seemed impossibly tall, and we imagined there were wild animals hiding up there. Emily made me go up first!"

"Want to climb up with me now? We can expunge your scary memories."

* * *

"Earth to Lori," Emily said.

"Sorry, I was just..."

"I know, a million miles away. You better not be worrying."

"No, just my mind wandering. Yesterday's drive wiped me out."

"Probably not just the drive. I'll drop you home. Take a nap before dinner. I can handle the rest of this list by myself."

Lori heard the teenagers in the basement. She tiptoed quietly upstairs, not in the mood to hear demands for rides or snacks. She was eager, though, to remember exact sentences that Brandon said all those years ago. He'd use certain words with her, to show her he knew grown-up things, not to boast, but because they had an understanding.

"Sure," she'd said to a teenage Brandon, "let's go expunging."

He laughed, before he scampered to the top and held out his hand. She recalled with a sharp jolt, all these years later, the heat of that first touch. She knew it meant something different than all the things she'd done with Bobby. Maybe because everything about the moment had seemed more mature, like she'd become a woman on that short walk in the woods. Maybe because she'd been wanting it for so long. Maybe because she knew nothing should happened, not with Sharon away, but still in the picture. Yet, Lori had brought him there.

They settled into the small, flat space in the crook between the rocks. Leaned back on their bottoms, shoulders touching, just

12

as she had with Emily when they were kids. She was nervous, just like she'd been with Emily. Wanting something to happen. Afraid that something might happen.

"So, this is the den of the wild beasts?" Brandon grabbed her side to tease her.

"It was really dark, not like tonight," Lori said, slapping back his hand. In fact, there'd been a gorgeous, almost full, ripe moon. Another detail that came back to her powerfully because she could recall that she would see Brandon's face in its unearthly glow.

She was sure they talked for a while. They spoke a lot that summer about what the future might bring. Living independently, meeting new people, facing a whole different level of school work and expectations. There was so much change around the corner.

"Will you and Sharon still, you know, go out, when you go to college?" It was a question Lori and been dying, trying, afraid, to ask.

"What about you and, what's his name?"

"That's not very nice of you. I call him guitar boy."

"Not to his face?"

"Of course not. To his face, he's Bobby."

"Will you?"

"Bobby wrote me song. He even sang it to me in front of his friends."

"At church group?" The smug tone wasn't like Brandon.

"Yes."

"How very teenage romance."

"Hey!"

"Just teasing."

"He was a good boyfriend."

"What do you mean?"

"He paid attention, you know, like he wanted to be with me, instead of his friends."

"I'm guessing you were a lot more interesting."

"They've been such a tight group since childhood. Always doing stuff together. Friends forever. I've never been part of anything like that."

"It's one of the things I like about you. You're an individual, maybe Bobby liked that too."

"I'm not sure what he liked about me."

"Really?!"

"He told me I'm pretty."

"Lori, you're beautiful. Don't you know that?"

"Emily's the pretty one."

"Who says?"

"And it's always been Sharon who the boys like."

"Sharon has a certain something…" Brandon smirked, but his look became serious as he turned to face Lori.

"It's more from knowing what boys want than from real beauty." He drew his finger through a strand of her hair, tucked it behind her ear.

"You are beautiful, Lori. I've wanted to be…with you…for a really long time."

She turned slightly, faced away, unwilling to meet his scrutiny.

"Look at me," he said, and when she didn't answer, "please?"

She gave him a side glance, without turning. He leaned down and kissed her thick hair. She kept it shoulder length back then. It was wavy around her face with auburn highlights. Brandon grabbed a handful, gently, and tipped her head back. He kissed her temple, brushed his lips over her eyelashes.

"It's something about those dark, brown eyes," he said, pulling back a little. He touched her chin to clinch her gaze.

"I could get lost in there."

Lori tried to smile.

"Come here," he said, and he swung her legs sideways over his, lifted her bottom into his lap, nuzzled her still downturned face with his nose until she softened, and his lips found hers.

It was Lori's first realization, she still remembered how it felt, not just in her head but with her body, that a kiss, lips and tongue,

14

ubiquitous features all, could have a particular and potent signature. Kissing Bobby was like cuddling a puppy, eager, playful, sweet. Brandon's tongue was assertive and purposeful, provoking essential juices and mingling their saliva to confirm a primordial match. His mouth became alpha to her omega, dominance and openness. He would have her, and she could have the starring role. His said all that with a kiss. It was crazy, and somehow true. It changed her.

Lori broke contact, to catch her breath. Maybe to find her nerve. Finally, she locked eyes onto Brandon's. If she had power, she should learn how to use it. Lori changed her position so that she was facing him, knees bent and straddling his thighs. She pulled off her t-shirt, slowly, with a new awareness of her capacity to arouse and direct. She tried unsuccessfully to unclasp her bra and doubted herself. Brandon reached back and quickly unhooked it. He let it slip off of its own accord. Lori sensed the cloth, falling against her skin, and then a sudden breeze on such a warm night. Her nipples were instantly erect. He brushed his thumbs across them repeatedly, harder with each pass. Every one of Lori's nerves felt electrified.

She became aware of a growing, hard pressure between her legs. Brandon was pulling at her shorts, fumbling at her waistband. She stopped his hand and stood up. Unsnapped, unzipped, un-rushed, she removed her shorts and panties herself. She nodded at him, and Brandon discarded his shirt. Still on the ground, he wiggled out of his jeans and boxers. He was searching his pants pockets and removed something, a condom, she realized.

She and Bobby never had to go there, and Lori remembered feeling both pleased and frightened. He had planned for this... for them. She took his hand and pulled him up to standing, got on her tippy toes to reach his mouth. Kissing hard, she nudged him with small steps back against the rocks, pressing into him. She liked the feel of his erect penis against her belly. It was powerful, and it tickled at a place beneath her skin, that was imploring, if a body could, for deeper satisfaction. She whispered in his ear.

"I've never done it."

He pushed her away too quickly. "Wait. What? You and Bobby...?"

"We didn't do it."

Brandon looked at her not understanding.

"I mean we did a lot of things. He, you know...touched me, all over, and...it was really nice... We didn't have sex."

"Why?"

"I don't know. At first, I wasn't ready, and he was okay with that. He'd done it before, and it made things too complicated, he said. Then, well, we got kind of smug about it, like maybe we were somehow superior..." Lori stopped abruptly. It sounded silly when she explained it to Brandon.

"We can stop."

"No!" She kissed him again. She didn't want to ignore that call from her belly, and farther down, that desire to be penetrated, not just rubbed against and touched.

He pushed her back gently. "Are you sure?"

Lori didn't answer. She nudged him to sit down. Then she climbed back on his lap, wrapping her legs around him. She kissed him for a while, made her tongue the aggressive one, swallowing his saliva. It tasted grown-up, as if the life he had lived gave him a certain flavor. She suspected she was also delaying the inevitable goal. It was becoming harder to avoid the insistent pressure against her bottom.

Brandon had dropped the condom package next to them. She picked it up and handed it to him.

Brandon handed it back. "You do it."

"I don't know how." She shifted back onto his thighs.

"It's not hard."

"Yes, it is," Lori said, staring at his penis. She remembered thinking that it looked so big. How was it going to fit?

"You're a comedian now?" Brandon asked, grinning as he unwrapped the package. "Just roll it over me."

With a little help, she got it on. "Now what do we do?"

16

"You stay on top."

"Really?"

"You can take me in as slowly as you need to."

"Oh...okay."

"And then I can look at all of you."

His voiced changed, Lori noticed, and his eyes too, like the way her dog looked when he was begging for dinner. She lifted up on her knees, took hold of him and guided him to her opening. She met a wall.

"Use your other hand and spread yourself open."

It was awkward. She slipped him in a little.

"Just use your hips, take as much of me as you can."

Lori remembered there was pressure, and pain, real pain, then it was more like fullness, and her hips started moving, almost without her willing them. He started moving too, and was grabbing at her breasts. She couldn't take her eyes from his face, so clear in the light of the moon. His blue eyes became small and dark, greedy. She could see when he came, more than feel it. His eyes opened wide and his lips formed a circle like he'd been shot. She abruptly stopped what she was doing.

"Lori, are you okay?"

"I'm fine. I mean, are you?"

"I'm better than that."

"Um, okay...good. That was amazing, right?" A dull pain had already started to spread through her pelvis.

"You didn't cum."

"Well, no..."

"I want to make you cum." Brandon had squiggled out from under her.

"I'm fine, really."

"Fair's fair," he said, smirking as he gently pulled her legs and she fell back to the spot where he'd just lay.

"I'm not fine unless you cum too." He looked so serious. Then he did things that surprised her. She still remembered. He had stubble on his face, which felt scratchy, at first, then she liked it. It satisfied a kind of...itch. Brandon knew places, and ways, to touch her and to then to stop, and then start again, that made her feel a whole lot crazy. His tongue seemed to be seeking more than just the wet, warmth between her legs.

When she thought about what he was doing, that he was tasting her wetness, that his mouth and lips and tongue were swallowing where he had just been inside of her, it felt taboo and shocking and..., secretly, thrilling. She tried to stifle a sudden, startling orgasm. A pleasure so intense, along with a sharp pang of embarrassment, maybe shame. She would spend years, she now realized, holding back, afraid of her power to enjoy sex that was dirty, defenseless, consummately brilliant.

He lay next to her after, and they watched the moon until, even on such a hot night, they felt a chill being naked. They got up and laughed to find sticks and leaves stuck to their backs. Lori was relieved that they could return to a playful normalcy, brushing each other off, tossing mislaid clothing, knowing, silently, that things would never be the same.

* * *

Why is this all coming back to me?! She was a married woman, herself the mother of teenagers. It'd been more than ten years since she'd seen Brandon, had a face-to-face conversation. He lived across the country in Seattle, with, if she recalled correctly, a live-in girlfriend. He had his own child, failed marriage, and shared custody with Jocelyn, the woman he'd started dating back in college when Brandon, Lori, and Jocelyn were all close friends. Another unsustainable triangle.

Lori told Brandon about her separation from Peter in a Facebook message, of all places. She wasn't even sure why, and so soon after. He responded quickly, though, and with genuine concern. Somehow, he'd gotten wind of her stopover with Emily and said he might be coming too, that he hadn't been home for the holidays in years and maybe he was due. Sitting down on the corner of Emily's guest bed, Lori decided she would drop by the McManus', not ask Emily to join her. Clearly Brandon was why she didn't tell her sister about her plans.

Chapter 4

Brandon's mom, Joanne, welcomed her at the door.

"Oh darling, how are you? Get in here out of the cold," she said as she pulled Lori into the small foyer and gave her a bosomy, reassuring hug.

"I know exactly what you are going through. Men can be such pricks!"

"It's good to see you too Joanne." Lori smiled, handing Joanne some fancy soap she picked up in New Hampshire.

"Thank you dear. You shouldn't have," Joanne said as she took a whiff of her gift.

"Mmm, lovely. Can I get you anything? Some eggnog? I made the good stuff, with rum."

"That sounds delicious, thanks." Lori was looking around hoping to find that Brandon was there, had, in fact, come home. He'd called it that, in his message, home, just like she did, even though neither of them had lived in their small town for so long.

"Your decorations are wonderful," she added.

"Thank you. I kept them up because my sister Patty and her husband are coming over tomorrow to finally exchange gifts. Sarah will be upset that she missed you. She had to get back to the City."

"I can't stay long Joanne. I kind of snuck out and left my kids with my sister. I just wanted to say hello and wish you a Happy New Year."

"Sit down, at least. Brandon and Fiona will be back in a minute. I sent them out to get some more ice cream."

"Brandon is here?"

"Yes, didn't he tell you?"

"He said he might be. I wasn't sure."

"I was shocked myself. They rarely make it. Fiona's mother makes such a fuss if Brandon takes Fiona away during the Holidays. I didn't believe it until he texted me that they were on the plane. They just got here yesterday."

There was the sound of a key scratching at metal.

"Honey, I didn't lock it," Joanne said in a loud voice as she moved quickly to the front door and opened it. "Here, let me help you with those."

"Mom, I've told you a million times, you've got to lock your door."

It was Brandon's voice. Lori recognized it immediately.

"Never mind honey, look who's…"

Before she could finish, Brandon had passed from the foyer into the living room. How long had it been since someone looked at her like that, like they saw her? His smile dazzled, as it always had, and contained a shorthand she remembered, saying all at once without words, it's so good to see you, sorry you had to deal with my mother, and wow, we need a few minutes alone.

He looked fantastic, tall and athletic. She was so used to a particular physique these days. That of her husband and her friends' husbands, all of whom spent way too much time at their desks and already, only in their mid to late forties, had hunched shoulders, paunchy stomachs, or deeply receding hairlines. Often, all of the above. Brandon strode over and gave her a quick, tight hug. Lori's head barely reached his shoulders and her neck bent up awkwardly.

He stepped back holding her arms as they exchanged glances. Brandon's hair was still thick and dark, if speckled with some grey. The quarter zip shirt clung to his muscled, broad shoulders, falling loosely at the waistband of his jeans in a way that indicated the abdomen beneath was trim and flat. She suddenly wanted to touch his stomach. When, recently, had she felt that? She smiled to herself thinking that recently would have to be defined generously to include, well, years. It'd been years.

21

"What are you smiling about darlin'?" Brandon asked, winking; he'd guessed correctly what his mother had called her.

"Nothing, you know, just a funny thought I had." Lori was thinking how different it felt when darling came out of Brandon's mouth.

"I'm gonna make you tell me later."

That smile again, like he was licking an ice cream cone. Then a teenage girl, with wavy blond hair pulled into a ponytail, appeared behind Brandon and kept walking, a book up to her face. Brandon dropped Lori's arms and turned.

"Fiona, please get your nose out of that book. I want to introduce you to someone."

Fiona looked up at Lori with direct, clear eyes. Lori felt a shock of recognition. They were the exact same shade as her father's.

"Hello there Fiona. I'm Lori," she said, holding out her hand, "a friend of your dad's."

"Very nice to meet you Lori," Fiona responded. The grownups in the room smiled at Fiona's older-than-her-age formality.

"I hope you had a Merry Christmas."

"I did Fiona. Thanks for asking. Whatcha reading?"

"Shakespeare."

"Seriously?" Lori stopped herself from making a joke when she saw Fiona's sincerity.

"I mean, that's great. How old are you anyway?"

"I'm fourteen, I'll be fifteen in June."

"Fiona," Joanne interrupted, "please go clean the mess you made in the kitchen. I want it clean for Aunt Patty and Uncle Don."

Fiona put her face back in her book and headed toward the kitchen.

"She's quite the chef," Joanne said. "She made us some biscotti from scratch, can you believe it?"

Lori turned to Brandon, her eyebrows raised. "You're going to have to tell me your secret."

"I don't take any credit. She's just a good kid."

"You know what, I should probably go," Lori said unexpectedly. "You guys are getting ready for company, and..."

It suddenly felt too much. Too abrupt an adjustment from her daydreaming just hours ago, about her first real sex, maybe her first real love, with this boy, who was now a man, a father of a teenager, and they were trading parenting quips.

"Don't! You just got here," Joanne said.

"I really should, my sister will be wondering about me."

"Well, if you have to. When are you coming back?"

"Everything's pretty up in the air, Joanne. I'll let you know. We can have lunch or something."

"That sounds perfect." She gave Lori another tight hug. "Please take care of yourself."

Why did every expression of warmth make Lori want to cry these days? When she turned to say good bye to Brandon, he said,

"I'll walk you to your car."

"Really, I'll be fine."

"I'd like to." Straightforward. It took Lori off guard. She nodded.

Lori had parked a few houses away. They walked without speaking until they reached the driver side door. Lori felt suddenly anxious, sensing an uneasy vibe from Brandon. Was it concern? Maybe chemistry? That had always generated as powerful a force between them as the energy they put into denying it. Romantic interest? Please, please not that, Lori thought, it's too soon, way too soon. She needed time to process the separation and Peter's betrayal, to figure out her next steps.

"Brandon, I..." There was a whole speech to follow. Brandon stopped her with a simple question.

"How are you, Lori, really? Forget the show you put on for Joanne."

"No, no I'm fine," she said.

He was looking at her again, with those piercing blue eyes, like she was the only person left in the world. It all came out, with tears and snot.

The unexpected shock at her marriage's ending.

Her fears about the troubling economics of life for a divorced woman, especially women like her who had stopped working to raise the children.

The worst part, the devastation it had caused her kids.

"I'll be doing something mindless," she said to Brandon trying discreetly to wipe her nose, "like loading the dishwasher, and my mind flashes to Ben's face when we told him. It just crumpled, in shock...and pain. I can still see it."

Brandon offered her a wadded- up cocktail napkin from his jean's pocket.

"I'm sorry. That's all I have," he said with that smile. It could warm an iceberg.

She blew her nose and then, like it was the most natural thing in the world, Brandon put his arm around her, turned her, almost imperceptibly, toward his body, enveloping her in a tight grip.

"I am so sorry Peter hurt you and your kids," Brandon spoke to the top of her head. "He's a fool not to see what he had. You were always way above his league," he continued, stroking her hair.

Lori suddenly felt something so unexpected, like his body was armor and nothing could ever hurt her again. She'd forgotten what it was to feel that, for someone else to give her strength and comfort. She looked up at him. How had she forgotten how strong he was; how being with him had once made her feel safe from dark woods and wild beasts? Safe enough to...

"I'm sorry Brandon, I've made a mess of your jacket. I must look terrible with my..."

"You look beautiful."

"I do not."

"You always do, especially when you're not trying."

"Brandon, I can't..."

He stopped her with his lips. At first, he just brushed them softly against hers, not breaking his hold over her with his eyes. He must have sensed something, some release or permission, and he kissed her. Not hard, but as if his lips could speak, conveying that he'd grant her anything she needed, his strength, his very breath. It steadied her.

When his tongue entered her mouth, she thought she might collapse from the straight shot of desire, right to where it mattered. As if Brandon's tongue controlled a direct link to her clitoris, audaciously short circuiting all preliminaries and sending electricity there. She was suddenly aware that she could orgasm, instantly, if she just increased her contact with Brandon's thigh. She pulled away to stand under her own control.

"Shit, what was that?" Lori brought her fingers to her lips to touch the burning rawness.

"That is that…," Brandon said, teasing out the third syllable. "That is what always happens, when we let it. Don't you remember?"

"Brandon. No. It would be too complicated. Your life's in Seattle and mine is in Maryland. I thought you had a serious girlfriend."

"Things happen, sometimes more quickly than we want or expect."

"No, they don't." Lori looked down at her shoes, shuffling them, like there was something that had to removed.

"Your life was just rearranged, wasn't it?" Brandon asked. It took Lori a few seconds to respond.

"Yes…"

"We can change things too."

"I should go now."

"Stop a second." Brandon lifted her chin, so she had to look at him.

"There's something I need to tell you. Something that I finally understand." His smile seemed a little sad. "It's the reason I came back to this place, for the first time in years."

"Brandon…"

"Just listen. Please," he added quietly, shifting on his feet as if searching for the right words. "I want you to know that…" His looked up again, his gaze raw and naked. "Lori, I've been searching for someone..., someone exactly like you, for as long as I can remember."

"Brandon, that's so... I don't know what to say."

"You don't have to. It's just..., I've wasted a lot of time not realizing that. You are everything I always wanted in a woman. No one ever measured up."

"Are you asking me...?"

"No. Just think about coming out to Seattle, for a visit."

"How could I? When would I?"

"Anytime. Just for a weekend. Promise me you'll think about it."

"Okay," Lori said. It didn't sound like a promise. She jabbed at her key fob to unlock her door. "It's getting late. I should go."

"I know." He touched her elbow and directed her gently toward the car door, opening it for her.

Lori got in and closed it fast. She didn't roll down the window, just drove away, giving Brandon a thin, scared smile.

Chapter 5

Lori knew she needed to get away, fast. To have the talk, with herself. The one where she remembered she'd only been separated from Peter a few months. She was going to be grateful for this time, if totally un-asked for. She would stitch together any pieces of her that were left, after the scavenging needs of Peter, and her kids, and everything about their life. No words came. There was just an unquenchable fire in her crotch as she tried to drive the car. Desire, murderous and all consuming.

She hadn't felt anything like it for years. It was a state of affairs she and her friends, suburban mothers all, tiptoed around delicately. Wanting to know if each was the only one not having much sex. Not really desiring sex, and not feeling anything when they did, finally, have sex. Despite what the magazines announced, no one Lori knew was getting it outside their marriage. They were resigned. Some even admitted to being glad that neglect had turned their shared beds into personal sanctuaries. One place where not even their husbands asked for or needed them. Somehow overlooking that they got nothing in return.

Clearly, they'd all forgotten. They must have obliterated from memory what wet, hot desire felt like because you wouldn't give this up. Not if you remembered it, even just a little.

* * *

Emily was straightening the kitchen when Lori walked in.

"Where'd you go sis? We thought maybe you ran away and left us the kids." Emily grinned as she rinsed the sink spotless.

27

Keeping an immaculate kitchen was something they'd learned from their father, who claimed to have learned it in the Army.

"I went to pick up some snacks for the ride tomorrow." Lori dropped a grocery bag near the door.

"I see you gave yourself KP duty," Lori said, chuckling. "I've yet to get my kids to embrace Kitchen Patrol. They'll put a glass or two in the dishwasher, but they don't get that it's a top to bottom commitment. You're not done until you've wiped every crumb off the counter and swept the last bit of dirt from the floor."

"Don't you think KP was best left behind?" Emily asked.

"No! It was one of the best things Dad taught us. My kids are hopeless to take care of themselves. I don't know how I let them get so spoiled."

"Stop! You've got enough to worry about. Don't give yourself another reason to feel bad."

"You're right. Sorry. Hey, I'm gonna pull our stuff together. We should get on the road early."

* * *

Lori closed the door to the guest room and stood there dazed. The drive back had been an awakening. There were so many memories contained in the short distance between the McManus's house and Emily's. Memories of her budding friendship with Brandon, when they hung out, so each could be close to Sharon, or so she thought. So many trips into their quaint downtown for pizza or ice cream. Hanging out at the burger place with the arcade in the back on Friday nights, until they were old enough to pass for nineteen with fake IDs and could go to the one and only bar in town. Then that miraculous first summer, and visits home from college, even later, finding places to be alone.

She and Brandon had probably walked every single street together, at some point. It was overpowering and wonderful, that her hometown, a place she had moved away from ages ago, and frankly discarded, was suddenly alive to her again, almost as if her life between then and now had simply slipped away…

* * *

The rest of that summer after senior year had been the most wonderful weeks of her life. Lori spent every moment she could with Brandon, talking, kissing, touching. All the world seemed bathed in golden sunlight, until Sharon got back. Brandon said he needed to make a clean break before he and Lori got together again. There were less than two weeks left of summer, and it'd seemed to take forever. Lori was eventually able to admire his sense of duty. Then, well…

She and Brandon barely had time to say good bye. Her college had an early orientation week and Lori was stuffing things into her parent's old station wagon when he showed up on her driveway.

"What are you doing?"

"Packing the car."

"I can see that. Why?"

"I'm leaving today."

"School doesn't start until next week."

"Mine starts tomorrow."

"And you weren't going to say good bye?"

"I didn't want to interfere with you and Sharon."

"Come on, Lori. I thought you understood."

"I do, I did, I guess it just took longer than I expected."

"So now what?"

"I don't know."

"Are we over?"

"I don't know."

Brandon grabbed her by the hand, led her around to the back of her house where he tucked her against the stone wall under the kitchen window, hidden. He kissed her, immediately opening her mouth with his tongue. There was that same taste of his saliva, of his whole being, minty this time, still, exactly, Brandon. Lori remembered the fascination she felt as her body parts responded. Breasts perking, belly twisting, pelvis throbbing, her... She'd moved her mouth away, confused at being simultaneously angry and so turned on.

"Brandon, we're both going away."

Brandon had changed his mind several times about whether to go to a State school or one of the private colleges that accepted him. Cost was an issue. She wasn't even sure what he'd finally decided.

"So?" He'd asked bitterly.

"I'm sure you want a fresh start."

"I want us. What we started. What I know you just felt."

"It doesn't make sense, not now."

"It did? Like a few days ago?"

"More like weeks."

Brandon made a face. "Sharon's parents were being awful, I just wanted..."

"It's fine. Look, I've been talking to my parents. They thought I was still with Bobby, and well, we talked about it being a new time of life, being available for a new type of relationship."

"That's bullshit."

"Not really... It makes sense."

Brandon looked at her, it was such a complicated look, sad, mean, still that hunger.

"Fine." He turned, walked around the side of the house and was gone.

Lori stood dazed. She had been thinking so hard about what she wanted. Bobby made things too comfortable, too easy. What she felt with Brandon was complicated, intense, a challenge. She felt inadequate. That gives him power. Too much power? What if Brandon was the best thing that ever happened to her? Lori had crumpled down against the stone wall and cried.

Chapter 6

Lori didn't bump into Brandon again, even that next summer. He'd finally broken up with Sharon, so there was no seeing him there. Neither tried to reach out. Lori returned to school. It was her first day back, sophomore year. She was in the quad checking out a student association fair. Brandon was suddenly standing next to her.

"Hey."

"Oh my god! What are you doing here?"

"I go here now."

"What?"

"Yeah, I transferred. The University was too impersonal, too many students. I wasn't getting into the classes I wanted, and..., Lori, are you okay?"

"Yes, I'm fine. I just can't believe you're here."

* * *

Lori insisted that they just be friends. So adamantly, that Brandon started dating other people. That was fine with Lori. There was so much besides sex that she needed from Brandon. It turned out the college was not unlike their high school, clique-y, with kids who had graduated from boarding school. They were smugly sophisticated, and at the same time, clueless. Suddenly, Lori had a best friend and a sparring partner. College, after all, could be a magnificent indulgence, even if you weren't a rich kid. When else was there time to act like every question mattered, consider every issue with stubborn abandon? When one of them found a worthy cause, they took it on together.

They had arguments. That was half the fun. Lori recalled an even split for whether she or Brandon thought they'd won. Funny to remember now. A running debate over whether or not one should have a child. Lori had an unwavering position, yes, a child is essential to the full experience of life. It always felt a little uncomfortable, anti-feminist, particularly against Brandon's insistence that having a child compromised the ability to accomplish significant things. Turned out, she suspected, they were both kind of right, and kind of wrong.

Lori and Brandon spent an inordinate amount of time together for two people that weren't dating. Late nights in the library, breaks in the student lounge, Friday nights at the campus bar. Girlfriends, boyfriends, others too. They built a circle of friends. Brandon liked to tease her, like about their friend who, Brandon insisted, had excessive feelings for Lori. Her eyes, they're driving me crazy. She has...such...knowing eyes! Brandon would mimic him. It became a joke. She wondered, now, how much others had noticed the stifled heat.

* * *

A night before spring midterms...

They'd studied especially late. Brandon offered to walk Lori back to her dorm. She unlocked her door, glanced around and invited him in. Brandon closed the door behind them. When she turned around, Brandon was as close as her own hand, rigid, like he was holding back a wild animal. He stared at her intently until he must have seen her eyes soften and say yes. He used everything, his hands holding her face tightly, the all-surrounding of his lips, his teeth biting gently, even the insistence of his saliva in her mouth, a taste, immediately, both familiar and knowing, to say, without words, I'll have you, and, somehow, possess me too. His thigh filled the space between her legs.

If he hadn't put his hand up her shirt, brushed aside her crapy, stretched out bra (because why would she put on nice under-clothes to study with her best friend) and started playing with her nipple, she might have grabbed his hand and put it there. Instead, she pushed her hips up hard and insistent against his crotch, a little surprised again to feel the size of his erection. She'd paused, she was sure of it, afraid to start something physical again. Afraid it would ruin a good thing. Afraid that friendship and sex always messed up both. She was afraid to ask for what she wanted.

Lori needn't have worried. Her baggy sweatpants made things easy. His hand, the one not busy teasing her nipple, ca-ressed her ass, finally cupping the fleshy curve at the bottom before sliding his finger past her soaked and slippery hole. He connected with the central point of her desire, of her entire being; the spot that'd been sending out a signal, in hopes of making con-tact, for as long as she'd fought to deny it. She nearly gasped, the gratification was so immediate. Like an itch someplace unreach-able, that gets scratched after clamoring all day. So much more thrilling, because that first-again, covetous, long-craved touch, meant there could be more.

Unbelievably, Lori's roommate chose that moment to return. They heard the key in the door and Brandon quickly pulled his hand from her pants. Lori straightened her clothes and smoothed her hair. It was obvious what'd been interrupted. A raw and ani-malistic smell had already permeated the small room. There was a funny, awkward moment where everyone half pretended that what had just happened hadn't really. Brandon hurried out, about as graceful as a frustrated runner tripped mid stride. Lori and her roommate laughed because it was public knowledge by then that Brandon was dating Jocelyn.

* * *

The interruption proved useful. Lori realized she had no de-sire to be the break-upper, or the other woman, not again. She forced herself to date other guys. It was never the same. Especially their kisses, tongues pickled in beer, darting and probing like dental devices. Brandon had shown her how a kiss should feel. They even had name for it, a private joke, their wolf-kisses.

Looking back, she wondered how she did it, kept things so cool when her body was hyper-charged by Brandon's presence. That spot, it ached and swelled whenever he was near, like an animal in heat. Whatever room they were in, she'd will it to empty so she could be alone with Brandon and he could slip his hand down her pants, tease and touch her the way he first did. The way she now craved. She could practically cum just thinking about it.

Lori got serious for a while with another of their friends. That didn't stop Brandon's smoldering glimpses whenever they were in proximity of each other, telegraphing that he reciprocated her body's feral call. She wasn't sure how Jocelyn tolerated it, except, even then she realized, the laugh was on Lori. Inevitably, Brandon walked out of those rooms with Jocelyn at his side. It was a game, or a serious competition. She was never sure if Brandon felt like the master or its victim.

Lori knew the board shifted when she and Brandon came back to their hometown for breaks, or for summer, later for more infrequent visits. They constructed a bubble in which other lovers did not exist. They would take the train to New York City. It was easy there to play by a private set of rules. Wandering bustling streets, Brandon would put his arm around her. The most normal thing in the world, yet it proved she was the coveted one. Guys, it seemed, would look away and women would glance greedily at Brandon as if at a handsome knight.

Heading back home later in the day, gently rocked by the movement of the train, Brandon would put his arm around her shoulder, let her head rest in the crook of his neck. She would relive the day's pleasures; the times she'd turned to point out something and found Brandon's hungry mouth; moments in crowded places where she could brush her breasts against his body; leaning back against Brandon while waiting in line somewhere, her ass tucked into his crotch, craving more, hoping there would be an opportunity. So often, one of them had something else to get to, papers were due, maybe Brandon had to check in with Jocelyn.

Lori never dwelt on that. Her frustrated desire would build so powerfully, it had a voice. A scream, at a silent pitch only Brandon could hear. Next, they would each be giving a parent some excuse to go out. They would meet in a darkened park or sneak back into her basement. When he finally touched her, unbuttoned her jeans and inched his fingers down, drew his finger teasingly through her pubic hair to play with her before sinking a finger deep inside, they both would moan, he at her wetness, she at the relief to have that desire finally assuaged. She could cum in that instant. She usually did, the first before they got into things further.

She probably could remember every place they fooled around. Playgrounds, a golf course, even the town reservoir. They'd almost slipped off the rocks and into the water half naked! It was always intense, furious, from the longing and the need for both to climax before their privacy was interrupted.

Once, when her parents were away, they did it in her parents' bedroom. He flipped her on the bed and took her from behind, so they could both face the mirror. She'd been fascinated to see her breasts bounce with each of his thrusts. Brandon had reached under her belly to play with her clitoris while they moved. That was the first time they came at exactly the same time. She'd watched their faces, mesmerized by identical looks of surprise and vindication, maybe even despair. It always had to end. Sometimes Jocelyn was waiting in the wings. Even if Jocelyn and Brandon had broken up for a while, other commitments, that felt like obligatory steps to becoming adults, pulled them apart.

Until—months, even years, would go by—the overpowering urge to re-connect. They would find the necessary time for smoldering stares, hands tentatively coming to touch under the table while they talked, working their way, slowly, through the things they each had seen in the world and thought were terribly wrong. How they might change things. Only then would they find some place, barely private enough, to satisfy the itch that built up slowly, painfully. The way untapped desire actually hurts the body, as well as some place deeper. They might get caught. She didn't care. Maybe she was even turned on by the possibility. She was with Brandon and he would defend her.

Those times, had they drawn an indelible connection between feeling vulnerable—both terribly exposed and fiercely protected—and deeply satisfying sex? She'd lost that with Peter and their oh so, careful and successful life.

When Lori and Brandon's lives shifted too far, maybe past any real hope of a fuller relationship, they still exchanged letters. It was as if Lori lived two distinct lives. One in which she studied, worked, even dated. There was a simultaneous universe in which only Brandon existed.

Lori saw the world in precise anticipation of how she would describe it to him. She picked up cards, and books, and trinkets along the way, gifts she didn't always send, but were intended for their private understandings. She was sure this way of seeing meant she lived more adventurously, experienced more deeply the beauty and romance of new places and experiences. Everything had heightened meaning, imagining how she would draw a picture of it, in words, for Brandon. It felt so long ago. How have I lived without?

Brandon's letters were filled with observations and ideas, tangled up with how much he wanted her. She would approach her mailbox with an explosive kernel of happiness and desire. The best was when a letter arrived at an inopportune moment and she had to wait to read it, carrying it around unopened, better than any tangible gift. She would re-read his letters endlessly, and his words were in her mind when she pleasured herself, sometime gluttonously. Does anyone send letters anymore? Oh god, Lori thought, she would run into a burning house to rescue her letters from Brandon. Were there any artifacts from her marriage she could say that about?

They'd slipped away from each other though, at some point irretrievably. She wasn't sure why. They married other people. Oh yeah, there was that, and jobs, and kids, of course. Life had a way of picking up the pace after taking those steps. Brandon seemed to end up living farther and farther away. Still, she stopped dead in her tracks when she received an out-of-the-blue, once every few years email or Facebook message from Brandon. She would read between the lines, trying to see if he was happy with his life. Perhaps he was telegraphing something besides the mundane details. She wondered how much of her own lonely truth she conveyed.

Maybe she should call him, Lori thought. Continue the dance Brandon started that night, as a middle-aged man, returned to the very streets their youthful passion had once claimed. She had Brandon's cell phone number from a quick Facebook message. She hadn't known it in ages. It wasn't the way they communicated. They'd tried the chatty phone call. Inevitably, it felt too...less than. Now they had smart phones. She could text him. Intimacy...at a safe distance. Maybe that could work.

Chapter 7

"I can't stop thinking about tonight," Lori texted Brandon, steeling herself against (or maybe hoping for) reasons why he wouldn't text her back. Almost immediately, he responded.

"Neither can I. I haven't had to hide an erection from my mother in a long time. Thank you."

"LOL! You're welcome, I guess?"

"My thanks are sincere."

"I'm sorry about how I behaved. I'm trying to sort out how I'm supposed to feel, who I'm supposed to be these days."

"No apologies necessary, baby. Oops, sorry, old habit."

"No apologies necessary" Wow. She'd forgotten he used to call her that. Seeing baby there on her phone, it sent a white, hot arrow through her heart, and well, someplace else.

"It's just, that kiss, I haven't felt, well to be honest, it's left me feeling more turned on than I've been in, like, a thousand years."

"You shouldn't have run away."

"It scared me. I'd forgotten how intense that can feel."

"Come back over. I'll sneak out and we can visit the playground, like old times."

"It's 30 degrees outside!"

"If I recall, environmental discomforts never stopped you before."

Lori could see, no feel, the heat of his mischievous eyes, his smirky smile, as she read his texts.

"I can't. I've got to spend a few minutes with my sister and get to bed so I'm rested enough for the drive back. I'm dreading it."

"Are you alone?"

"Yes."

"Do something for me."

"What?"

"Just touch yourself."

"No!"

"Why not?"

"I don't do that anymore."

"Really?!"

"I thought it was something we're supposed to outgrow."

"Why in the world?! Now you've gotta do it. This counts as an emergency. I'll talk you through."

"Wouldn't that be, like, sexting?"

"Exactly like sexting," Brandon replied.

Lori didn't respond immediately, she felt, suddenly, in over her head.

"So, you've heard of it?" Brandon texted a minute later.

"Don't get all smug on me. I know what sexting is. I have teenagers, if you recall."

"So, your kids sext, and you don't?"

"I don't think sext is a word and, ewww, I hope not!"

"Which part are you aghast about, your kids doing it or you not?"

"I should probably go."

"Just try. I dare you. Touch yourself."

Lori's hand felt like it was not her own, wanting to do something while her brain was yelling S.O.S. He'd directly challenged her, just like he used to, in all their college skirmishes and crusades.

"You still there Lori?"

"Yes, I'm here."

"Touch yourself, baby." That word! It cut a straight channel to her clitoris, again.

"How?"

"Are you still dressed?"

"Yes."

"Those jeans look great on you."

"They're falling off me."

"Even better, you can reach in and touch your pussy without taking them off."

Pussy! Really?! It was not a word Lori used, that they'd ever used, as close as they'd been. It got her wondering. What did she call her vagina when she was trying, granted a rare occurrence, to be flirty and casual? Her vjayjay. It was good enough for Oprah. That didn't really send her, and she could just imagine the teasing she would get if she shared it with Brandon.

"Baby, you still there?"

"Yes, I'm here." Maybe baby is what she should call her vagina because whenever Brandon said it, something happened. How can one word make me feel adored, safe, stripped naked, and ravenous—all wrapped in a bow?

"Where'd you go again?"

"Nowhere."

"Unzip your jeans."

"Okay." Lori didn't, though. She was too busy wondering at what point Brandon's telling her to do things by text, and her responding by text in addition to trying to do the things he was asking her to, was going to become unmanageable. She thought about asking Brandon. He texted first.

"You chickening out on me?"

"No! Just thinking about something."

"Stop thinking!"

"As if!"

"Tell me if your pussy's wet."

Lori put the phone down this time. How come when Brandon uses pussy it seems loving and incredibly hot? She'd considered the word kind of crude, and misogynistic, always shielding her daughter from it.

Stop thinking! She took a deep breath, put her hands down the front of her jeans. She hadn't even unbuttoned them, assuming it was just a word game they were playing. Not that it mattered. She could fit in both hands. With one, she pushed aside

40

her panties, feeling a little anxious. What if her sister came up, or the kids burst in with some imagined need? She couldn't believe how aroused she felt. She brushed her clit on the way to seeing whether or not she was wet. That alone nearly gave her an orgasm.

"I'm wet." She was glad texting did not convey her raspy breathing, or the fact that she was soaking.

"I thought you'd be. I'll leave you alone while you take care of yourself. Tell me when you cum."

She glanced at the door, shit, no lock. I'll be quick. It took only seconds. It hadn't happened like that in ages. She was soaked with a silky moisture that made her feel, this is easy, not such a chore, to get off. She fast forwarded through their times together, imagined it was Brandon's finger moving inside her curling out dripping with her juices, his thumb rubbing her own wetness around and around with pressure on her clit while he sucked at her nipples. She nearly screamed when she climaxed. Then remembered where she was and drew in her moan. Her entire body continued to feel the aftershocks. She wasn't sure she could stop herself from doing it again, immediately, especially as she imagined Brandon waiting, want to know that it happened. She texted him quickly while she caught her breath.

"I did it!"

"Did what?" Brandon texted back immediately.

It took her an extra second, "you know."

"You've got to say it."

"I came."

"How was it?"

Lori was struggling to find words to describe her body's urgency, it's eagerness for more. She was even starting to touch herself again, when her sister called up. Shit!

"Lori, come down and have a last glass of wine with me and Thomas." Lori texted Brandon that she had to go.

"Okay," Brandon texted back. "I'll try not to punish you for leaving me hanging."

Chapter 8

The next few weeks were awful and wonderful. Brandon texted her, not all the time, just often enough to keep her phone nearby, and a part of her perpetually hungry and distracted. She was learning about Fiona, his work, and life in Seattle. It was almost like they were strangers, newly dating, getting to know each other for the first time. Sometimes his messages were playful, hinting at sex. As evasive as she tried to be about the intensity of her feelings, Lori was hooked again on the rush of desire.

That switch had been turned back on. Suddenly, all she could think about was sex. Everything she read or saw on TV, the men she passed on the street, things sniffed in the air or brushed up against innocently, it was all immediately, shockingly arousing, in a way that could not be ignored.

She started to plan for moments in the day when the kids would not be home. She felt like a teenager again, almost. She was shy touching herself, only in her bed, under the covers, and not until after the mailman came by. She didn't want to feel like there might be someone at the door when she was playing. She couldn't even name it masturbation. She kept doing it, though, to sexual fantasies she hadn't conjured up in years.

She'd forgotten how satisfying it was to bring herself to an orgasm. The first touch of her clit, an immediate zing of incitement, quickly spreading out from that spot of searing thrill to a deep fluttering bliss in her entire pelvis. She could feel her muscles opening to the velvety touch as she fingered herself, reticent at first, then it was two fingers, necessitated by her body's insistence that it feels its own clenching purposefulness.

It occurred to her that this was the reason we outgrow our horny, young selves. Otherwise, nothing would get done. Here she was in middle age, a mother of hormonal teenagers, hornier than ever. This can't be okay. It had to be affecting her behavior with the kids, her general state of mind. Maybe she should go to Seattle, for one weekend. Just for the sex. Anything to get past this frantic, gratuitous self-pleasuring.

* * *

It's a straightforward enough proposition, Lori tried to convince herself. A visit to an old friend. A friend with benefits. Isn't that what kids called it these days? The problem was, nothing between she and Brandon had ever been simple. If it became something more, it wouldn't end well. Lori couldn't get past that fear.

She imagined telling Emily, or Jeanette and her other friends. She knew what they'd say without needing to hear. It's too soon. They'd tell her she was lonely and missed having someone. It's to be expected. They would warn her it was too easy to fall into a relationship with someone she'd known since they were teenagers. People always idealize their first love. A rebound affair, they would call it. Those never work out. They'd urged her to go out and have a fling, just to get it over with it. Why do it with someone three thousand miles away? That's just crazy.

If it got serious with Brandon, Lori knew the situation would get worse. Lori's kids, their father, her life was here. A cross country relationship was doomed. If Peter got wind of it, shit, just when they'd started to negotiate the terms of a separation. Almost twenty years of marriage..., Lori could write the script. Peter's guilt would immediately be replaced by self-righteousness. See, we were both unhappy. Go have your bi-coastal fling, he'd tell her, with the guy he always, always, suspected she preferred. The one who got away. But do it on your own dime! Don't drag in the kids.

* * *

They all had a point, Lori knew it, even Peter. She'd be giving him a bargaining chip. If she went to see Brandon, it wouldn't just be for a weekend. Their life lines were too deeply incised, with too many intersecting points. She'd get pulled in, kids and everything, try to blend the whole damn thing. She didn't know how to do it any other way, and they couldn't pull that off. Not against Peter. Not for the long haul. No f'ing way.

Lori forced herself to picture it. Did she really want to destroy their friendship with that bad ending? She and Brandon never had any closure, just a kind of fade. If she was honest, she'd never stopped comparing the life she had, to the life she could have had with Brandon. It would have been more passionate, more meaningful, just...more. Lori could keep those dreams intact, filled with possibility. They were some of her best ones. An actual relationship with Brandon could never compete.

It was safer, and smarter, to accept that her less-than-fulfilling life was where she belonged; these kids, their school and activities and friends, her utter devotion to it all, and to this town of theirs, in the shadow of the Nation's Capital, even with its pretensions, and judgy-ness, and outrageous cost of entry. Lori wasn't willing to put her financial and emotional status, or her kids' stability, at risk.

Lori didn't, of course, discuss any of this with Brandon. She kept the banter pleasant, even when he sent insightful or sexy messages that reminded her how good it might be. Lori censored those feelings. She was good at that. Like when she turned away from a beautiful summer evening, infused with the smell of her jasmine bushes, and fireflies twinkling in the trees, shut the back door anyway, because there were dishes in the sink and laundry in the washer.

Eventually, that switch turned off again. The grabbing lust subsided. She took longer to answer Brandon's texts. His rejoinders were shorter. Pretty soon he got the message and stopped writing.

Chapter 9

Lori was discovering that being a single mother was even harder than being married to a workaholic. Peter's clients still demanded all his time and attention. She could no longer imply, though, that she might just do something reckless, if he didn't get home, immediately. Funny how that went. His threat was locked and loaded, deployed just once—decisively. He had no sense of brinkmanship. Lori guessed he didn't have to. Their division of labor—after all, somebody had to stay home and raise the kids while the other went out and earned the money - had somehow stripped her of will power and conviction.

Then Peter had the chutzpah to claim an upcoming trial, work around the clock, blah, blah, blah. He didn't have time to get the kids' bedrooms ready at his new house even though he'd found time to secretly rent it before his decampment. Ben and Catherine were only going there a couple of Saturdays each month. He tried to take them out to a dinner once a week. They were usually back before she got any respite. Lori knew they needed to talk about a real schedule. The kids, though, seemed to prefer living at one home. They were doing okay, their teachers and her family kept reassuring her. That was all that mattered.

* * *

"Have you worked out a schedule yet?" Jeanette asked.

Lori was having coffee with Jeanette, as she'd been doing every Tuesday, at Jeanette's insistence. Lori knew Jeanette was worried that she might be falling apart, and Lori appreciated the attention, even if Jeanette wasn't always helpful. How could she be? Not in their competitive town where even the best of friends felt the need to measure and compare against an increasingly unattainable ideal of success.

"Next weekend, they go to Peter's from Friday night to Monday morning. He says he can get them to and from school, and he wants to do that two, maybe three weekends a month depending on work."

"Are you okay with that?"

"I think so, at least for now. It feels like too much time away, but it won't amount to anything. He'll keep them once a month, maybe. It means I can keep things steady for the kids through the school week."

"You get the hard parts, you realize that, right? He gets to be Captain Fun."

"I know. I want to minimize the impact. I'm trying to be accommodating so Peter will focus on finances. I've got to figure out how quickly I need to get a job."

"Do you have to rush into that?"

"I don't know. It'll be a huge change for the kids."

"Kid's adapt."

"I guess. That's just one item on my long list of worries."

"What else?"

"You know how people have to do lists?"

Jeanette nodded.

"Well I have a list of how do you… Fill in the blank." Lori paused to sip her coffee.

"It's terrifying. How do you lease a car? The minivan lease is up next month. Peter told me to get another one. I don't think I've been in a car dealership in fifteen years. The sales people will be fighting over who gets to screw the unsuspecting housewife."

"What?!"

"Wait, no! Your mind's in the gutter. I just mean they know a sucker when they see one. I have no idea what a car should cost."

"Want me to ask Richard to help you?"

"Going car shopping with your husband sounds even more humiliating."

"Richard would eat it up."

"Ach, I don't know. How much do I spend? I've got no idea what my income will be."

"Can't Peter just buy you a car?"

"I asked him. He said it's going to be my car. I should learn how to do it."

"What else is on your list?"

"This thing called searching for employment. Apparently, I need to set up a Linkedin account and upload a resume and have a social media networking strategy. I don't think I've looked at my resume in ten years."

"Why don't you give yourself a few more months before you start thinking about that."

"Okay, then what about health insurance? I can COBRA once the divorce is final. It costs a fortune, though, and eventually it runs out."

"You've got a while before that happens. Can you write yourself a reminder to worry about that, maybe a year from now?"

"You know what I really dread?"

"What?"

"Going to the pool this summer."

"Why on earth?"

"The pool is for intact families. Mothers sitting around half watching their kids while they gossip and shop online. They can do that because they have husbands who want to take care of them, not dump them at the first itch. I don't belong there."

"Of course, you do. You're not the first divorced woman in this town, you know that, right? Certainly, you're not the only person in an unhappy marriage."

"Sometimes it feels that way. It feels like people are looking and talking."

"Sweetie, that's all in your head. If they are talking, it's to avoid admitting their own problems, which are likely worse."

"Jeanette," Lori took a breath, "I know you're trying to be helpful, and you're saying all the right things. I even know most of it is probably true."

"It is true."

"This endless loop of worry just keeps circling inside my brain. I don't even realize that I'm listening, except suddenly, I forget where I'm driving, and I stop in a panic when I'm, like, buying milk."

"Go away for a few days when the kids are with Peter."

"By myself?"

"Sure."

"I haven't gone anywhere alone in twenty years."

"Go to one of those fancy spas in Virginia. Let them pamper you. No thinking for a whole weekend."

"Come with?!"

"No way. I go nowhere except games and tournaments since Jonathan made the travel soccer league."

"So, I should go off and have a good time while everyone else dutifully takes care of their children?"

"Why not. Go someplace really nice and charge it to Peter's credit card."

Lori made a face.

"Look, from everything I've read, your financial circumstances will change, and not for the better. Women get the short end in divorce. Even if you end up better off than most because of Peter's earnings, he'll still become wealthy, and you, well, may not."

"Thanks for the optimism," Lori said, silently adding non-divorced friends' casual smugness to her list of worries.

Not that Jeanette was wrong. Jeanette had the benefit of an intact family, and Lori had been reading those same depressing articles about her doomed financial prospects.

"I'm just saying, use Peter's money while you can. Get away from the worries for a few days."

"I'm not sure I can."

"Google some places. See if it changes your mind. Or sign up for match.com. Go on a date. Maybe that will help."

Chapter 10

Lori tried. First with the few obligatory set-ups by friends and acquaintances with men she was expected to like. These dates were as much fun, and one-sided, as sitting in the dentist's chair, or watching a rare sporting even with Peter. Mansplaining, that was one of those newfangled words that made perfect sense to Lori. Her dates seemed to assume, no career, no brains, certainly nothing worthwhile to add to what Lori could hardly bring herself to name a conversation. Lori had started to slip out of early from PTA meetings before someone could ask for her permission to give her number to their recently divorced brother-in-law.

* * *

There was an entire book club devoted to Lori's potential new love life. It was a group of women who'd met years before on the elementary school blacktop. To a one, they had given up a career, and they met every few weeks, during the yawning hours in the middle of the school day. They'd start with the book they'd assigned themselves, before moving on to a never-ending discussion about kids, and husbands, and the unexpected, very real confines of their lives.

These women were well educated, well-traveled, devoted to their children, and, since they were honest with each other after so many conversations, and salads and, lately, bottles of white wine, could admit, bored, some days out of their skulls. And afraid. They could already feel their children leaving them behind. Then who would they be? Each had stopped working long enough ago to be incapacitated by thoughts of stepping into the real world again. They fretted about it, a lot, actually. Though lately, Lori's specific fears and challenges had been appropriated as the club members' obsession. They encouraged, and were proud of, Lori's baby steps in considering work again and dating. Not that Lori felt she had much choice.

Last month, they opted for another bottle of wine, popped open someone's laptop, and helped Lori beef up her rather pathetic online dating profile. It was the most animated gathering she'd been to in years. When Lori read the words again later, she was struck by how they'd created an idealized version of a suddenly single, interesting, and brave woman. As if, despite her obvious pain, they perceived her dislocation as a way to imagine a new beginning (for themselves?) with an idealized man. He would be handsomely aged, already wealthy enough to give her (them) all she (they) desired.

Whatever the crazy methodology, she posted the new profile and the results were an immediate boon. Her inbox greeted her daily with suggestions for personalized matches, and, after playing with some winks, Lori paid for the premium service to send and receive messages.

The men sounded thoughtful and funny and genuinely interested. Some were even good looking, if profile pictures were to be believed. She had six dates in twelve weeks and realized about twenty minutes into each that the guy only wanted sex, or at least a blow job, in exchange for the privilege of being asked out at her advanced age, what with young women being how they were these days. She'd almost taken a vow of celibacy. It wasn't worth the effort, or, frankly, the humiliation.

* * *

Then she met a gentleman—at the neighborhood pool of all places. Samuel. Never Sam, he told her. Lori was playing a silly game in the pool with Catherine. It'd been a tough summer. At that moment, though, she and Catherine were their old, close selves. Besties having fun. Samuel had watched them for a while. Lori noticed. He noticed that she noticed. Eventually he came over and squatted at the side of the pool. He came right out and asked, "I see you're not wearing a ring. Are you married?"

It took Lori off guard, so she said yes when he asked if she'd like to get coffee. She gave him her email address thinking, it's the local pool, it's safe, he'll probably never contact me anyway. He sent her a message immediately, threw out a few things about himself and asked about her. It turned out they had a lot in common; growing up in the suburbs as part of close knit families; parenting two teenagers, though his were both boys, a little older than hers, and spent half their time with him; hints on the horizon (his closer) of parents' failing health, soon to be sandwiched between competing needs of the young and the aging. Samuel ran marathons and took his boys skiing out west every spring break.

Their emails were an unexpected, fun challenge for Lori to match Samuel's humor and intelligence. Within two weeks, Samuel had taken her to coffee and lunch, then a fancy dinner. He dispersed information subtly, but it was clear he was broadly educated, well connected, and monied. When Lori made a self-deprecating comment, Samuel quickly pooh-poohed it. He thought she was a catch. Not only available, smart, attractive, and interesting. It surprised Lori. She'd believed those things about herself once. Why had that changed? The ladies in her book club were thrilled.

Nothing much physical had happened yet, though Samuel was clearly interested. He was already talking about plans for a weekend away. The more she thought about how much she should like Samuel, how they would be a perfect fit, the more she didn't. It didn't. Was it his age? He'd definitely started aging in ways she hadn't. Wasn't that what her friends were advocating—wealth and the freedom to enjoy it that came with maturity? Maybe it was just basic chemistry. None of her molecules were clamoring to collide, transfer energy, make heat with Samuel's. That hadn't been a requirement for ages, though.

A relationship with Samuel is a good thing, Lori told herself.

They would enjoy friends in common. Hell, they probably already had some. The Washington, DC area became a very small place at a certain income level. They'd have solid conversations and enjoy sophisticated, middle-age activities. Their kids might even like each other. She knew Ben regretted not having a brother he could wrestle with as their primary form of communication. She would never have to worry about money. She paused on that one, and that Samuel resided where her life had long taken root.

Why then, when she was with Samuel, did her thoughts wander to her to do list, her grocery list…, to be honest, thoughts about Brandon, comparisons to Brandon? Brandon who lived as far away as someone could live without crossing an ocean, and she wasn't even sure how he made a living out there.

Lori said yes to more dates. They made out on Samuel's designer couch in his beautifully appointed living room. She felt as clumsy as a middle schooler, awkward, and overly aware of the mechanics involved in touching unfamiliar hands, and lips, and tongue. It was okay, nice enough. Samuel was pushing hard for her to commit to a weekend. They couldn't find a mutual time when both sets of kids would be with their other parent.

When he tried for another dinner date, Lori had conflicts. She had a lot on her plate with her kids, and maybe needing to find a new place now that she was considering letting Peter buy her out of their house. A couple more legitimate reasons why Lori couldn't meet him for the next two weeks, and Samuel sent her an email saying it was obvious they were seeking different things. She let go of the neatly packaged possibility, despite that it left her feeling a little empty and disappointed when Samuel's emails no longer appeared in her inbox. Still, Lori felt stronger for her decision. She would learn something from Peter's leaving, about the dangers of settling.

* * *

Lori found herself googling weekend specials at places in driving distance. Wasn't that what Jeanette had suggested, an all about me weekend? The Homestead Resort popped up. A grand dame hotel that reeked with elegance. It wasn't too far, and they took exceptionally nice care of you. Lori remembered from when she'd been there with Peter and the kids on one of his law firm's retreats. The biennial event always felt like a less-than-adequate apology to families for depriving them of a spouse or a parent; maybe it was a bribe.

I can be more creative! The thought of traveling somewhere, anywhere, alone, though, was almost too much. Not to have to agonize over the decision about rooms. Were three rooms too extravagant, or instead each kid with a parent? Would that disappoint Peter? To think only about what she might want. The freedom was unnerving.

It's only a weekend, stop sweating it. She could carve out almost four days if she planned right. She'd never been to Charleston or Savannah, cities she heard had loads of charm. The kids always made a face when she suggested them. Either one was an easy flight and she could pay with some saved up airline miles.

Somehow, though, without seeming to think about it, she was staring at a computer screen comparing flights and airfare from DC to Seattle. She could leave around noon on a Friday two weeks from then and take a red eye back that would get her home before the morning school bells rang. She bought the ticket, just like that, without checking with anyone. She felt proudly independent, until it occurred to her that Brandon might have other plans. She hadn't texted or talked to him in months.

Chapter 11

I'm coming to Seattle." Lori texted Brandon, recognizing that a call might be more appropriate. She told herself she didn't want to put him on the spot.

"If you're in town, I'd love to see you, if you have some time."

"What!?" Brandon responded within seconds.

"I've got a weekend without the kids, I thought I'd take advantage. Obviously, if you're busy or will be away, I understand. Maybe you could give me some ideas for things to do."

"Lori, are you coming to Seattle, or are you coming to see me?"

"Both, I guess. I don't want to interfere with your plans."

"If you're coming to see me, I have all the time in the world. I'll re-arrange any plans and I would hope you'd stay at my place."

"I can stay at a hotel, really. I don't want to take you away from Fiona."

"If you are coming to see me, I'll make sure Fiona stays with her mom. Are you?"

"I've never been to Seattle, I've never been to the Pacific Northwest. There are things I'd like to see," Lori texted back, frustrated with Brandon for forcing the issue.

"If you're coming because you're in desperate need of sightseeing, I can book you a hotel room," Brandon responded, followed by an annoying winking emoji.

Lori paused, thumbs poised, not sure what to say next. Brandon got there first.

"I just want to know your intentions, Lori. A few months

ago, I was pretty sure I'd lost you. Forever. Just when I thought I'd found you again. I can't go through that again."

Lori's thumbs remained stalled over the phone. She and Peter had played that game for so long, verbal evasion around seething resentments and private anger. She'd forgotten it was possible, maybe even desirable, just to state how you feel and ask for what you wanted.

"I'd like to see you."

"Almost good enough, baby."

There it was again, that word and the immediate physical response in her belly, butterflies, and below, a surge of desire.

"I'm coming to see you."

"Excellent! Was that so hard?" Another winking emoji.

Damn him. "Yes, it was actually."

"I hope it gets easier. Stay at my place, okay? It'll be like old times, without Joanne checking on us, unless you want me to invite her. She'd be on a plane in a New York minute!"

"LOL, no."

"Which part no?"

"No to Joanne, I'd love to stay at your place."

"Great. I can't believe you're coming!"

* * *

Lori found herself floating through the next weeks. She wanted to tell Emily, tell Jeanette, tell somebody about her plans. She stopped herself. Lori knew it was better to have a secret. So, she took innocuous steps, started to pack a little bag in her closet, some pretty clothes she hadn't had a reason to wear. Maybe she'd buy some lingerie. It was so nice just to pack for herself. Travel always involved four suitcases, rounding up what Peter and the kids might need for every possible contingency, and then throwing her things together at the last minute, inevitably forgetting something important.

"What's the weather like out there?" Lori texted Brandon. "I'm trying to figure out what to bring."

"Perfect Indian Summer weather," he responded almost immediately, "and BTW everyone's very casual here."

"I don't need to pack anything fancy?"

"Nope. Nothing much at all."

"Not sure what you mean? Is there something in particular I should bring?"

"LOL. No. I'm hoping you'll be naked most of the weekend."

"Oh."

"Not what you had in mind?"

"I didn't say that, just catching up I guess."

"I've missed your beautiful body. A weekend's not much time and I want to see it as much as possible."

"That's sweet of you to say, Brandon. It's not the same body, you know. I've had two kids."

"Don't do that."

"I'm just trying to keep your expectations reasonable."

"That doesn't sound like much fun."

"I'm serious Brandon!"

"What are you serious about?"

"You've been divorced for a while. You've had lots of girlfriends I'm sure. I haven't been with anyone except Peter since we married. I'm not sure I'll be very good at, you know, that stuff."

"What stuff? 😊 😊"

"You know what I mean."

"It's not just sex I want, Lori. It's you."

"You say that."

"You gotta stop. Want to know what I've been fantasizing about?"

"I guess so."

"Love the enthusiasm!"

"I'm sorry."

"Don't be. I've been picturing you a lot from behind."

"Oh, great!"

"Don't you know how sexy you look that way?"

"Not really."

"I would love to look at you after a good fuck. Running my

finger down your long, curved back, right down to your beautiful ass."

"I'm sure it's not so beautiful anymore. And really, fuck?"

"It's a good word. Sounds exactly like it should—big, loud, fun sex. What word would you prefer?"

"I'd prefer make love."

"That sounds a little delicate for what I remember us doing."

"You still remember us together? Being like that?"

"It's all I've been thinking about since you said you were coming."

"I've been thinking about it too."

"Can't say the word yet? ☺ It's okay. Fucking's not all I've been thinking about. Remember how I loved to brush your hair away from your neck and kiss the soft skin there? Why'd you cut your hair?"

"I don't know. It's easier to get out of the house in the morning." Lori inadvertently pulled at a piece of her cropped hair, as if to stretch it.

"I loved when it was long and wild looking."

"I loved when you stroked my hair. It felt like an instantaneous sync, no matter how long it had been since I'd seen you."

"I could have touched it all day."

"Do you know how hard it was? The way you made my body feel when you came into the room and I couldn't do anything about it because you were with a girlfriend or someone else was around?!"

"It was hard for me too."

"Idk. It couldn't have been the same. I felt crazed. Like if you didn't touch me, you know, down there, I was gonna die."

"You're adorable. It was the same for me, when you would show up with one of your boyfriends! I never wanted you more intensely than when you were with someone else."

"Wonder what that says about us?"

"Gluttons for punishment?"

"Catholic guilt?"

"Exactly."

"If you want it too much, it can't be a good thing, right?"
"LOL."
"Kinda dumb really."
"Let's change the story."
"We should at least try to enjoy a weekend without regrets."
"I will if you will."
"LOL. I promise to try."

Chapter 12

The days leading to Friday were unbearable. She went through the motions of homework, carpooling, the mass of electronic paperwork her kids' lives seemed to require. Meanwhile, a stranger hung around who dabbed on anti-aging cream night and day, bought new panties and a sexy bra. Treated herself to a bikini wax, something Lori hadn't done since spring break in college.

Finally, it came. She felt like a spy, secretly stashing her suitcase in her car the night before. She got up earlier than the kids, showered, shaved, put on makeup. That got Catherine's attention since Lori usually drove her to the bus stop in raggedy pajamas.

"Why you all dressed up mom?"

"I'm meeting a friend downtown, from my old job. I thought I should look the part."

"You're not going back to work, are you?" Catherine asked sounding grouchy.

"Not yet, sweetheart. I'm just having lunch. Though I'll have to at some point."

"Then, like, who will pick me up and stuff? I do not want to get stuck going to the after-school club. Only losers do that."

"Please don't get angsty on me, Catherine. This is hard for me too."

"I'm not getting angsty. I just don't see why you have to go back to work. Things are fine the way they are."

"Things are going to change, sweetie, I'm sorry, they just will."

"Why?" Lori sensed that Catherine was getting teary. "I really like that you're always home with us."

"I love being home with you, but if your dad and I get divorced, I'm going to have to figure out how to support myself."

"Then don't get divorced. Please. Don't." Catherine's last words came out like a sound from a wounded animal.

"Oh sweetie, I wish it was that easy." Lori chocked back her own tears. "I really do."

"Did you tell Dad to leave?"

"Of course not!"

"So, tell him to come back. Dad should be with us."

"I'm sure he wants to… It's, well, it's complicated."

"Why? It doesn't have to be." Catherine's tears had morphed to anger.

Lori couldn't answer Catherine. She felt a sudden wave of anxiety that left her near paralyzed. She pulled to the side of the road as someone honked behind her. How can we be doing this to our children? How could Peter not have talked to her first and tried to worked things out? She tried to calm herself. She could see that the bus was already there, idling.

"I want to talk more about this Catherine," her voice was shaky, "I really do, but the bus is here."

Lori pulled out erratically and then into the parking lot.

"Do you remember you're going to your Dad's house this weekend?"

"Yes," Catherine answered with a snarl.

Lori took a steadying breath. "I'll drop your stuff off later today."

"I want to go home first."

"Your father and I already made a plan. He'll get you at school."

"I don't like his house. It smells gross."

"He's just going to live there a few more months, and it's only a few days. I'll see you Monday, right after school. I promise."

Lori's, I love you got lost to Catherine slamming the car door. Lori watched the bus pull away, waiving stupidly in its direction even though Catherine would be busy greeting her friends. Lori sat there, in her crookedly parked car, until she got her tears under control.

* * *

At the airport an hour later, the stranger had returned, walking with confidence Lori didn't quite feel, in heels way higher than Lori was used to, and with more cleavage than she'd shown in years. Lori felt men's eyes on her. It was odd and exhilarating. Five and a half hours, locked in a pressurized tube, hurling across the sky alone, and all communication cut off... God, the luxury of it. Lori relished the unexpected insight, until anxiety crept back like a sneaky rat each time she revisited her conversation with Catherine. She downed a quick glass of white wine at a terminal bar before boarding.

Lori read a little on the plane. Gradually, she fell into daydreaming, mostly about those first seconds when she would see Brandon again. She pictured it like in a movie. She'd say something clever and he would laugh. She'd flip back her head, try to get a little movement from her too short hair, and he would pull her into an embrace, his hands at the small of her back, lips on lips, her foot lifted daintily.

* * *

Lori was startled awake by the hard impact of airplane wheels on a runway. She must have fallen into a deep sleep. She'd slept so little in the days preceding, and then a daytime glass of wine. What a lightweight. Lori quickly grabbing up her things. Walked determinedly through the terminal, until her legs suddenly turned to mush, muscles liquified by a volatile mix of anxiety and eagerness.

She hit the ladies' room to use the toothbrush and toothpaste she'd put in her pocketbook, at the last second, when it occurred to her she should. She applied some lip gloss. Rarely did she put on lip stick during the day and Brandon was never a person who'd wanted her to change. Lori peered into the mirror at almond shaped eyes that were dark, intense..., maybe even beautiful. She glimpsed her flushed cheeks, shiny, bemused lips, startled by the sensation of not being sure who was looking back.

* * *

She was about to text Brandon where to meet when she spotted him, leaning casually against the wall, just past the sign that said, No Return This Exit. She had a moment to catch him unaware, enough time to notice that he'd worn a sports coat for her, over a black t-shirt and jeans.

She saw another woman taking a second look at Brandon. He's here for me. Lori allowed herself that pride, before she stepped in front of him, smiling awkwardly, not sure how to compose her face. She held onto her handbag white knuckled tight. He didn't move, just looked at her the that way he did, like she was the only person in the airport, the entire world, his warm, teasing smile spreading slowly to his eyes.

"Hey," she said, finally, with a too squeaky voice.

"Hello." He reached out and touched her cheek, then put his fingers slowly through her hair.

Something in her shifted and Lori felt herself collapse from the release of her weeks long expectations. Brandon caught her, held her to his body with one arm across her back, his other hand holding her head sideways to his chest. Even though she was closer to his height in heels, Lori still felt the comfort of fitting snug inside the dimensions of his body. "I'm so glad you came," he whispered, his chin tucked down to her ear. Brandon let go only after a few minutes had passed in silence. Then, he took her hand.

Chapter 13

The highway from the airport took them north in the direction of the city of Seattle.

"Oh my god, look at those mountains. Wow."

"That's the Olympic Range, over on the Peninsula. They'll be even prettier when the snows fall."

Quickly then, they were passing right through the heart of downtown.

"There's the Space Needle!" Lori said, remembering that she wasn't just visiting Brandon. She was seeing a new city.

"Yup."

"Look at all those sailboats. It's such a pretty scene." Just at that moment, a small seaplane took off, then another landed. "I didn't realize Seattle was on the water, with all these, you know, seafaring activities going on."

"It's very lively here. Lots of outdoor activities."

"Wait, I thought it rains all the time," Lori said, sounding genuinely confused, looking through the front window at blue sky, no clouds in sight.

"It's our little secret. We try not to tell. Actually, Seattle can have spectacular weather in the spring, summer, and fall."

Lori was avidly scanning the view. "You get mountains and sea, all in one view. That seems kind of greedy."

"People here like to think they're just more deserving."

Lori laughed, and continued to take it all in as they drove over a large bridge and exited the highway, navigating a dense neighborhood of eclectic styled houses with intricate rock gardens and Japanese style fences.

"It's so different here from where I live," she told him. "I inhabit the land of the center-hall brick colonial, on a quarter acre plot, with a row of red azalea bushes under the front windows." Lori smiled as she pointed out a house painted three different shades of purple.

"You're really going wild, in DC, if you paint your shudders blue."

"They might just be U-Dub fans."

"U, what?"

"UW, University of Washington, that's how we say it."

"Oh. Cute. So, we're still in Seattle, you know, like, actually in the City? It doesn't feel like a city."

"Yeah, Seattle's mostly residential."

"Look at that," she pointed through the front windshield, "are those the same mountains?"

"Nope, we're heading east now. Those are the Cascades."

"You get two mountain ranges? It's starting to feel unfair!"

Brandon smiled at her and turned his eyes back to the road. Lori got quiet. This wasn't the conversation she expected. She felt silly playing the role of unschooled tourist.

"We're here." Brandon pulled up to the sidewalk in front of a small, craftsman style bungalow with a porch that spanned the width of the house.

"Ohhh...I've always wanted a porch with a swing," Lori said getting out of the car.

"That was at Fiona's insistence. When she's was about six. It's been well loved ever since. I get sad thinking about her not wanting to use it anymore."

They approached the house, Brandon jiggling his keys to find the right one.

"Welcome." He pushed open the wide, wooden door.

"It's beautiful," Lori responded, reflexively, and, she realized quickly, it was true. Bright and light, slightly modern furniture, and not a lot of clutter. She couldn't say the same for her own house. There was a bowl of wildflowers on the entrance table.

"Do you always have fresh flowers?" Lori raised an eyebrow.

Brandon smiled but didn't answer.

"It's not what I expected."

"You were remembering my dorm room, perhaps?"

"Perhaps."

"Fiona runs a tight ship. No letting me slip into bachelor pad hell."

"I like your daughter." It felt weird to say that, daughter. Of course, she knew Brandon was a father, she a mother, and still someone else's wife. The reality, though, was at odds with her desire to go backwards, if only for a weekend, to a time before they were any of those things.

"Can I get you something?"

"No, I'm fine. Maybe just a glass of water."

"You must be starving. It's a long flight."

"I'm a little bit hungry."

"I'll get you a snack. We can go someplace later for dinner."

Lori continued to examine Brandon's living room while he disappeared into the kitchen. She immediately fell in love with the stone fireplace and wood slab mantel. On the walls were black and white framed photographs, quirky compositions of Fiona, at different phases, each iteration catching the thoughtful, straightforward personality that Lori glimpsed during their brief meeting in New York. She sank into a sleek but comfy leather chair. Brandon returned jacket-less, with a plate of cheese, dried meats, and fresh bread that he put down on the coffee table. He sat in front of her on the ottoman and handed her a glass of ice cold water.

She pretended to be interested in it, looking down, feeling suddenly reluctant. Brandon reached over and tipped her face up with his finger, gently nudging her chin. Then he leaned in and kissed her, opening her mouth wider with the pressure of his lips. His tongue moved over her teeth and deeper into her mouth exploring with the confidence that it had been there before. Lori's restraint was faltering. No matter how reticent her brain, her body had been on tenterhooks, craving his touch for weeks. She met Brandon's tongue just as he pulled back.

"I have wanted to do that for so long," Brandon said shaking his head. "I can't fuckin' believe you are here. Excuse my language."

"Me either. Please don't stop."

Brandon's lips moved quickly to hers again, this time his tongue was more aggressive, pulling her close with his hand against the back of her head, his fingers tangled in her hair. He cupped her breast with his other hand. Lori gasped at the electricity of his touch.

"Am I moving too fast?" Brandon pulled away again. "It's just...I've been wanting this for so long."

"Believe me, it's all I've been thinking about." Lori looked down again. "It's just, I don't know, I'm still feeling a little shy."

"Look at me." He waited until Lori glanced up, then he leaned in and kissed her mouth with deliberate and tender movements. "See," he said releasing her, "I can do slow. How about a glass of wine?"

"That would be great."

"White or red?"

"Either is fine."

Brandon disappeared into the kitchen and came back with two large goblets of red wine.

"Was it hard to get away?" Brandon asked as he handed her a glass and sat across from her on the couch.

"A little," she said, after taking a large gulp, "Peter needs a lot of written instructions when he has the kids."

"Really? He always struck me as a smart guy."

"He is," Lori frowned, "though you can only be smart about the things you pay attention to." She took another big sip.

"Is that what went wrong?"

"Let's not go there," Lori said. The wine had already gone to her head.

"I want to backup." She got up from the chair, put her glass down on the table and sat next to Brandon on the couch. Lori put her hand on his thigh, looking at it there, not at him. She was still nervous, and there was a question that troubled her.

"Have you been with a lot of women since you got divorced?"

"Only a few," Brandon answered. "It's hard when you have a kid, and, I don't like starting at the beginning. I know people say it's the newness that's sexy for most people. I don't like not knowing, all the guessing and games."

"I haven't enjoyed the dating much."

"You must have lots of men interested." He drew her face toward his again, played with a tendril of hair. "You're so beautiful."

Lori had been noticing only the lines and spots, signs that she was closer to fifty than forty. To have someone look at her as if she was young again...

* * *

When they kissed this time, both their tongues darted and parried, encircling like birds in a courtship dance. The action was all in her mouth. Everything she felt, was in the space between her belly and crotch. The place her body always flipped and contracted when she was anxious or excited. This had an edgy thrill of desire mixed in, like a fire inside her.

She turned fully to face Brandon, brought her knees up and under her, pushed his shoulders down toward the arm of the couch, noticing how strong his arm muscles felt. Before long, she'd flattened herself, rubbing hard against his thigh to generate some amount of satisfaction, unable to wait for him to touch her there. Brandon surprised her by pushing her away and slipping out from under her. She sat up on her knees.

"I want to see you." He kept eyes locked on hers, watching. He waited. She wasn't sure what to do.

"Show me," he said finally.

Lori had worn a button-down shirt. She imagined it would feel sexy to be unbuttoned. She was going to do the unfastening, apparently.

Emboldened by need, and the look on Brandon's face, she suddenly believed she could look sexy, slowly fingering the edges of the buttons as she pushed each through its slit. She slipped off her sleeves, all the while watching Brandon watch her. She was glad she'd bought a new bra, transparent and gauzy, the material scratchy against her nipples. Lori suspected they were hard and brushed her finger against one, just to see. She made a noise she didn't recognize, a guttural sound that Brandon repeated, echoing voices as they faced each other.

Brandon brought his hands to her breasts and cupped them. He pushed the inner edges of the bra away exposing her nipples, his thumbs passing over each one, catching on their hard edge. There were two distinct gasps, and Brandon's mouth was on hers, quickly moving. He kissed her neck, her décolletage, pushing her breasts together, his face in her cleavage, breathing in deeply.

"God, you smell good."

Then his mouth was on her breast, sucking and gently biting at her nipple.

Lori wanted to be free of her jeans, free on anything between her and Brandon's body. She still feared showing more of herself, the stretch marks and loose tummy flesh, a gift from giving birth that kept on giving. Brandon opened her jeans. He pushed them down over her hips and she squirmed out of them entirely, her panties coming off too. She sat back on her shins to feel less exposed.

"Yours too," Lori said, her ragged voice surprised her.

Brandon lifted off his t-shirt. She had to admire the way he'd stayed in shape. His pectoral muscles were flat and squared with just the right amount of sexy, trimmed chest hair. Something to play with and feel against her skin. He stood up and pulled off each of his pants legs without breaking eye contact. The flesh remained taut even when bent at his midsection. He wasn't wearing anything else.

"No briefs versus boxers debate for you?"

"I go commando about half the time."

"Good to know," she said, and he was standing in front of her. Lori was looking directly at his penis. It was long, hard, curved up and slightly bent to the left, exactly how she remembered it and she couldn't help smiling.

"Are you laughing at my cock?"

"No, no, not at all. It's just so good to be like this again. Can I say hello to...should I call it your cock?"

Brandon laughed hard. "If you'd like. We would both be delighted."

Lori stroked her finger lightly along the bottom of his shaft, until she reached the head of his penis and circled the flared edge with her finger adding pressure. She could hear without looking Brandon's sharp breath in.

"Hello old friend," she said still not looking away from his... She couldn't help thinking about what her son once called it, his trouser snake, she smiled again.

"What are you laughing at?!" Brandon stepped back a little.

"Nothing! Come here," Lori said, willing him back with her eyes. She cupped his balls and tugged him gently toward her, took him in her mouth so he wouldn't move away again. She moved up and down his shaft, swirling her tongue around its head. Looking up at Brandon, she wanted to see him watch her, watching him, her mouth wet, in a circling O. She read need and pleasure written on his features. It drew pulled her into the moment. No more thoughts of home.

"Come with me," Brandon said abruptly, pulling out of her mouth. He took her hand and led her through the dining area, and down a hallway into a room that was dark, shades closed, with the gentle glow of flickering candles.

"When did you..."

Brandon put his finger to her lips, "it's your turn." He brought her to the edge of the bed and gently sat her down. She tried not to slump to hide her breasts. Brandon lifted her chin. With his other hand he licked his thumb, reached down, and rubbed it in a circle around one nipple and both were hard again.

It seemed impossible to remain shy when her body was so alert to Brandon's every movement and touch. Brandon raised himself above her and pushed her back on the bed. He brushed his lips against her diaphragm, tickled her naval with the tip of his tongue, moving down he planted kisses along her linea alba. They locked eyes and she wondered if he could see in her the things she was desperate for him to do and see also that she was afraid. He pushed his hands against her inner thighs, sensing, perhaps, her remaining resistance. It had become her habit with Peter, to close herself off in order to avoid sex.

"Relax, Lori," Brandon gently whispered, spreading her legs wide, and taking in her sex. He ogled her so appreciatively, it was torture.

She watched him kneel. His tongue found her clit immediately. She gasped, taking a breath after neglecting to breathe, her head fell back. His tongue seemed to be everywhere at once and then back, exclusively, on the one place where her relief was so much stronger than any qualms about whether her body was still attractive or if she would be good at this anymore. She came quickly, rising up from the bed crying out ohmygod, her entire abdomen clenched around the sensation of release.

"Good, I want you to be loud."

Lori felt herself dripping. She couldn't believe how wet she was. It'd been such a long time since her body, her pussy, just say it Lori, had responded so generously and Brandon's mouth and chin were glistening. She wiggled backward, not exactly trying to escape. Brandon stayed with her, his body over hers, knees locking her hips, hands holding down her forearms bent back by her head. His swollen, hard penis, its soft head, both were playing with her clit now, a touch, fire, then his hips pulling back. She lifted hers, chasing contact, demanding its return.

"Tell me what you want me to do." His voice was different, throaty, almost inhuman.

Lori shook her head. Why was it so hard? Was it only that stranger who could comfortably say words like pussy and cock?

"Just say it."

"I don't know, enter me," she barely uttered the words.

"What do you really want? I want to hear you."

"Fuck me." It seemed impossibly loud.

"That's good." He was pushing his cock inside her.

"Your pussy feels incredible." Brandon's voice was strangely pained.

Then he was kissing her, his tongue inside, his hips thrusting. Lori could taste herself on him, in her mouth, almost like he was fucking her in both places. His orgasm brought her to another climax. It surprised her that it happened, another so quickly, and nearly at the same time as Brandon's. They froze for a moment, Lori intensely aware of the aftershocks of her organism clenching around Brandon still inside her.

"Shit," he said and collapsed on his back next to her. "I haven't cum that fast or hard in a long time."

They were both still, looking at the ceiling, breathing hard for a few moments until Lori curled into Brandon's body, wrapped her arm and leg around him, traced the veins in his upper arm. She couldn't believe it, her sex, no, her pussy, that was exactly the right word, was acting with a will of its own, pushing up against Brandon's thigh, already wanting more.

"You're still the hungry girl I remember." Brandon's face had a look of such contentment.

Lori turned away abruptly to hide unexpected tears. It'd been so long since she had felt matched delight, and the exquisite reciprocation of desire. It stung suddenly to be reminded of her deprivation.

"Lori? Is something wrong?" Brandon wrapped his body around her back, tucked her shoulders into his arms.

"It's hard to put into words," she said.

"That's okay." Brandon held her tight.

She was grateful he didn't push her to explain. Instead, he kissed her hair, paired his breath with hers. She thought they might fall asleep, but she felt his cock hardening against her tailbone. Still facing away, she adjusted her body, took hold and directed it inside her. With her thumb, she pushed just the head in and out, feeling the ridge of his penis catch against the hard edge of her opening. She was surprised by what her fingers stumbled on, her down there lips beyond soft, swollen and silky slick.

"That's good. Play with yourself," he whispered, while grinding against her.

They stayed like that, spooning, not seeing the other, their hips moving in tandem until she came again on the edge of sleep.

Chapter 14

Lori woke, uncertain, for a moment, where she was. Brandon was curled around her from behind, still holding her tight. She listened to his steady breath, could feel it blow softly across her shoulder. Tears welled again. When had she last spent the whole night, any part of the night, tucked into someone's arms?

Lori reluctantly extracted herself, though, because she really had to pee. She climbed awkwardly over Brandon to get to the open side of the bed. Thankfully, a couple of candles remained lit and she made her way through the unfamiliar room and into the hallway. She could see through to the living room dimly lit by the glow of street lights and she noticed Brandon's t-shirt on the floor.

She went and pulled it on. Passing over her nose, she breathed deeply to smell his smell, just like she used to with her kids' clothing. A stolen snuffle as she gathered up miniature shirts and jeans and sundresses, hoping in those whiffs of sweat, spilled food, and grass stains, that she might catch hold of their fleeting joys. Brandon's scent was different, still familiar, the aroma of deep compatibility. Can smell reveal such a thing? Her nose detected a trace of Brandon's cologne, woods and leather—something almost animal like that she remembered well. It felt intoxicating to know he was so near.

On route back to the bedroom, Lori took a quick glance at her phone to make sure there were no texts from the kids. Jeanette was inviting her to see a movie. Lori would have to make up an excuse. It was three am, she noted, six in the morning East Coast time. That seemed to trigger her appetite, and Lori poked through Brandon's refrigerator. She spotted a container of Greek yogurt.

After several wrong picks, she found the drawer with the silverware, leaned against the countertop, removed the cover and, half aware, started to eat. It seemed a sudden recognition, her bare feet starting to feel the cold of the floor, that she was three thousand miles away from her kids, had just slept in a man's bed, not her husband, a strange bed, but one that felt, well, kind of like, home.

Brandon appeared, then, as a shadow at the kitchen entrance. He turned on the light. When she flinched, he quickly adjusted the dimmer. He was as naked as he'd been in bed, yet she felt like she was seeing the all of him, for the first time. Brandon was tall and thin when they were young. Clearly, he worked out now. Just the right amount. Not over the top muscles, like some boys gave themselves, looking awkward and bulky, arms so thick they no longer rested comfortably against their bodies.

She appraised Brandon, trying not to look obvious, the sculpted shoulders and biceps; slim and strong-muscled legs, relaxed at the moment; a well-defined stomach, no six pack. Still, there were indents in all the right places, highlighting musculature and triangulating his sweet spot which, with a quick glance, revealed a three quarters erect penis.

"What you lookin' at?" Brandon asked smirking.

"I'll assume that's a rhetorical question."

He laughed softly, such a warm, cozy sound in the dark, early morning.

"Have you been up long?" He walked over, tipped up her face and kissed her on the nose.

"No, just a few minutes. I was suddenly wide awake and hungry!"

"Jet lag can be tough, and we forgot to eat." Glancing at the yogurt in her hand, he said, "you probably need something more than that."

"I just wanted a little something. This is perfect. It's my favorite brand." Lori took another bite. "Want some?"

"Sure."

She scooped up a spoonful and fed it to him.

"You look good in my shirt, by the way, very, very sexy."

Brandon's mouth was half full, so the words sounded slightly garbled and sweeter.

Lori gave a twirl to acknowledge his compliment, then made a slight curtesy pulling out the bottom hem. With her bowed head, she could see that her legs still were still shapely, extending down from where the bottom of the shirt hit high on her thighs. She was frowned, though, when she looked back up.

"Peter hated when I wore his clothes."

"Why?"

"I don't know. I told him I did it to look sexy. He said he didn't like people touching his stuff."

"Wow. Whatever. Okay." Brandon leaned back against the countertop, so they were side by side. "Were you thinking about him? About home?"

"Actually, I was thinking about how strange it is to feel so comfortable, here with you, in your bed."

"Why strange?"

"It's been so long since we've seen each other, been together, or even talked. Our real lives, you know, our grown-up lives, happened without each other. I thought you'd feel like someone I don't know." She glanced sideways catching his eye.

"You don't."

"That's the thing about us," Brandon said as he put an arm around her, "we knew each other before we started making up shit, before we did all the stuff that was expected of us." He touched her cheek and turned her face back to him.

"I bet I know the real Lori, the one maybe no one else knows."

"That's interesting," she said shifting from his gaze, because I'm not sure I know who Lori is anymore."

"You knew back then."

"Did I?" She looked at him again fiercely. "I can't remember it at all."

"You were so smart, Lori. You were gonna save the world."

"Wow. I don't know if that should make me laugh or cry." She turned away, said nothing for a while.

"You know," she said finally, "I always felt most alive when you and I were fighting some cause, being big fat pains in the world's ass. In the end, though, you scared me."

"What? How?" He backed off the counter, so he could regard her directly.

"You were uncompromising," she said, "and restless. I was afraid where you would take me."

Brandon gazed at her not understanding.

"I guess I wanted my fights to be manageable, family friendly affairs." Lori smiled, even as she shook her head. She'd never quite put those old feelings into words before.

"Instead, I've managed myself into, what? Boredom? Irrelevance? I don't want to sound melodramatic. I just don't feel like there's much left that's me anymore."

"You're an attorney. You went to one of the best law schools in the country."

"Yeah, great. My point exactly! I can hardly call myself that these days."

"Stop that. Education doesn't just fade away, not unless to you let it. You're a mother too. That's the most important job, even if our hypocritical society only pays it lip service." Brandon lifted her chin, forced her to look at him.

"You're right. Being a mom has been my greatest happiness…, and my undoing." She looked down again, went back to a silent place. After a few moments she spoke to him with puzzlement.

"I still can't believe you have a kid. You were so adamant you didn't want that."

"I surprised myself," Brandon said leaning back again against the counter. "I think the reason I said those things was because I was afraid. My parents weren't great role models. I didn't want to repeat their mistakes."

"Our kids will say that about us one day. You know that, right?"

Brandon laughed, "it's true." He paused, seeming to elicit a memory.

"One day, I'm sure it was more gradual than that, but I only remember waking to a sudden, overwhelming need to have a child. It felt like the most important thing, more important than having a wife, though one kinda went with the other."

"Is that why you married Jocelyn?"

"It was a big part of it. She and I had been on and off again for so many years by then. We either had to break up for good or get married. Never the best circumstances to say, I do." He gave her a sad smile. "Of course, you were already taken."

"Were you ever happy as a couple?"

Brandon gave a tired sigh. "Yea. Maybe. Sometimes. Let's save that conversation for daylight. Do you think you can sleep a little more?"

"I think so."

"I'll take you out for coffee in the morning. Have you heard we have a very intense relationship with our coffee in Seattle?"

"I've heard something about that."

The brief banter made Lori feel light on her feet, and sleepy. She followed him back to the bedroom. Brandon lifted the covers for her, climbed in after, tucked her shoulder under his, her head under his chin, his other arm wrapped around her. Lori was sure she must have tossed and turned, gotten hot and thrown off the covers as she often did, yet Brandon was still holding her just as faithfully when they woke.

Chapter 15

They had coffee at a neighborhood cafe. There were three or four places they could have chosen, each with a distinct feel, none she'd heard of. Brandon just raised an eyebrow when she asked if they were going to Starbucks. Thankfully, she'd put on her shortish yoga skirt, with exposed zipper pockets, and her heels. She didn't look quite so suburban mom, if not exactly matching the hipster vibe around her. Lori found a table while Brandon went to order. She felt anxious again, wondering when the adventure would wear off and they'd run out of things to say.

On her last date night with Peter—it was a homework assignment from their very brief encounter with a marriage counselor—she and Peter struggled to find things to talk about. Lori certainly felt it as a struggle, making opening gambits with topics unrelated to Peter's work or their kids. Each fell flat, unreciprocated, the failed conversations accumulating like a bunch of rain clouds stalled over their small table at the restaurant. When she brought up her concern, hesitantly, the next day. Peter was incredulous. We went on a date. He snickered a little at the word. We saw a movie and had a nice bottle of wine. So, they didn't talk a lot. Why is that a problem? Lori hadn't been sure which of them was right.

* * *

Brandon handed her a mocha coffee made with the cafe's homemade blend of chocolate. On the top of her drink, the barista had made a beautiful heart shaped design with the latte foam.

"That's so pretty! And you remembered I'm a chocoholic!"

"I remember a lot."

"You make that sound like a bad thing."

"Not at all." He sat down next to her. They glimpsed out the cafe window as they sipped their coffees.

"Do you remember that night we all hung out together," Brandon asked eventually, "a few months before you got married? You, me, Peter and Jocelyn."

"Yeah, I think so. Jocelyn and Peter met for the first time and really hit it off, right? Comparing notes about their proper New England upbringings."

"That's the night."

"We were living in Northern Virginia. We'd just moved, and you were visiting Sarah. You came over to see our place."

"I'm pretty sure I came to see you."

"You know what I mean!"

"Do you remember that you and I went outside?"

"I remember the townhouse we rented. It had a tiny backyard that you could get to from downstairs, and a little deck off the living room upstairs."

"You said you wanted to show me something you'd planted, I don't know, some nonsense. The minute you got me out under that deck, you kissed me."

"Oh my god, I did that didn't I?"

"I figured, if we're playing that game, I had my tongue down your throat, my hands all over you. I loved how quickly your nipples got hard, and then I grabbed your ass before you could pull away."

"And Peter and Jocelyn were inside, right upstairs?"

"They were."

"Wow. That was ballsy."

"Do you remember what you asked me?"

"Brandon, it was like twenty years ago."

"You said please don't let me marry Peter."

"I did not say that!"

"Yes. You did."

Lori stopped talking. She took a slow sip of the mocha, her eyes focused on the frothy milk heart stretching apart. She looked up to find Brandon waiting for her to speak.

"I did say that," Lori voice was very quiet. "I remember. How could I not have remembered until now?"

"I don't know."

Lori made a strange noise, trying to hold in tears, pain, regret, she wasn't sure, though it must have suggested she was about to faint.

"Lori, what is it? Are you okay?" Brandon grabbed her shoulders.

"Why?" Lori said with the little breath she could manage.

"What? I can't hear you."

"Why did you...let me...marry him?"

Brandon looked sickened then. "I don't know. After the sneaky kissing, we went back inside. We each went back to being with the other person we belonged to. I know I drank a whole lot more. We said our good nights, and two weeks later, Jocelyn and I got your wedding invitation in the mail."

"It wasn't always terrible, you know."

"What wasn't?"

"My marriage. For a while, it felt like we were building something."

"I know that. It's probably why I didn't do anything to stop you. That, and I couldn't bring myself to hurt Jocelyn. We share that gene."

"Which one?"

"The nice gene. No, the guilt gene."

"So, we both got married because it was hard to say oops, sorry, made a big mistake?"

"Actually, as much as I didn't want to, I liked Peter. He seemed like a solid guy. He made a good case about why he became a lawyer. He was going to apply to be a prosecutor in a year or two and stop defending corporations. It was obvious he couldn't believe his good fortune that you agreed to marry him." Brandon shrugged. "How could I deny him that? He was damn lucky, and he said he knew it."

"When you visited that time," Lori sat back, remembering, "I was working day and night at the law firm. I was surprised how much I liked it. You had to be quick and tough and smart—and I liked succeeding, even if I secretly worried I'd sold out. Peter and I had our secret weapon, we would leave to do good work once we'd paid off our student loans, bought a little house, started a family." Lori paused to look directly at Brandon.

"I just wasn't sure...you and me, together... We were dreamers." Lori's voice drifted off. "I didn't think we'd be able to pay our bills."

"You weren't wrong, Lori. Honestly, some months I still struggle to make ends meet."

"Peter and I got seduced by success." Lori looked down feeling the shame of it. "Peter never left the law firm. I guess you know that," she said looking up again. "I tried to keep up with what was expected after Ben was born. It was impossible. I had divided loyalties, and that wasn't a tenable position for either side. So, I quit. They kept promising Peter more. Turned out he was very ambitious. Nothing in our life was balanced or equal after that." Lori stared into her cup of coffee as if there was an answer there.

"Maybe I got dull and distracted at home with the kids," she continued. "I certainly failed to anticipate that Peter's striving would annihilate his generosity and kindness." Lori glanced up at Brandon, surprised to be finally understanding the things she was telling him.

"We have a lot of money, Brandon. To be precise, Peter's made a shit load, and there's almost no charity or joy in spending it."

"Lori, honestly, I don't know what to say. Who knows if it could have gone down differently. It doesn't sound like you were the one who sold out." Brandon gulped his last bit of coffee.

"All I know is right now, I want to take you back to my place and start making up for all this fucking, wasted time."

Chapter 16

By the time they got back to Brandon's house, Lori felt the awkwardness creep back from the divergent paths their lives had taken, and all the years they'd been apart. She followed his lead, kicking off her shoes at the front door. When he took her hand and led her through the living room, though, Lori side stepped into the kitchen, and rummaged through the cabinets for a glass. She moved to the sink, filled it, took a gulp, finally turning around to find Brandon there, surrounding her, with barely a hair's breadth between them. Brandon watched her take another long drink, then he took the glass from her, set it on the counter, rested his hand there. Lori was looking at her toes.

"Don't tell me you're turning shy again?"

"Maybe."

"Are you worrying about something?"

"No. I feel comfortable here, actually, with you."

"Then what is it?"

"I don't know." She looked up finally. "It's embarrassing to say. I'm not used to so much sex."

"You're joking?"

"Not really."

"You loved sex. My horny girl, I called you."

"I remember that!" Lori smiled, but it faltered.

"Honestly, no one would describe me that way, certainly not Peter."

"Forget him."

Brandon moved his hand from the counter and grabbed Lori's lower back tightly to press her hips against his. Leaning down, his lips opened hers, his tongue filled her mouth, so tight against her, he barely left space to breathe. He brought his other hand to wrap her throat, not chocking Lori, but possessive. When he finally released her, he asked,

"How does that make you feel?"

"Like I'm twenty years old again."

Brandon brought his hand to her belly, spreading his fingers just below her naval. She could feel the heat from his hand through the thickness of her skirt.

"I mean here," he said. "How does it feel here?"

"It feels great."

"No. Really tell me. Describe it."

"I don't know. I don't have words for this anymore."

"Try. Close your eyes."

"Alright. It feels, well..., liquid-y hot, like your hand is turning my insides into molten chocolate." Lori smiled, kept her eyes shut, concentrating.

"There's almost pain, too, an aching, no, more like an emptiness that needs filling. I can actually feel the inside of my body, straining against your hand, waking up from some long-imposed confinement."

"Does it make you want something?"

"God yes, there's that itch, no, that's not right exactly, that sweet place that can barely stand the wait to be touched."

"Keep your eyes closed." It sounded more a command than request and one her body dare not ignore.

Time stopped, every nerve in her body centered on that one infernal spot. Brandon put his knee between her legs, separating them. He took his hand from below her belly and lifted up the front of her skirt to the edge of her panties. He slipped his hand inside them, pausing for a moment, pressing the palm of his hand against her pubic bone. She could feel his warmth.

His other hand was no longer at her back. Brandon wasn't kissing her, or touching her anywhere, except his hand on her pussy. She kept her eyes firmly shut. She was sure his were fixed on her face. His middle finger brushed through her pubic hair, like a thing unto itself. It touched the flesh of her other lips making them tingle and swell in response, finally granting her the exquisite relief of finding the center of all her longing. That one finger was like a snake at play with what was, Lori was sure, her plump, engorged clit, announcing its readiness like a baboon's red ass. Lori pressed her back against the counter edge, using its solidity to curl every muscle in her pelvis around his finger on her clit.

She knew she was still holding back, a part of her trying to disengage, as if her pleasure sensor was not quite convinced it was programed to feel this good. Brandon must have sensed it too. His finger moved away for a moment to find her wet hole, in and out, its own delicious reward, he captured her juices, anointed her with them. Then his thumb played fast and hard on her clit and moved away again. His middle finger curling out, sloppy with wet, slowly circling her clit, teasing, hard pressure and friction again with his thumb. It was near agony.

He seemed to want to build arousal, layer upon layer, to see how powerfully he could make her cum. Her orgasm was a slow burning eruption, her mouth curled in a circle of ecstasy, sucking in breath, slowly growling out a word, or maybe a sensation. She worried she might be drooling, fuck it, ingrained caution finally lost to the singular sensation of release.

"Brandon, how the... Shit!" Lori opened her eyes in an effort to rectify her incoherence. Brandon's eyes shone as if reflecting wildfire.

"Do you know how turned on you just made me?"

"I'm not sure I'm responsible for anything that just happened."

"You're wrong baby, come here."

Brandon's mouth was on hers again. Without stopping he pulled up her skirt, then yanked her panties down over her hips. He picked her up, sat her on the edge of the sink. Only then did he leave her mouth alone. She caught her breath while he unbuckled his belt, slipped off his pants. His cock already stiffly perpendicular as it pushed out from under his t-shirt. She lifted his shirtfront to enjoy a view of his stomach and the sexy triangle of muscles that lead down from there to his erection.

"You look so great." Lori was smiling approvingly.

"I love the way you're looking at me, but what I really want to do right now is to fuck you. Are you okay with that?"

Without answering, Lori put her arms around Brandon's waist, lifted her face to his, opening her mouth to present him full, wet lips. She reached down and grabbed his ass with both hands. His tongue and cock seemed to penetrate her at the same time, thrusting from above and below, a sensation of simultaneous fullness in her pelvis and her mouth.

Brandon's hard thrusts ground her into the sharp edge of the sink as her brain unconsciously hummed hurts so good. He groaned a loud fuuuuuuck, as he climaxed, and Lori tightened around him, her pussy responding to the continuing reverberations of his eruption. She could feel his hot cum shoot into her, adding to her own wetness soaking his cock. The kitchen filled with a pungent smell of something better than any food.

When Brandon pulled out, Lori's butt slipped into the sink. They collapsed in laughter. Such a profound release. Lori could feel her brain shift from the eviscerating tension of climax and settle into its fuzzy afterglow. She was suddenly certain that everything in her life would be better because of what sex with Brandon had given to her body, and her self-esteem.

Then exhaustion, the jet lag and chopped up sleep, caught up with her. Brandon suggested a nap on the couch, and maybe a fire.

"I know it's sacrilege; it's sunny outside, but how 'bout it?"

"That would be perfect. I love fires," Lori said. "Catherine and I make them a lot, after dinner. Well, we press a remote control and flames appear."

Brandon raised his eyebrows.

"I know. It's cheating. It's fast, though." She laughed. "We put a little blanket in front of the fireplace and make some hot chocolate, like were camping." She looked away as if to picture it. "I think there was maybe one time in the past five years when Peter got home in time to join us. He promptly took up the whole blanket, fell asleep, and started snoring. Catherine and I found another place to drink our cocoa." Lori turned back to Brandon.

"I'm sorry, do you mind me talking about them? Him?"

"Of course not." Brandon took her hand and led her to the couch.

"Does Fiona like to make fires?"

"Absolutely, that's why I built this thing."

"You built this?"

"There was the chimney and a hole in the wall. I did the stone work and the mantel."

"It's beautiful. It was the first thing I noticed when I came in."

"That's what I was going for."

"I don't remember you being so handy."

"Sure, you do. Every summer, my mother gave me a project to do on her house or yard. You'd walk by and if we were outside, you'd stop to talk to me, and which ever cousin she corralled into helping me that year."

Lori nodded as she sat down on the couch, suddenly able to conjure the scene Brandon was describing.

"I know I sound like a broken record. You remember a lot."

"About you, yes."

"It bothers me that I don't remember as much. I don't even know what you do for a living. Why don't I know that?"

"Maybe you never asked." Brandon sat down next to her.

"Last I knew you were studying for a Masters Degree in a really hard subject, like physics or something, right?"

"Close. Philosophy, and a PhD."

"You made it through?"

"I did."

"That's impressive. Do you teach?"

"I did, for a while. Turns out I don't have the temperament to spend all day in a classroom, even if I'm the guy standing in the front. The work wasn't, I don't know… I like to get my hands dirty, and the students…. No one was discussing it yet. It was already there, though, the coddled entitlement. It was a hard job to love."

"So now what do you do?"

"Guess?" He flashed a mischievous smile.

"You didn't go to law school without telling me?"

"No. I work with a lot of lawyers."

"Ach."

"No, the good ones."

"There are good ones?"

"You know there are. I work for the FBI. I'm a field agent."

"No! Really?"

"Does that surprise you?"

"Sort of, I guess. Not really. You were always defending the underdog."

"Now I go after the really bad guys."

"Is it dangerous?"

"Sometimes, yes."

"Do you like that?"

"Most days, I love it. Turns out I'm a bit of an adrenaline junkie."

"It sounds hard."

"No two days are ever the same. I like that. Lately I've been dealing with some awful criminals. You have to learn not to let it in too deep. That part's tricky."

"What are you working on?"

"Human trafficking. We're trying to identify and interrupt major rings moving in and around the West Coast. Some days, I swear, I don't want to let Fiona out of my sight."

"Oh my god, I can imagine."

"We've got a case right now... Never mind, I'll tell you some other time. I don't want to ruin our day. I should take you out to a nice lunch. You must be starving."

"I think I will be."

"You didn't eat last night," he sounded concerned.

Lori simply felt horny, that was the only word for it. Why did I give that up, and so willingly?

"Well, you did kind of feed me." Lori grinned. "I can't believe I'm saying this. I'd like some more of that."

"Ahhh," he laughed, "but you need real food. I want to take you to my favorite restaurant. Italian with a Pacific Northwest twist."

"If you insist," Lori smiled, "actually that sounds great."

"Sleep a little first."

Lori lifted her legs to the couch, tucked them under her while Brandon covered her with a blanket.

"I'm going to go grab some wood," a smile replaced Brandon's look of concern, "and make you a real fire."

Lori was asleep before the first flame flickered.

Chapter 17

When she woke sometime later, she didn't immediately see Brandon, so she went to take a shower. Lori turned the water cold for the last few seconds, and stuck her face straight under the nozzle. She needed to slap away the jet lag, the post-nap fatigue, and the feeling that she was still in one of those long, lovely dreams you desperately want never to wake from. She put back on the short skirt she arrived in, without the leggings. Lori wasn't quite sure if she looked sexy or silly.

"I think I'm too old to wear a mini skirt," she said when she walked back into the living room and found Brandon on the couch enjoying the fire.

"Out here, there's no such thing as too anything, you'll see. Anyway, you look hot. Your legs are still incredible."

Lori made a disbelieving face.

"Really, you look great."

* * *

The restaurant was on Capitol Hill. Lori loved the energy of the place, streets filled with art galleries, restaurants, and hip looking bars and also lots of people walking their dogs or out with babies in strollers like it was a regular afternoon in the neighborhood. It was near impossible to find a parking space, though, and they had a bit of a walk to the restaurant. Brandon put his arm around her shoulder as soon as they hit the sidewalk. Lori was suddenly nineteen again, walking with Brandon around another city, with no place to be, no one she was responsible for. It was, for a moment, as if no time had passed. She put her arm around Brandon's waist to show this new world he belonged to her. Lori's hand hit something large and hard at his hip.

"What is that?!"

"A gun."

"You have a gun with you?"

"Yes."

"Do you always bring that along?"

"Always."

"Hmm. I'm not sure I'm comfortable with that."

"It comes with the territory."

"Do I have a say?"

"Sorry, no."

"Really?"

"Really."

"Okay, I guess, for now. I think I want to talk about it."

"Can we put a pin in that for later?"

Lori smiled at the expression. "Sure. Let's enjoy dinner without getting into our first argument."

"It wouldn't be our first."

"We argued about pretty much everything, didn't we? I'd forgotten. It was fun, though, right?"

"You kept me honest, except when you were being a pain in my ass."

She walked through the restaurant door Brandon held open for her, smiling at the memory of her old self.

* * *

Brandon ordered Manhattans, in old fashioned glasses not martini.

Lori raised an eyebrow, "whiskey in the afternoon?"

"It's dinner time on the East Coast."

"True," Lori said.

Brandon offered her his bourbon-soaked cherry when Lori made a fuss over how delicious it tasted. He even asked the waiter to put an extra one in her second drink. It'd been a while since Lori had drunk anything besides wine. She felt tipsy by the time they finished pasta, short ribs, and salad. Brandon offered to get the car.

"Don't be silly. I'm fine. The walk will be nice after all that food."

They strolled back through pleasant side streets. At one intersection, they had a straight shot view toward Puget Sound. The sun was moving behind the Olympic mountains, framing their silhouetted peaks and shoulders with a blush of pale orange. In the forefront, was the flying saucer shaped glow of the Space Needle. Lori stopped to take it in.

"This City gets more than its fair share of scenic beauty."

"You'll have to visit in the winter, when everything's shrouded in clouds and drizzle," Brandon chuckled, "then see if you still think so."

They were approaching the car. Two people were next to it, Lori thought a man and a women. It was hard to tell they were so bedraggled. Suddenly, the one who looked more like a man lunged at the woman. The woman screamed. Brandon instantaneously thrust Lori back from him.

"Get behind a car," He said in a sharp tone, without raising his voice or looking back.

She did as she was told. Brandon walked toward the pair without hesitation.

"What's going on?" He asked.

"Nothing," the man replied.

"He's trying to kill me," the woman screeched.

"This ain't your business." The man was squaring his shoulders and angling his body in Brandon's direction.

"You need to walk away from her. Now." Brandon's voice was uncompromising.

"She owes me, and I told you this ain't your business."

Lori saw the glint of something in the man's hand. Brandon must have seen it too and he moved in front of the woman as if to shield her. The man lunged at Brandon. Lori meant to scream, she was sure of it. Before any sound came out, Brandon had dropped his weight, locked the man's arm with the back of his own, grabbed the back of the attacker's knife hand with his other hand. Brandon stepped back with one foot, spun his body suddenly to the left and the attacker was face down on the ground, his knife somehow in Brandon's hand. Lori uttered a weak gasp. Brandon planted his knee firmly on the man's back and held the attacker's arm behind his back. It looked painful. The man seemed in shock, and the women's hand shot to her mouth. Lori turned toward Brandon. He remained calm, his voice quiet, but menacing, as he ordered the man not to move.

"Call 911," he said to Lori while the woman yelled obscenities, seemingly at everybody involved, "and Lori," Brandon said, "stay where you are."

Lori fumbled at her phone as the woman turned to walk away.

"You need to stay right where you are, Ma'am," Brandon told her. She began cursing directly at Brandon, still, she stayed put.

They all remained frozen in their places until a patrol car pulled up, fairly quickly, Lori noted, with lights and sirens. Two officers jumped out and took control of the would-be attacker. They handcuffed him and put him in the back seat of their car. Brandon showed one officer what Lori assumed was his badge and they spoke briefly. The other officer tried to talk to the woman. She puckered her mouth like she might spit at him. It didn't seem like the way to behave when you had just been rescued from serious harm.

Lori was relieved to see that Brandon was heading back her way. She tried to say something to him. Her mouth was dry and, she realized, her whole body was trembling.

"It's alright. We can go now," Brandon said.

He put his arm firmly around Lori's shoulder, guided her to the passenger side of his car, opened the door and almost shoved her in. Just as quickly, he was around the car, in the driver's seat, and starting the engine. He accelerated out of their parking spot and they drove without speaking for what seemed like a long time. Lori stared straight ahead. The suddenness of the incident, and their silence, made her feel as if she'd imagined everything.

"I am so sorry," Brandon said.

"It's okay. You…, it just surprised me."

"I should never have let that happen. We could've come back later for the car."

"He was threatening her with a knife."

"I risked your safety. I would never have forgiven myself."

"I'm fine, really. You seemed to have the situation well under control. It was…well, remarkable." Lori looked down at her hands in her lap. They were still trembling.

"Nothing is ever totally under control, but I know what you mean." Brandon glanced over at her, "you're as white as a ghost." With one hand remaining on the wheel, he drew her close and held her awkwardly still constrained by her seatbelt.

"Let me get you home."

Chapter 18

"I think you need a shot of whiskey," Brandon said when they were safely back in his house.

"I think I've had enough for one day."

"I'm gonna have one." Brandon went to the kitchen, came back into the living room sipping something golden brown from a well filled glass.

"It's the good stuff," he said, a brand I just discovered, Envy of Angels.

"Great name. I don't usually drink straight whiskey. On second thought, though, I'll have a sip."

Brandon handed it to Lori and sat next to her on the couch. She liked how heavy the glass felt in her hand.

Wow, that's really good." She handed it back. He gestured for her to have another sip.

"Does that happen a lot?" Lori asked.

"God no. I mean, it could. This city practically invites the homeless to move here. There are so many people on the street with serious mental health issues. I usually avoid going downtown, unless it's for work."

"That's sad."

"It's being realistic."

"You may have saved that woman."

"People can be very unpredictable. There's and old cliché; sometimes even the worst swordsman can beat the best."

"You had your gun."

"I never want to use my gun, Lori."

"Really?" Lori looked puzzled.

"Really."

"I'm glad you helped her."

"She'll be back on the street tonight fighting with some other guy for a way to get high. There's just not enough resources, and sadly some people are beyond help."

Lori took another sip of the whiskey and handed it back to Brandon.

"I think it was good what you did out there. It felt real. The world I live in, people are so busy showing off their impeccable lives. None of it's true, under the surface, and, still it's exhausting to keep up."

"And I thought my job was hard." Brandon gave her a searching look, "you realize your describing Plato's cave."

She smiled back, suddenly remembering long ago college nights, studying, talking, always hoping that Brandon would reach out for her.

* * *

They stayed quietly on the couch, passing the whiskey glass between them.

"I liked you out there." Lori finally broke the silence.

"What do you mean?"

"You were strong, in charge. I knew you'd keep me safe."

"I'd never let anyone hurt you."

"I know that." Lori turned her body toward Brandon, bent one leg up over his lap. "The incredible thing is, I've always known it," Lori said looking directly at Brandon. She brought her hand to his cheek, stroked the edge of his jaw. "Somehow, I let myself forget how good it feels to trust someone that much."

Brandon put the glass down on the table beside him. He gathered her body the rest of the way over so that she was kneeling on his lap facing him. Their eyes locked, then his lips were on her, eyes and lips and throat. He quickly lifted her arms and pulled off her shirt. He pushed away the cups of her bra, tucked them under the swell of her breasts and stopped, it seemed, so he could appreciate the sight, until his tongue, sharp as the edge of a sword, found her hardened nipple. Brandon pulled away again with a sweet, wicked look on his face.

"Do you really trust me?"

"Apparently with my life." Lori grinned.

"Let me try something." His look was so direct, intense, eyes not so much watchful as smoldering.

Lori drew in her smile. "What do you mean?" She asked, suddenly alert, like a rubber band had been snapped against her diaphragm.

"Whoa Lori, I didn't mean to scare you."

"I'm not scared."

"You're reminding me of Fiona's pet turtle, out exploring and then, boom, something frightens him and all the exposed parts retreat into its shell."

"Oh, come on." She shifted off him and slumped onto the couch instead.

"No really, you changed so suddenly."

"It's just, I don't, me and Peter, we didn't, you know, try stuff. We kept it very...regular."

"No porn?"

"Once in a blue moon, if we were in a hotel."

"No toys?"

"Toys? No."

"Role play?"

"No way!"

"That's sad."

"It is what it is."

"You were okay with that?"

"I was too exhausted, or annoyed with Peter, to really care."

"I don't believe you."

"No, really, it was fine."

"I could feel you holding back this weekend. I thought you were holding back from me. I think it's yourself."

"You got your therapy license, when?" Lori tried to sound

teasing. She really just wanted to shift the conversation away from her feelings of inadequacy.

"It's just, you're so sensual, you've always been. I want you to feel that, without inhibition."

"Maybe I was, once."

"You said you trust me, right?" He asked with a childlike intensity, pivoting on the couch to look directly at her.

"Yeaaaah." Lori drew the word out exposing her uncertainty.

Brandon picked up and handed her the glass. "Finish that off."

The name of the whiskey seemed suddenly ironic, do angels really envy the bodily pleasures they've lost? Lori took a gulp and put the glass down with a bit of a flourish, flashing Brandon a see, I can be game smile. He got up from the couch, took her hand, talking as he led her to the bedroom.

"You said you liked me out there, right? In control."

"Yeeeah, I said that."

"Did you mean It?"

Lori paused, questioning herself. "You know what? I did. I do!"

"Okay. Let me be in charge."

* * *

Lori stood watching in the doorway. Brandon moved around the room, like he was setting a stage. He drew back the comforter and propped some pillows. He went to his drawers and rummaged as if looking for long lost items that'd gotten buried under underwear and socks. He dropped a pile of black leather things on the corner of the bed and Lori felt her legs trembling. He came back to her, unsnapped the clasp of her bra and pushed her skirt and panties over her hips and legs, dropping all her clothes in a pile.

"Lie down," he said, "on your back."

Lori did as she was told, fearing she looked like a trapped

animal. Her eyes darted, following his actions and betraying her anxiety.

"Don't be afraid. I just want you to feel pleasure without policing yourself."

"Exactly how are you going to do that?"

"Give me your arm." Brandon was sitting next to her still fully clothed.

Lori held it out to him tentatively. Brandon strapped a leather cuff around her wrist.

"What are these for?"

"You'll see. Let me have your other arm."

She complied. Then he got up and moved to the bottom of the bed and placed a cuff on her right ankle. Lori shifted her left leg away from him.

"Don't worry, I'm not going to hurt you." He gently pulled back her leg and cuffed her other ankle.

"Are these toys?"

"More like props." Brandon reached down, and a rope materialized, tied to the corner of the bed. How did I not see that?

"Wait."

"It's okay."

"What if I don't like it?"

"You'll tell me right away and I'll stop."

Brandon worked his way around the bed, connecting ropes at each corner bed post, attaching them with clips first to the loops on the wrist cuffs, then to the ones on her ankles. He tightened them slowly, still they tugged her legs wide apart. Lori felt utterly exposed and tried to bring her legs together, ignoring that the obvious physics of the ropes and cuffs made it impossible.

"Aren't you going to get undressed?" Lori asked.

"This is all about you right now," Brandon said, though he pulled his shirt over his head.

"You look sexy shirtless."

"Let's not change the subject," Brandon said teasingly.

He climbed up on the bed and over her body. Lori opened her mouth for a kiss. Brandon ignored her. Instead he brushed his lips slowly, fluttering lightly across her breasts, then licked, slow and deliberate, around each nipple, all the while looking up to watch her. If he wanted her to squirm under his gaze and attention, she was, on the inside, as she couldn't much move her arms or legs.

His tongue moved down, circling her abdomen, dipping into her belly button. He moved down further, no longer looking up at her, and blew air gently across the top of her pussy. Her entire body shivered. His tongue moved through her pussy lips. She liked the feeling, like he was out on a leisurely Sunday walk exploring, but a pressure was building in her lower belly. Then, the tip of his tongue connected sharply with her clit. A sensation of pleasure so acute, it was not unlike pain.

She wanted to touch his head, lace her fingers through his hair so she could direct him to stay on her, right at that spot, or move his lips away, if it was too much. She was abruptly reminded of the cuffs. It was unnerving not to be able to control, even a little, what Brandon was doing with his mouth. She couldn't help moaning.

"That's good. Let yourself feel everything."

His tongue was moving around her clit with a broad, hard pressure that felt bruising, like he was splitting her open. She could feel her pussy dripping, and instinctively tightened something inside but his tongue entered her, cavorting against her retracting muscles, lapping her up, his saliva mixed with her juices. She could feel her muscles clenched.

"You're holding back again. Why?"

"I don't know. It feels so good. I'm kind of embarrassed, I guess, by what's happening down there."

"You've got nothing to hide from me," Brandon said. "I want to savor you."

"Really?"

"Don't you know how good you taste?"

When Lori shook her head, Brandon stuck his finger inside her. Another shock of pleasure. He pulled it out and brought it to her lips.

"Try it."

Lori turned her face away. Brandon's other hand gently forced open her lips, and he put in his finger. She tasted sharp, tangy. Brandon opened her mouth wider with his thumb.

"Suck me," he said.

She started to and he pushed his thumb in further, toward her throat, like a cock in her mouth, almost making her gag. She wanted to move, to pull back his hand and panicked a little when she realized again that she was helpless.

"Relax," he said gently." Go with it."

Lori took a deep breath and concentrated on the feel of his thumb, rough against her tongue, the taste of it, earthy with a hint of pussy. She relaxed her throat, let his thumb take over, her tongue following it, sucking as if a child again, enjoying the sense of fullness from the saliva filling her mouth. Inside her pussy was still clenching and releasing, mimicking her mouth. Both were hungry.

"That's it." He moved his thumb against her teeth forcing her mouth open wider. "I want to try something else."

Her whole mouth tensed against his fingers. He stroked her cheek.

"You'll like it, I promise," he said. Then he climbed off her, off the bed, leaving her still splayed and vulnerable.

* * *

Brandon was back at the drawer, rummaging until he took out something silver, smallish, shaped like an egg. A compact vibrator Lori guessed. When he turned back she was glad to see his erection pressed hard against his jeans.

"Now this is a toy." He pressed a button on the small box attached with a cord and Lori heard a low hum.

"I'm hoping this will break down your defenses." Brandon remained standing and put the ball against one of her palms.

She could feel it vibrate.

"That tickles."

He placed it against her nipple. The sensation made her abdomen clench, more excitement than pleasure, like being in the back of a car going over a bump in the road. Then, he walked to the bottom of the bed, kneeled on the mattress and put his hand against her thigh, not letting her legs close, even the little bit allowed by the play in the ropes created as they loosened. He held the shivering ball directly against her clit, delivering an immediate gratification. A bazillion fingers creating infinite pulses of melty, delicious sensations deep inside her body. She was defenseless, and, instinctively, fought to shift away. Brandon held the vibrator tight to the spot. She came quickly.

"Oh, fuck! What the...!"

"You've got more in you," he said as he put the ball back on her clit.

Lori couldn't help pushing up against it, rhythmically humping the ball in his cupped hand, coming over and over. It was unadulterated sensation and abandonment. She could actually feel the letting go; the muscles and nerves in her body finally driving a truck right through the stop sign in her brain. She vocalized deep guttural moans, then screams of delight. She heard the sounds almost as if from another person in the room. Making noise felt so unfamiliar. Finally, she uttered,

"Stop, please."

Brandon turned off the vibrator immediately and threw it aside. He faced Lori and unzipped his pants, watching her watch his cock popped out of his jeans, all swollen red head and hard shaft. He bent and gently kissed the flesh of her inner thighs. He climbed on the bed and moved over her, knees on either side, his erect penis bobbing and grazing in the path left by his planted kisses up her torso, between her breasts, finally her lips.

"Your body was meant for this."

Lori was shaking her head, "I don't know...," even as her abdomen clenched, greedy in response to the alternating brush of soft head and hard cock pressing against her.

"You did know, you just forgot." Brandon spoke kindly, as he moved off of her, circling the bed to unclip the ropes.

Her limbs each fell, heavy and numb. She put her hand against her breast to ground herself in the pounding of her heart. Brandon had returned to the bottom of the bed, standing directly in front of her, his eyes blazing, almost scary, like an animal preparing to devour her.

"Do you know how turned on you just made me?" It was the second time he'd asked her.

Maybe Lori was starting to believe it. Before she could say anything, he was inside her. He lifted her legs over his shoulders as Lori buried her face in the crook of his neck, absorbing his increasingly fast thrusts and penetration deep into her abdomen. She was suddenly aware that you can hear sex. Not just the thumping and bed springs, but all its particulars. The friction created, the slapping of flesh, the slurpy wet sound of his balls against her soaking hole, even the release of air from her pussy, almost like a small farting sound, she thought, shocked for a nano second. She was too far gone to be embarrassed.

Brandon lifted up from her when he came, with a long, drawn out grunt, holding himself over her, arms locked, head falling, eyes clenched, as if he wanted to remain in that moment forever. He finally opened his eyes and a slow, broad smile spread across his face. He pulled out and flopped down next to her. They held hands, both quiet. The immediacy of their mutual release receded, and Lori felt a little flustered.

"I want you to know, I wasn't passing gas when you heard that, well, farting sound."

Brandon laughed.

"What? It was weird. It came out of my pussy, I think."

"I take it you never heard the term queef?"

"Um...no."

"It's a vaginal fart."

"Seriously, there's a word for that?"

"Yup. Hey, do you smell that?" Brandon asked.

"I told you I did not fart!" Lori released his hand and slapped his side playfully.

"No, it's a good smell."

Lori sniffed at the air, a sort of sweaty, yeasty pungency filled the room, like the smell in the kitchen earlier, only stronger. "What is it?"

The smell of sex."

"I like it! I really do."

Chapter 19

Lori woke the next morning to find she'd wrapped herself tightly around Brandon. Her head rested on his chest, her hand on his abdomen rising with each breath. Her knee was tucked inside Brandon's legs pushed up between his legs. The rough scratch of his short hairs was reassuring; unexpectedly, and deeply, grounding after so many months feeling unmoored. Except, she realized, her arm resting below her body had fallen asleep. She should get the blood flowing, or she'd have terrible pins and needles. Lori didn't dare move, or risk breaking the spell cast by their entanglement.

She and Peter inevitably slept like quibbling siblings who'd drawn an imaginary line down the middle of the bed. It was crossed rarely, and only if certain unspoken conditions were met. She'd wanted the demarcation as much as she hated it. On her long list of grievances was that Peter only reached out to touch her when he wanted sex, the completed act. She turned her body away from him more and more. Her anger at his unwillingness to grant her small acts of affection, to simply hold her in bed, or stroke her hair, had gradually supplanted desire. Lori lavished affection on her children instead. She still sometimes engaged in an elaborate bedtime ritual with Catherine, tickling each of her arms and down her spine and the backs of her legs. That was a one-way street.

She'd nearly forgotten that affection can be grown-up, mutual, the spark of desire. Lori moved her hand down from Brandon's abdomen, brushing over his erection, rock hard even in deep sleep. She smiled remembering a silly expression, something about an erect cock first thing in the morning being at a full salute. Lori coddled his balls, embracing their heft. It felt a small way to return the favor, the sheer joy of being coveted that she felt in Brandon's arms.

She couldn't help recalling it was Sunday morning, the last day of her visit. If she was home, she and the kids would probably be finishing breakfast. Always pancakes on Sunday. Plain for Ben, blueberry for Catherine, usually chocolate chips for their friends who slept over. Catherine loved to tell them that her mother made the best pancakes in the world because it was her great, grandfather's secret recipe. Emily and Lori laughed over how each of their kids claimed the same kernel of truth. She wondered if Peter was trying to keep up the tradition.

Lori suddenly missed her children deeply, with a pang of guilt, realizing she'd not thought about them much in the past few days. It would be good to see them the next afternoon. Ben liked to walk home. She might get Catherine straight from school rather than wait for the bus to drop her. Then again, she nearly blurted it aloud, I'm going to miss this.

She snuggled closer to Brandon her hand still cupping his balls. He stirred, tightened his hold on her, rubbing her arm as if to assure himself that she was really there. He kissed the top of her head, breathed in deeply, seeming to fill himself with the smell of her hair. They remained like that for a long moment.

"I like how you're holding me," Brandon said finally.

"I like it too."

She lifted her face to Brandon's and he kissed her forehead, the tip of her nose, then her lips. His touch made pieces of her soften and swell. She tipped her head back down.

"Have you been up awhile?"

"Just a little. Still on East Coast time, I guess."

"You've been thinking, haven't you?"

"A little."

"About what?" He kissed her hair again.

"Oh, nothing much. About you. My kids. That I miss them. How complicated we just made things."

"So really, nothing much." Brandon removed his arm, so he could pull himself up, half seated, on the bed. He looked amused, and a little anxious at the same time.

"I'm sorry. It's just that first thing in the morning is my absolute, very, best time to worry." Lori smiled weakly. She pushed herself away from Brandon, sat back on her calves, turned to meet his gaze.

"You're worried already?" Brandon sounded a bit surprised.

"Yeah, kind of. Aren't you?"

"No."

"I'm already thinking about how much I'm going to miss...," Lori spread her arms gesturing around him, her, the bed, "all of this. I guess I was thinking it would be a fling, for old time sake, you know, get it out of our system. Now, it's feeling like so much more, and I'm..."

"I didn't invite you here for a fling," Brandon said, interrupting.

"Please don't be angry. I was... Didn't you just want to satisfy some ancient curiosity?"

"No."

"Then what were you thinking? We have kids, responsibilities. You have a job. We live thousands of miles apart. I can't figure out what, no, how, we're going to do it."

"It?"

"Us, I mean us."

"Let's go back to why you're here. Is your curiosity sated? All flung out?"

"I didn't mean that was the only reason." Lori felt too quickly shifted from the comfort of Brandon's body, to the brunt of his irritation, yet she'd started them down this path.

"It's just, I can't see where we go from here."

"Apparently, nowhere."

The words cut deep, colliding with her sudden, desperate need for Brandon. Despite that they'd been apart for so long, and all the obstacles she still couldn't see her way around.

"No! That's not what I'm saying."

"What do you want Lori?"

"I want you! Something, anything, with you. I mean, we've only had these few hours and already, you've helped me remember so many things that were important, that I just put aside, so easily, I..." She was tearing up. Lori clenched her eyes shut. She didn't want to be pathetic after acting like she didn't care. Why do I have to be such a hot mess?

"We have history, Lori, serious history. I wasn't looking for a nostalgic fuck."

"Ouch."

Brandon seemed not to have noticed her tears.

"I'm not here to congratulate ourselves for finally seeing how good we could have been," Brandon continued. "We're middle-aged..."

"That's not true."

"I'm not saying we're washed up." He was looking at her again, as she was trying casually to wipe her eyes. "Or that we can't keep fucking wildly." If he was trying to make her feel better, it was working.

"You know," Lori interjected, still trying to comprehend her befuddled mood, "if we had gotten together back then, maybe things wouldn't still be good with us." She grimaced. "Look at our marriages."

"I think we'd have been good together...," Brandon said slowly, "always," he added with raw tenderness.

"What if it's the screw ups that got us here?" Lori asked desperately, as if trying to salve her painful regrets.

"Listen to me." He put his finger to her lips. "We can't ever know." He reached for her hands, clasped them tightly. "I just don't want us wasting any more fucking time." Brandon's look was intense, both pleading his case and broadcasting desire. Lori decided to try and forget her myriad what ifs and how's, for the moment.

"So, let's not," Lori said.

She got up from her knees enjoying that in this position she was a whole head above him. Lori took back her hands, grasped Brandon's face, brought his lips up to hers and kissed him fiercely.

* * *

How could Lori already be seeing this city, Brandon's city, grown dark in the rearview mirror. It seemed like only minutes ago that they were heading in the other direction; a moment ago that she was entranced by unexpected scenery and what the weekend might bring.

During their last moments of intimacy, Lori perceived the shift and contraction. Jettisoned from the languid, time-shifted weekend—she never really knew, nor cared, what time it was—she cowered now in the face of neglected needs back home, and her anxiety about how to speak with Brandon about what, if anything, would be next.

Lori said nothing. It felt cramped in comparison to the easy silences they had shared the past few days. The car was racing past Boeing airfield. They'd be at SeaTac airport soon.

"Brandon, I'm not sure what to say, or even, what to think. I…"

"What do you feel, Lori?"

"Too many things. That's the problem. Like I've been in a dream, and… that I'm finally, thankfully, awake. It's been so long." Lori was looking down, moving her head slowly.

"I can't imagine not being with you now that I've found my way back. How can I? I don't know when I can get to Seattle."

"I'll come to you."

"Really?!"

"Will you have me?"

"God yes! Please. When?"

"I'll talk to Jocelyn about the schedule. Soon. I promise."

They were suddenly stopped in the departure zone. He walked around to her side, opened the door for Lori and grabbed her bag from the back seat. He led her up to the curb, depositing the bag next to her. Brandon brought her in close. Somehow, he conjured a bubble of calm, while cars pulled in, fought with each other for space, and scurried away again. She wanted to get small enough to fit inside his jacket pocket and stay there, unencumbered for a while longer.

"Sir, you have to move your vehicle." Brandon didn't respond. He just held her. "Sir, you need to move it now." Brandon planted one hard, last kiss then released her and walked to the other side of his car. They locked eyes as he opened the driver's door, raised his hand in a gesture both of connection and parting. He lowered his hand to the car roof, lowered his gaze, slid back in, and was gone. Lori took the handle of her bag, dragged it behind her as she stumbled into the tumult of air travel.

Chapter 20

"Catherine, get down here now! You need to eat breakfast and I don't want to miss the bus."

"Okaaaay. I'm coming." Catherine came out of her room and yelled back down to Lori standing at the bottom of the stairs.

"Where's your math homework? Bring it down with you."

"OMG. Why are you so stressed out?" Catherine asked jutting out both her arms and neck to fully demonstrate her annoyance. "You can just drive me to school."

"I'm not driving you. That's why there's a bus, and I'm not stressed out. I have other things to do today besides schlepping you."

"Whatever." Catherine mumbled as she turned back toward her room.

"Don't whatever me. I can see your eyes rolling from down here."

* * *

The weeks had been difficult since Lori returned from Seattle. She often woke in dread of the day. Catherine was being a pill. God, that is something Eleanor would say, but it was true, and an unwelcome change. Catherine had never been the most organized child. She struggled with reading and school work generally. While Lori worried constantly, Catherine had been perfectly happy knowing she was good at the things she loved; dancing around her room, drawing characters in her sketch book, being a good friend.

112

Lately, though, not a day went by when Catherine didn't have a fit because she lost a book, forgot an assignment, failed a quiz. The mean girl stuff at school, who was in or out, or clawing to be readmitted to the constantly reconfigured cool clique, all of it recorded, discussed, shared via their phones, in ten-minute updates. It was making Catherine a beast to live with. It would drive anyone crazy, Lori thought, not that it helped her deal with Catherine's tantrums.

Ben, meanwhile, had simply shut off, pulled down the blinds, and put up the gone fishing' sign. She really needed to ask around for a good adolescent therapist. Maybe Emily would have some advice.

Lori's attorney was nagging her to come up with a budget, so she could finally negotiate a financial settlement with Peter. The status quo of the past year was going to end soon, the entirety of their marriage now reduced to a spread sheet—what she needed, what he owed her, divvying up the stuff that remained.

At the same time miseries long, fixed inside her were loosening their hold. She felt—it was so simple and strange—happy. She and Brandon already had a lovely routine, taking advantage of the three-hour time difference. After getting through her get-the-kids-up-and-out obligations, she would text him, she suspected waking him. He always said he was already up. They would chat for a while, until it was his turn to get Fiona to school. She liked that their talking was texting, fearing, perhaps, that his voice would be too arousing, or that lulls in actual conversations would expose their relationship as a one-weekend fling.

Lori kept her phone always in her sight line, something she repeatedly asked her kids not to do. With texts, though, she could keep Brandon near. She was paying attention again—to an interesting discussion on the radio, or the crazy sounds some birds make.

Last week, when she was rolling out the bins on yet another garbage night, she spotted a magnificent full moon. It was late, she'd nearly forgotten to put them out, and she was half-asleep, still the moon caught her attention. It was huge, perfectly round and fat, floating through lazy, drifting clouds. In all the hundreds of Tuesday evenings that she'd put out the trash (noticing that at her neighbors' houses it was the man's responsibility), she'd never seen such a moon. It occurred to her that, despite the time difference between their two coasts, the way it usually made her connection with Brandon feel slightly askew, tonight he would be able to see the same moon, at the exact same moment.

"Step outside," she texted Brandon, "hope it's not cloudy there."

"Nope, beautiful night," he texted back immediately. "What am I looking for? Oh wait, the moon, right? Gorgeous. Smooth and pale and round. It reminds me of your beautiful ass."

Chapter 21

She'd become one of Pavlov's drooling dogs. The slight reverberating knock of the bamboo chime meant that a text from Brandon had arrived. The sound came to her ears. She felt it in her pelvis, the whole area buzzing, achy, wet, even if he was just commiserating about running errands during rush hour.

"I've been thinking about you all the time," Brandon texted her.

"I'm thinking about you too. About how much I miss you."

"Me too. Thinking about your body. Miss that too. Taking care of yourself?"

"I'm doing my Get Amazing Abs video!"

"Great! But not what I meant😺."

"How's work?"

"Just got in. Have some tough interviews to do in the next few days."

"Good luck."

"Thanks. I've almost got dates tied down to come to Maryland."

"OMG. Really? When?"

"The third Friday after next."

"I'll make sure Peter can take the kids. Things will be decorated for the holidays. We can take a drive to downtown DC."

"I'm not sure I'll want to leave your bed."

"Even to eat?"

"I'm hungry for only one thing these days" ☺😺.

"You must be starving."

"I am. Can you FaceTime tonight, I need to see your pussy."

"No!"

"Please, baby."

That word. He knew how to get what he wanted. "Text me when you go to bed. No video. We can text."

* * *

She put on a little mascara and lip gloss before she went to bed, just in case. This is crazy. She set the alarm for two am, eleven pm his time, so she wouldn't miss his chime. She sat on the edge of her bed and took off her pants and panties. Reaching for her pajama bottoms stuffed under her pillow, she paused to imagine Brandon's searing gaze, and left them there.

She removed her top, unclipped her bra and slipped under her covers. The sheets felt cool and light against her naked skin. She couldn't remember the last time she'd slept in this bed naked. With Peter, after sex, they put night clothes back on, even though their kids had long stopped coming into their room fresh from a nightmare.

Staring at the ceiling, Lori touched herself gingerly, finger to one nipple to see if she could bring it erect. She sensed wetness down below. The heavy ache of desire, that sat perpetually lodged in her pelvis, was even more pronounced. She'd wait...to really touch. For Brandon.

* * *

"Lori, you awake?" She saw the text as she crawled out from sleep, blinked a few times, had patted beside her to find the chiming phone

"Almost ☺." She texted back, after propping herself up on the pillow.

"Are you naked?"

"Jumping right in ☺. Yes I am."

"Good. Are you wet?"

"Can't I ask first how your interviews went?"

"I didn't wake you in the middle of the night to talk about work."

"A girl can ask for a little verbal foreplay 😊."

"Since you won't let me see you, I was gonna talk you through a quickie and send you back to dreamland before you were even awake."

"That could work."

"So, are you wet?"

Lori knew the answer. She checked anyway.

"Yes, I'm wet."

"Soaking?"

"Yes, actually."

"Do you have a vibrator?"

Lori paused, embarrassed to state the truth, aware that as a modern woman she should have one.

"No."

"We have to do something bout that ☺."

"I know ☹."

"No worries. I'm gonna call now."

"Okay, I guess."

"Don't sound too enthusiastic ☺."

"I'm just, you know...my kids are..."

"Do they sleep soundly?"

"Pretty much."

Suddenly, Lori's phone was vibrating, A moment of small talk, before Brandon said, "put me on speaker."

"I did. Can you hear me?"

"Loud and clear. Now touch yourself."

"Okay, okay, bossy," she said with a small laugh. "Don't say I didn't try to have a conversation."

Lori reached for her vagina, touching herself gently, not saying anything.

"Are your legs open?" Brandon asked.

"No."

"Then imagine me climbing on you," he said, "kneeing your legs apart."

Lori made a small sound.

"Good, baby. I'm holding your arms to your sides, so you can't squirm away."

It was a bit disappointing, Lori realized, that Brandon couldn't see the effect of his words, how her knees drew up and spread open.

"What are you doing now?"

"I'm touching myself."

"How?"

"With my fingers."

"Fast or slow?"

"Kinda slow still."

"How does it feel?"

"Fine."

"Fine?"

"Good."

"You gotta give me a little more."

"I'm too self-conscious. I thought you were going to talk to me."

"Alright." Brandon paused. Lori heard his breath, could sense him composing his battle plan. "I'm brushing your beautiful breasts with my lips; can you feel it?"

"Yes."

"Now I'm kissing down your soft belly," Brandon stretched out the words, "there, and there, and there..."

They fell distinctly onto Lori's ears, like eager caresses. "Until I reach your pussy."

Lori sucked in a moan.

"I'm nudging my nose..., right between those pussy lips." Brandon's encouragements spooled out like tempting morsels. "Can you feel me?"

"My god, it's like you're actually here. I think I just felt the stubble on your chin."

"That's it, go with it. Your pussy is so pink and swollen. I'm burying my face in that hot, wet cave. Can you see it?"

"I want to touch you."

"Imagine that you are. Now I'm drinking your pussy juice. Rubbing it all over my mouth and chin. Do you remember how good your pussy tastes?" Brandon asked, his voice suddenly rushed.

"I think so."

"Taste it. Are you touching your clit?"

"Yes," Lori grunted, barely able to answer.

"Touch it the way you like to. Think about my tongue right there, circling. Now I'm putting my finger in you."

"I can feel that." Lori's voice had changed, deeper and raspy, she could hear it.

"Next time, I'm going to fuck you so hard with my fingers." Brandon words came fast and thick, genuinely eager. "Your pussy gets so ready, inside and out."

Lori's moaning was audible.

"Good Lori. Make all the noise you want. Do you have your fingers inside?"

"Yes, one, the other's busy someplace else."

"You're incredibly hot when you pleasure yourself. Can I watch you next time?"

Lori heard the desire in Brandon's question, but she was beyond answering. Her orgasm came quick and hard, so much stronger than her usual masturbatory releases. Lori's whole body tensed and arched off the bed as if necessary to contain the long grunt of repletion that wanted to escape her mouth but might wake her kids.

"You still there?" Brandon asked, then after a few moments. "Lori?"

"I'm here," she managed to say. "Just catching my breath." She could hear Brandon's soft laugh.

"Thank you," she said. "That felt so good. I have so much pent up desire. I'm like, buzzed, down there, all the time, Brandon."

"Down there?"

"Don't make fun of me! I'm serious. I don't remember ever

being like this. I'm thinking about you, us, this, all the time. I'm worse than a teenage boy. All I want to do is stay in bed and get off. I can't get things done."

"I want you to tell me exactly what turns you on."

"Brandon, I can't, I've got to get some sleep."

"Not now, when I'm with you. I want you to tell me all your desires."

Lori was at her kitchen table, the day before Brandon was due to arrive, warming her hands around a mug of mocha latte she'd made with their custom installed espresso machine. It'd been another unpleasant morning with Ben. Lori detected something like scorn when she tried to talk with him about his plan of attack for a research paper. A break from her kids was long overdue.

She gazed out back, thinking one more day, as her eyes scanned all the work she'd invested in that yard. Lori could identify every plant she'd added to create a color palette, height and texture, even winter interest, something that payed off this time of year. Emily taught her that trick, be sure to plant a few things with redeeming value, evergreen shoots or bare red branches, to give beauty when everything else is shriveled and dead. Funny, she never thought of herself as a gardener, yet how many hours had she spent digging and transplanting, weeding, watering and tending?

She turned back to what was inside. Her home was filled with pretty things. No grand gestures, just objects gathered over the years, from the few places they'd traveled, or street art fairs, the kids' best work, only things she could bear to be broken. They'd renovated the house a few years ago. Turned it from an ordinary colonial into something bigger and nicer, not too imposing. She and Peter had agreed on that. There were still some unfinished spots. Right before the separation, Peter had been talking about buying a real piece of art work to fill the empty wall in the family room. Something more impressive for when potential clients or his partners came over for dinner.

The house was Lori's, for now, until Peter's lease was up, and he moved back in. Her decision to let him buy her out was as hard as she could imagine. Her kids came home here from the hospital, and walked to and from its welcoming front door on their first days of school. They all agreed on the one perfect spot for the Christmas tree. Fish and turtles and a beloved iguana were buried in the backyard.

New and stubborn facts, though, had replaced these cornerstones. Ben and Catherine hated staying with Peter at his rented house. He'd never have the time to make it, or anyplace new, feel like home. Besides, Lori thought, who am I kidding. Even with alimony, she'd have a struggle each month to pay the mortgage.

Lori sipped her coffee, trying to get motivated to do what needed getting done. Errands and chores, PTA projects she had promised to help with, and Christmas was around the corner. The holiday season seemed to arrive earlier each year, with all its hundreds of extra items to make, order, buy, and remember. Things that all fell to her, that had always seemed so important.

Instead, she sat wondering what Brandon would think about her renovated kitchen. It could be in a magazine. High end appliances. Custom cherry cabinets, he'd have to appreciate those, an island of granite. She laughed remembering a remark a friend made, as she was wiping off counter tops after their two families had dinner. Her friend knew she was supposed to adore her ocean of granite. She complained with something close to bitterness, that the countertops were so time consuming to keep clean and shiny.

Lori had started looking for a new place she could afford with the money Peter would pay her to leave what was once their home. There was one house she liked enough. Nothing fancy, certainly no granite, but close enough so her children could walk downtown without her worrying. She appreciated that from her own growing up. Back then, parents barely knew where to find their offspring and they hardly seemed to care.

Lori panicked occasionally about the responsibility of owning a house in her own name. Still, she daydreamed the life she might create there. Lori permitted herself to imagine it included Brandon and Fiona, painting them into imagined scenes of domestic comfort and happiness. At the same time, Lori couldn't help wondering, a tight band of guilt forcing the air from her lungs, how unfair it must seem to Peter. That his punishing hours and never-sending stress were still what provided her this second chance.

* * *

"Emmy, I'm going a little crazy, call me." Lori left Emily a voice message which Emily returned in about forty-five seconds.

"What's going on?"

"Sorry to be melodramatic. Am I interrupting anything?"

"Nothing that can't wait."

"Well, for one thing Ben hasn't said a kind word to me in weeks. Actually, I'm not sure he's actually spoken to me except to answer a question."

"That's right on schedule."

"Is it the divorce?"

"Maybe, some of it. They also get pretty smug and secretive after sixteen. Is he spending time with Peter?"

"Peter's managing about a weekend a month and dinner maybe once every other week."

"That's not a lot of time. Even if Ben's not talking to you, I'm sure, deep down, he appreciates that you're there for him day in and day out."

"It feels awful to say this. Sometimes, even though Peter's basically blown us off, it's like Ben's on his dad's side, like they agree that what I do around here just isn't that important."

"That's crazy."

"It's the feeling I get...that my status as a homemaker disgusts Ben at the moment."

"Let him see what happens if you stopped."

"I know. Still...it hurts."

"This too shall pass."

"Can I ask you something?"

"Sure."

"Did you ever feel guilty getting money from your ex?"

"Whoa. Where'd that come from? No! Not for a second. Don't tell me Peter's gotten into your head about that."

"It's just..., he does have to work really hard."

"You don't?"

"It's different."

"Not really. He could never work the hours, succeed like he has, without you, keeping twenty-four seven, all the other never-ending shit together." Emily paused, Lori could hear her frustrated sigh.

"He wanted it all, Lori, the perfect family and the perfect career. You're as much a part of his success as he is, and you're still giving him that to boot."

"Do you think that maybe, I mean, that Peter did me a favor by leaving?"

"What?! What's really going on Lori?"

"I spent a weekend with Brandon."

"Wait, who? Brandon McManus?"

"Yeah."

"Wow! When? I thought he lived in Seattle."

"He does. I went out there a few months ago."

"Really? Shit. How was it?"

"Weird. Intense. Amazing."

"There's always been some kinda crazy chemistry between you two."

"Actually, he's coming here this weekend."

"Like tomorrow? Shit! Sorry, I already said that. So... what is this?"

"I don't know. We met up when I came to your house at Christmas last year."

"You're kidding. How did I not know that?"

"I didn't say anything. It was unexpected, and it seemed too soon. Talking to him, even for that short time, it brought back so many feelings, and all the what ifs. I tried to avoid it, even though he asked me to visit him."

"He did!?"

"Yeah. I talked myself out of it. Too many complications, too much distance, and the feeling I was going backwards, I guess. Brandon, us, the possibility, it was background noise that wouldn't go away. Finally, I thought I should just go, get it out my system so I could move on, but…" Lori breathed deeply.

"Oh Emmy, when I was out there…the old stuff was all still alive and well, that primal connection, and who we've each become, that fit too, maybe even better."

"Whoa, Lori. Look, I really want to say, enjoy it. You absolutely deserve that. You've got to be careful, though. Do you hear me?"

"Maybe," Lori answered weakly.

"Promise me you'll take things slow. You might expect it to be easier the second time around. You've lived, you've learned. That's the thing, believe me. The prior wreckage sloshes around on deck, just waiting to knock you down."

"I don't know, Emmy." Lori paused for a long moment. "It might be too late to jump out of the way."

Chapter 22

Brandon told her not to bother coming into the airport, just to pick him up at arrivals. Lori was grateful, driving gave her something to do. She wouldn't have to walk on her rattletrap legs, weak with anticipation. All week her stomach had been in turmoil, chasing butterflies. She engaged auto pilot to get through the routines with Ben and Catherine, hoping they wouldn't notice. Meanwhile, Lori labored over the details. What should we do? What will we talk about? Where will we sleep?

* * *

The arrivals area was congested with tourists and business travelers. She spotted Brandon immediately, taller than everyone else. Amidst the hustle, he stood in an aura of self-possession and calm. Parts of her shifted immediately, a buzzing and wetness responding to his presence even though she was still several car lengths away. She pulled up, got out, and he was suddenly next to her, at the back of her car where she fumbled at the hatch back. Brandon ignored the open space. He collected her into his chest with both his arms clasped at her back. He kissed her so hard their teeth clanked. When his tongue filled her mouth, her whole body softened. You're really here. She momentarily forgot were here was. Someone honked. Brandon pulled back to look at her, his smile spreading.

"I guess we better move," he said, finally throwing his duffle bag into the back and slamming it shut.

"Yes," Lori said, touching her lips, smoothing her skirt. She

125

got in, put the car in gear, tried to focus on the exit signs. It'd been awhile since she picked someone up from the airport. She could feel Brandon's eyes, as disconcerting as being in front of a camera, taking all of her into sharp focus.

"God, I missed you," Brandon said. He put his hand on her thigh and squeezed. Lori grasped the steering wheel harder.

"I missed you too." She turned quickly to see his face. "How is Fiona?"

"She's good."

"Does she know where you are this weekend?"

"Yes. She said to say hello."

"That's sweet of her. I didn't tell my kids. It seemed too soon for them. I'm sorry. Is that okay?

"Of course, Lori."

"It's just, Ben especially, he's been so remote. I'm worried about him." Lori started scanning the road signs trying to find the right place to exit. "Give me a second to figure out where I'm going."

"Sure." After a few minutes he asked, "does Ben know that Peter left you?"

"I'm not sure. We gave them the, we've grown apart line, you know, it's nobody's fault bullshit. I think he knows what happened. Dad moved out. I was the one falling apart. I didn't always hide it so well."

"It must be hard for a son to watch his father cast his mother aside. How does he process that betrayal?"

"I never thought of it that way."

"He's with you most of the time, right? It's easy to blame the available parent."

"I know. I thought he'd appreciate me more, instead, he seems to think everything's my fault. He's actually kind of mean sometimes."

"He's at a tough age. Starting to imagine what love might look like. Does he have a girlfriend?"

"There's a girl. He's trying."

"Maybe that will help."

"Or make it so much worse. Teenage emotions, they suck."

Lori was talking about Ben. For a moment, though, she remembered her own heartache, the hurt like she'd been socked, crouching behind her parents' house. How can it be that Brandon's here with me again?

"So, when were you last in the DC area?" She asked, after a long pause.

"Not since Sarah moved away."

Lori glanced around her. It was pretty enough, this part of the world, certainly a lot of trees and open space, but nothing special, just an ordinary kind of niceness.

"We can visit downtown, do some sightseeing," she said. "There's some events going on at the Mall, and this one gallery I love. It's in a house, well a mansion really, off the beaten path. I would love to show you. Oh, and I researched some new restaurants. I haven't been into the City in while. There're tons of new places we could try. I've been feeling guilty, lately, that I don't take my kids down to the museums like I used to. My friends used to tease me about how much I did with my kids. I was like, hey, they're only young once, and isn't that why I gave up my career, to nurture and enrich their lives?"

Brandon squeezed her thigh again.

"I know, I'm talking too much. I do that when I'm nervous."

"No Lori. You can never talk too much for me. I was just thinking, or we could stay in bed."

With those few words, and the electricity of his hand on her skin, Brandon managed to flip that switch in her brain. All the energy she'd used for distraction was re-directed to her erogenous zones, maybe had been there all the time. She'd just talked over it.

"Have you missed that?"

"God, yes," Lori said and quickly glanced from the road to his face wondering if the lust that had consumed her these past weeks was evident on her own.

"I don't know which is more confusing, that all I can think about now is sex, or that for so long I didn't think about sex at all."

"I still find that hard to believe."

"I swear, desire, lust, gone, for the past few years."

"You were okay with that?"

"I guess so. There were so many people needing so many things from me, even sex felt mostly like someone else's need."

"What do you need?"

"You, wanting me. That feels so good."

"You deserve more than that."

* * *

She barely recalled how. Suddenly they were on her street, in her driveway, the garage door opening as if by magic and swallowing up the car. She turned off the ignition, turned toward the back seat to grab her handbag when Brandon's lips were on hers. His hands dug deep in her hair, his tongue full in her mouth as if to safeguard her really being there.

"Wanna go inside first?" Lori said, breaking from Brandon to catch her breath.

They entered through the basement to find it cold and dark. She led Brandon to the stairs. He took her arm and turned her back. His eyes were fiery, his mouth more a grimace than a smile.

"It's warmer upstairs," Lori said with an awkward half smile.

"I can't wait a minute longer," he said, and then her clothes were coming off.

He pulled her skirt down, yanked at her panties, blouse up and off. Brandon unsnapped her bra and then slowed down. Slipped off each strap, one at a time, letting them drop down her shoulder and fall off. He stared at her, fully naked, like he'd just been presented with a delicious spread of food.

"You're so beautiful, Lori."

It was a startling revelation—Lori felt, not past her expiration date, as she feared, but like someone worth admiring. Lori was about to she tear up, not again! She raced towards Brandon, instead, grabbed at his t-shirt. He worked on his belt, slipped off his pants. Naked too, he backed her against the wall at the bottom of the staircase, pinned her arms to her side.

Brandon was inside her so fast it shocked, ignited, brought

her pussy insanely alive. She was acutely aware of the head of his cock breaching the opening of her vagina. She could feel every inch of his erection, like sparks firing against the membrane inside her, as he thrust, over and over. They both came, breathing hard in tandem, stuck together as the continuing pulses of her pussy contracted around him. He stepped back to look at her, his eyes suddenly sweet, all tension gone.

"Better?" She asked.

"Much better, thanks. You're so wet. It's incredible."

Lori gave a small chuckle.

"You better not be laughing at me again."

"No! No, it's just something I worry about?"

"What! Why?"

"I don't know, sometimes I imagine my body might have dried up, or forgotten what to do."

Now it was his turn to laugh. "Believe me. Your body was made for this."

"I still can't wrap my head around that." Lori's gaze turned coy as she looked around her. "We were always good in a basement, weren't we? Hiding from our parents?"

"I remember it well."

"We're the grown-ups now," Lori said, pushing herself off the wall and twirling her arms out wide. "We can screw anywhere!" She grabbed his hand. "Let me show you the rest of the place."

"Can I walk around naked?"

"To mark your territory?"

"Something like that."

"Go for it," Lori told him, and she grabbed up his t-shirt and led him upstairs.

* * *

"Are you hungry?" Lori asked, slipping on his shirt at the top of the stairs. "I made us some food. I just need to warm it."

"That'd be great. Nothing but peanuts on the plane. I think I'll go back down and put my pants on if we're eating."

"Not on my account."

"I have a rule about wearing pants when I'm around hot food."

"If you insist. On your way back, can you grab a bottle of wine from the butler's pantry?"

Brandon raised an eyebrow, as if smirking over butler's pantry.

Lori shot back at look. "Don't worry. There won't be one in my new house. It'll be back to a crappy, old kitchen in anything I can afford."

When Brandon returned, he stood across from her on the other side of the kitchen island. Working to uncork the wine bottle he asked her,

"Does that bother you?"

"What?"

"That you have to leave this place for something less nice."

"A lot less nice," Lori said, pausing with her hand on the knob of the glass front cabinet. "I don't think so...no," she said after a moment, retrieving two wine glasses and handing them to Brandon. She looked around her kitchen.

"On second thought, maybe a little. I like to cook." Lori gestured around her, like one of those booby blonds modeling merchandise on the Price is Right. "This is a really nice kitchen to cook in."

"It is beautiful. Probably better for me that I never got used to anything like this." He handed her a glass of wine.

"Here's to cramped and outdated kitchens." He lifted his glass to hers.

Lori put a plate of food in front of him, another next to it. She came around and sat down at the bar stool.

"The entire house is beautiful," Brandon said, sitting down.

"It's funny," Lori paused to sip her wine, "I really wanted you to see what I'd built here, even knowing I have to let it go."

"I would've been fine not seeing it, especially knowing that you're being forced to leave."

"Not forced exactly... I guess you and I should have talked

about this. We could have waited for you to come east until I moved."

"I didn't want to wait any longer, Lori. It's just, I'll never be able to make you anything like this."

"I don't need this, Brandon."

"There are other things I can give you, I hope, but not this."

Lori put her fork down, turned to him. "I need you, baby. This...," she looked around her, "is just stuff."

"Let's see how you feel in a few months." He kissed her nose. "I do like it when you call me baby, though."

"Oh my god, when you say that to me," Lori puckered her lips, sucking in her breath, "it turns my insides to jelly."

"Does it now baby..." He drew out the syllables with a devouring look. "Can I take you to your bedroom and lick your marmalade pussy?"

Lori burst out laughing.

"I wasn't trying to be funny," Brandon said, grabbing her hand as he walked them toward the staircase.

Chapter 23

"I was thinking we should we use the guest room," Lori said, pausing at the top of the stairs.

"No. I want to be where you've left your scent."

"My room is where I slept with Peter," she said with a pained expression.

"So, let's expunge him."

Lori's face lit up at the shared memory, grateful, too, that it was made long before she knew Peter. She turned them toward her bedroom instead, stopped at the threshold. The room still felt complicit, so she turned off the light.

"Turn it on, please. I want to see you."

Lori flipped back the switch, at a loss for what to do next. Brandon stood before her and lifted his t-shirt up off Lori, then he sat her on the edge of the bed.

"Lie back," he gently nudged her shoulders down. "I've missed the taste of you."

Lori remained propped on her elbows. She wanted to watch Brandon's mouth on her, to see if he truly enjoyed doing those things; she didn't quite believe it. There he knelt, though, muscled and sexy with only his jeans on, looking at her pussy like it was a great big ice cream sundae with a cherry on top. He nudged her legs apart and stippled her inner thighs with kisses.

She could think only about how good it would feel when his tongue finally connected with what, she suspected, was her already inflamed clit. Tucked within her pussy's folds, was the morsel that remained on high alert, that zinged with pleasure where her jeans rubbed her crotch every single time she moved; that buzzed, hot and wet, with each staccato chime signaling a text message from Brandon. All her weeks of longing wrung out and concentrated in a small locus of unadulterated desire, there. She thought it might just burst forth with an orgasm at his slightest touch and then, he bit her thigh! Hard enough, she guessed, to leave a mark. Instead of pain, her pining intensified.

"Brandon, please."

He looked up at her while he blew air lightly over her pussy, mad desire searing his eyes.

"What do you want?"

"Lick me, fuck me, something, anything, please." The last word came out like a plea for mercy.

Still he teased her, licking the inner folds, his tongue in and out of her, swallowing her juices greedily, making her wetter still. She'd never felt so conscious of her vagina, how she could sense it grow fleshy and ripe when he sucked her with abandon; how responsive it/she was to another person's rousing, his stiffening erection, her muscles clenched and throbbing in anticipation.

She groaned with as much relief as euphoria when his mouth finally focused on that blessed spot. The papillae of his tongue, the scratch of his stubble, rough against soft, all heightening her bliss. He stayed on her when she tried to wiggle away, shocked by the intensity of what she was feeling. Her orgasm came in clenching waves, with a brand-new sensation, like she'd secreted something. Lori tensed, fearful she had urinated.

"What's wrong?"

"Nothing..."

He followed her gaze to a wet spot on the bed.

"I'm so sorry," Lori said.

"Why sorry?"

"I think that I...peed."

"I think you squirted."

"What!?"

"It's a good thing."

"It is?"

"I'll explain later. Right now, I've got to fuck you. You're incredibly hot."

He lifted her entire body onto the bed, one knee spreading her legs apart. His mouth was hard on hers forcing hers to open. His tongue, keen and insistent, was unabashedly slopping with saliva and the residuals of her pussy's fluid. It felt like they were fucking with their tongues and it immediately brought her back to a state of high arousal. He slid inside her, lifting just one of her legs over his shoulder.

"I want you to feel me, all the way inside you."

"I do."

"Tell me what it feels like."

"You feel huge."

"Do you like it?"

"God, yes. I feel possessed."

"Are you mine?" Brandon asked, while his cock continued to make deep incursions in a staccato rhythm marking each of his questions.

"Yes!"

"Say it. I am Brandon's."

"I'm Brandon's."

"Do you want my cock?"

"Yes!"

"Say it. Be loud."

"I want you inside me." Lori felt like she was screaming.

"What do you want?" He was humping her now with quick, penetrating thrusts.

"I want your big...hard...cock, inside me." She said each word slow and clear, with a voice she did not recognize, looking right at Brandon, so he would know exactly how she felt.

Brandon gave way to a final, deep irruption. "Fuuuuck." Then he stilled, remained above her, his body shuttering while Lori felt the hot jet of cum coating her inside.

She waited until their breathing had settled to something approaching normal. Lori was tucked under Brandon's shoulder, her eyes fixed on her hand feeling the beat of his heart.

"What do you mean, I squirted?"

Brandon cocked his head, so he could look at her. "You've never squirted before?"

"I've never even heard the word. Are you making it up?"

"No. It's something that happens for some lucky women. The glands inside the vagina fill up during arousal and..."

"You know this, how?"

"There's this thing called the internet." Brandon grinned. "More importantly, did you like it?"

"It was...kind of weird, I guess. I'd have to say it felt good, almost like an extra perk in the process. A genuine release."

"You've really never felt it before?"

"Never!"

"Want to see if you can do it again?"

"I don't know. I probably can't have another orgasm for a while."

"Women can cum over and over again. That's your gender's greatest asset."

"Really? Our greatest?"

"Well, one of your best."

"Maybe some women can..."

"You've done it before, I...," Brandon said.

He stopped abruptly and jumped up from the bed like a kid on Christmas morning.

"Wait here a sec. I've got a present for you."

He was back in a flash with his duffle bag. He plopped it on the floor, unzipped it, and pulled out a box tied with a ribbon.

"Something every women deserves." Brandon grinned as he handed her the gift.

There was a picture on the box. It looked like a hand-held microphone.

"I'm confused. Are we doing karaoke? I have a terrible voice, you know that."

"No! It's the Magic Wand." Ta da was implied by his grin.

"What?!"

"It's a vibrator. So much better, I'm told."

"I'm not going to ask."

"Good! Now where can I...?" He held up the plug.

"Behind the bed."

"Get comfortable," Brandon said as he fiddled to get the plug in the wall socket.

Lori slid back into the pillows, propped up to get a better look. Brandon sat back on the bed, device in hand. It had an elongated, large ball on the head of a long handle, humming at what sounded like an incredible rate of speed.

"It's awfully big."

"Give it a try." He handed her the buzzing wand.

"You're gonna watch?"

"For now."

"Okay." Lori sounded skeptical.

She examined the thing until Brandon made an impatient sound. Then she touched it lightly to her vagina. The hit was immediate and intense, a hot surge of indulgence like she'd never experienced.

"Shit," she said as she pulled it away.

"You, okay?" He sounded concerned.

"Yeah..."

"Then don't stop," Brandon urged.

"If I keep going, Brandon, I may never stop." Lori already had a premonition of the device's potential for addiction.

"Let's see where it takes you." He took the handle from her and placed the head on the hood of her clit.

Lori's head snapped back against the pillows. If she wanted to think about what was happening, what she wanted to have happen, she was out of luck. The sensations were so heightened and fervid, inhibitions simply fell away. Her knees fell open. She was clenching her ass muscles rhythmically as she lifted her hips, grinding against the device as Brandon held tight.

"Good girl," he said several times.

Lori could barely hear him. Ripples of hot sensation were all encompassing, intimate, compelling her alone. She felt her breasts, rubbing the edge of her wrist against a hard nipple. Her mouth was curled open, as if she needed something to suck.

"Here," Brandon said as he inserted several fingers.

She was vaguely aware of a slurping sound, as she consumed him. She wanted everything rock solid against her body. Her eyes teared, not from emotion, from the onslaught of impulses wracking her body. The sound she made, when she came, was not quite human and there was a gush of fluid as if her climax was coupled with an ejaculation. Lori's head hurt immediately. She needed to catch her breath, but Brandon held the devise tightly against her. More spasms of satiety came in waves, even more intense, with more rushes of fluid that gave each new orgasm its own reward.

"Stop Brandon! Enough!"

He turned it off, the room suddenly silent except for the sound of her raspy breathing. Lori fell back onto the pillow. Grabbed at her head.

"You okay?"

That sweet sound of concern again. Lori would never tire of it.

"I've got a massive head ache. Ohmygod that was incredible."

"Let me get you some water." When Brandon came back from the bathroom, handing her a cup, Lori was already sitting up examining a big, wet spot on the sheet, still puddling in places.

"Did I do that?"

"It's all you. Lori, that was incredible! Your squirt reached your feet and I could watch it flow down to your asshole, like a river through a gulch."

"I love when you talk dirty, like a mountain man," her smirk faded to a frown.

"You're sure it's not pee?"

"I'm sure. You can smell it."

Lori realized that she could. It filled the room, different from the smell of sex she'd hit on in Brandon's kitchen and bedroom. This time it was earthy, slightly brackish, like coffee, or mammals rutting in the damp early spring.

"Did you like it?" Brandon asked.

"Yeah, a lot, actually. It's a whole new level of enjoyment. Explosive is the only word I can come up with."

"It was beautiful to watch," Brandon said.

"Really? I think I might have been drooling, and if I'm not mistaken my eyes rolled back into my head. I must have looked like an animal possessed!"

"You did bite me."

"I did? I'm sorry. I had no idea."

"You're very oral. Did you know that?"

"What does that mean?"

"You like something in your mouth."

"I do?" Lori registered the information as familiar, from a time way, way back. It made her want to reclaim something. She put down the glass and rolled to the edge of the bed.

"So, I like something in my mouth?" She asked with as teasing a tone as she could muster.

"Yes, you do," Brandon said responding to her shifting mood.

"Then come here." She drew Brandon closer, tucked her left leg in and around him so that he was standing between her legs. His hard penis lined up perfectly with her mouth. She loved how it swelled and tightened, ready to burst out of its skin.

"Something like this?" She asked, looking up at him, as she began to lick his erection, a big, delicious lollypop.

She longed to see his eyes answer to her tongue. The look of gratification made her horny, her fingers tickling his balls while her tongue swirled around the head of his cock. When he moaned, she took all of him. She moved her lips over his shaft, letting saliva freely pool and spill from her mouth, covering his cock in wetness, while her thumb and finger circled its bottom, moving her mouth so he filled it entirely, deeply, slurping too, then up and down, everything faster and noisy.

"I'm going to cum in your mouth."

He said it with a question mark. Lori didn't stop, didn't move her head, just grabbed his ass checks, pressed him closer. Everything tensed.

"Fuuuuuuuuuuuuuck."

Lori looked up at him swallowing and grinning. His cum was thick, tasting sharp in its unfamiliarity.

"I love how you say that, when you climax," she said, rubbing the remnants of his ejaculate around her lips.

Brandon sat down next to her, and fell back onto the bed. Lori curled up to him.

"So that was good?" Lori asked, walking her fingers around his chest.

"That was fucking incredible. I loved how you made my cock so wet. You..." he stopped and kissed her nose, "are full of surprises."

"I surprised myself," Lori said looking up at Brandon. Your penis is really big, you know that, right?"

"I think I'm about average."

"If you say so." Lori made a face. "I was close to gagging a few times. The more I realized how much I liked it, the more my throat relaxed. I liked it, a lot, actually."

Brandon turn to her, kissed her hard.

"Thank you," he said.

"Anytime."

"Be careful what you say."

Lori laughed as Brandon fell back again. She loved these moments right after—deep contentment, bodies awash with pleasure, brains primed for playful conversation. Eventually they shifted their position to be fully on the bed, their heads tucked into the pillows. Brandon brought the sheet up over them. He asked if he should get up and turn off the light.

"Not yet." She snuggled under his arm listening to him breathing.

"So, do a lot of women...what did you call it?"

"Squirt."

"Yea, squirt."

"Some. It's a very coveted skill."

"Really?"

"You should ask your girlfriends."

Lori couldn't imagine broaching the topic with any of them.

Chapter 24

She woke the next morning to an obnoxious brightness from the light they'd left on and the rays streaming past the shades they'd forgotten to close. Brandon was comatose. It was still early, and she remembered the three-hour time difference. Another of the many complications of this relationship, she thought, as she got up and closed the blinds.

She planned to make them a nice breakfast, but decided to climb back in bed and close her eyes for a few more minutes, enjoy the effortless comfort she only felt when she was snuggled tight against Brandon. He lifted his arm and curled it around her shoulder even though he seemed to be sound asleep. She felt for him, a full erection, of course. She rested her hand on top.

The next thing Lori knew, Brandon was kissing the top of her head. It seemed like only a few minutes had passed.

"Morning, sleeping beauty."

"Morning," she said. It looked very bright outside even through the shades. "What time is it?"

"Eleven-thirty."

"What?!" Lori shot up. "I never sleep that late."

"You have someplace to be?" It sounded rhetorical. The corners of Brandon's morning smile spreading up to warm his face.

"No, it's just..."

"Put your head back down. I like it there," Brandon said tucking a bit of hair behind her ear as she lay against his chest. "You can put your hand back too."

"You had quite the erection first thing this morning."

"I must have been dreaming about you."

God, she loved his sexy smirk.

"You know you can climb on top," Brandon said. "Use me anytime you want, even if I'm asleep."

"Funny."

"I'm serious."

"Right," she didn't sound convinced. "Are you hungry?"

"Not for food."

"You want more of that, already?"

"It's been over twelve hours."

Lori shook her head, grinning though, at his energy and audacity.

"Fine," Brandon said. "I'll take a shower and we can eat." Before he got up from the bed, though, he drew his fingers slowly through the rumpled tresses of her hair. Lori leaned into it, moving her head against his hand, like a luxuriating cat.

"I hope you grow your hair out again."

* * *

Lori got up once she heard the shower water running. She lifted the shades and examined for a moment her tree filled backyard. It was one of the reasons they'd bought the place. So many trees, and two of the them perfectly spaced for a hammock they inherited from Peter's parents. She'd read so many story books to Ben and Catherine out there coasting on its light, lazy roll. With a wistful sigh, Lori turned away, went into the bathroom, brushed her teeth, rinsed her mouth. When Lori lifted her head from the sink, Brandon was standing behind her, naked and dripping wet. He stared at the her through the foggy mirror.

"Look how sexy you are," he said.

"Look who's talking."

"It's never the same as a woman's body."

Lori made a questioning face.

"You know that, right? How sexy you are?"

"Yes, well, maybe..."

He shook his head unbelieving and commanded her not to

move as he grabbed a towel, drying off while he went into her bedroom. He came back with her desk chair and placed it on the floor. After looking in the mirror, he moved it back a bit.

"I want you to see yourself." He wiped away some of the steam, put the towel on the seat of the chair, and sat down.

"Here," he said patting his thigh.

Lori walked over, leaned down to kiss him. He turned her, instead, so she was facing the mirror. He sat her on his lap. She glimpsed them together, her naked body with four arms and two heads, his appearing to sit on top of hers. She was going to say that they looked like a parody of a Vishnu statue, but Brandon seemed so serious. He leered at her in the mirror, looking back at him. Kissed her shoulder with open lips, both soft and hard against her skin, then licked off some of the water that had dripped from his wet hair. She turned to kiss him. He stopped her.

"Just watch," he paused. "Release the untamed beast."

Lori wasn't so sure. Her eyes bore into the mirror as Brandon smoothed the palms of hands across her breasts pressing them inward, then slowly drawing back, fingers spread, catching her nipples between them. She watched herself thrusting breasts forward to meet his unyielding pressure. Eventually, he licked one thumb casually. Still looking at her through the intermediary glass, he spoke to the face in the mirror.

"I'm going to give you a THO."

"What?!"

"A titty hard on."

She laughed as he brought his wet thumb to her nipple, circling it with his finger, as if around the lip of a goblet to coax the glass to sing. Her nipple rose erect, the other joined in, made hard as if by magic. He pinched and pulled at them. Lori watched her lips purse to say "ouch." No sound came out. It didn't really hurt, just a brief sharpness that intensified the pull of desire spreading open her pelvis. He moved his finger between her breasts, drew a line languidly down her torso, making a side trip around her belly button and explored the one dark, round mole on her hip bone.

Her pussy was calling to him. He increased the pressure of

his hand as he neared her pubis, spreading his fingers over her mound. She watched his middle finger work its way playfully, deliberately, toward its goal. When he reached her clit, she regarded how her mouth soften and fell open. He fingered her, and she saw the changes caused by lust. The whites of her eyes disappeared, her irises turned almost black with an unexpected, feral hunger.

It became increasingly difficult to focus her attention on the mirror. She caught sight of her legs falling open to welcome his finger further inside her, moving in and out with deliberate care, like she was a sacred vessel. Brandon using her own wetness to anoint and tease the nerve endings on that tender spot. Lori's eyes slipped closed. Her hips moved up and down, ass clenching and bumping into his erection. His fingers were so adroit, seeming never to do to same thing twice, always bringing her to that exact precipice, the brink of oblivion. She willed herself to slow it down, to open her eyes.

She barely recognizing the face in front of her, still Lori watched, intrigued, as her own hands grabbed his shaft and tugged it forward. She studied her fingers toying with the bulbous head of his member as she guided it just inside her, then out again, hungry for the hard rub of it against the edge of her opening. When she couldn't stand it anymore, she rolled her hips, took all of him inside, grinding on his erection. His features were contorted in pleasure. She increased the pace, fascinated to watch it all, until something in her brain shut off, and her titillation sharpened and peaked. She felt a disintegration, like a falling star, hot, bright pieces of her floating down until extinguished, at least that's what it felt like. At that moment, she couldn't really see anything.

* * *

They were finally having breakfast. During her turn in the shower, Brandon had gone to the kitchen and made fresh lattes, apparently undaunted by the complicated apparatus. He'd gathered some things from the refrigerator and pantry, and they sat at the table in the nook, surrounded by windows, framed by her trees.

"People always say it's kind of like being in a tree house," Lori said, "though the kids desperately wanted a real one."

"There is something of a thrill to being off the ground."

"Peter refused to build them one. He said it wasn't safe."

Brandon made a face. Invoking her not-yet-ex seemed to put a lid on the conversation. They leaned in, instead, to scoop up yogurt, berries, and granola, munching like hungry, contented bears.

"Did you know your marriage was in trouble?" Brandon asked, eventually, sitting back in the chair.

Lori thought for a moment. "No and yes. I knew I wasn't happy. I lost something essential when I stopped working. I think Peter wanted me to go back, and maybe I should have." She shook her head slowly.

"I'm absolutely positive he would not have worked any less or picked up the slack at home." Lori's features scrunched into a question mark.

"Who was going to raise the kids?"

She wasn't asking a rhetorical question. It had troubled Lori lately, the sense she got from Peter, as they negotiated custody, that he had been doing her a big, fat favor to let her stay home and take care of their children.

"I did keep working after Ben was born, and it felt like I was always missing an important meeting or deadline, because Ben was sick, or was at the cusp of a baby milestone. I didn't want to just hear about it from the nanny." Lori slumped back in her seat, picking at some berries.

"It was so hard disappointing colleagues when I missed work, and then feeling guilty about Ben, when I was at the office. After a while, we didn't really need the money I was earning. We had a new baby by then... It just seemed predetermined that I should stay home."

"Wasn't Peter glad that you were willing?"

"I thought we'd agreed that a parent raising our kids was undeniably better than hiring out the job, and we were lucky we could afford my staying home." Lori felt a sadness speaking about their missteps.

"Before we understood what was happening, Peter was all work, I was all about the kids. It rarely felt like we were building a family, or a life that had any common threads. That made me so lonely...and angry, and it hurt the marriage, I guess, more than I realized."

"Did you fight a lot?"

"No. Never, really. Our marriage seemed about as good, maybe better, then the couples we know. All the husbands work long hours." Lori grimaced.

"How else can we afford our entitled lives? Everyone we know believes their kids' burnished self-esteem is the highest priority, and that the moms should jump through hoops to make that happen. Our lives seemed to operate like everyone else's. All parties to the contract feeling overly stressed, under-appreciated, and vaguely thwarted."

Brandon grimaced. "That sounds awful."

"Our friends are all still married." Lori shrugged. "I know a lot of them aren't happy. Damn it if they don't stick with the program for the sake of the family's finances and their kids' success, maybe just for loyalty. I feel like people look at me and ask themselves, how could she do this to her kids?"

"You shouldn't give a fuck."

"You're probably right."

"You have to live like you only have so many fucks to give." Lori laughed.

"Really! I just read that somewhere. Isn't it great?"

"How old was Fiona when you and Jocelyn separated?"

"About five."

"Just a little girl. I didn't know that. You always shared custody?"

"Actually, Jocelyn left us a couple of times."

146

"You mean, moved out before you separated?"

"No. After we divorced. She traveled for long periods to pursue her dancing career. She once left for an entire year."

"Brandon, that's awful, I had no idea."

"It was really hard on Fiona, obviously. I had to keep working, always struggling to find good child care. That cost dearly. I nearly lost my house."

"Shit."

"Yeah."

"So that's why you and Fiona are so close?"

"I guess. There's a lot of things I can't give her. You should've heard the argument we had over why I wouldn't buy her Uggs." Brandon looked at Lori only half smiling.

"I bet Catherine has a pair."

"No comment."

"More than one?"

"I said, no comment."

"Fiona knows that I won't ever not be there. We live in the city mostly so I'm never far from her school and activities. I don't want her to miss out. I tell myself that's all that matters." Brandon stopped speaking for a moment, drawing imaginary lines on the table with his finger.

"I feel I let her down. The public schools are dangerous. I'm gonna have to figure out something else for her soon, if I can afford it."

"Can't Joanne help with tuition?" Lori asked.

"Maybe, a little. The work, the parenting, the money, or lack thereof, has nearly destroyed me a few times."

"I just do the parenting and it's sucked the life out of me. I'm not sure how you can do it all."

They paused to sip coffee, each considering what the other had said. Lori noticed the trees as they swayed, the hammock rocking, ghostly vacant.

"Do you ever regret it? Having Fiona?"

"Not for a second."

"Me either." She took another sip.

"It's funny, way back, when I struggled with whether I could really be with you, I thought being a parent, a desperate, devoted parent, was the one desire you and I would never share."

Chapter 25

Lori felt like getting out of the house to stretch her legs; anything not to get lost in pointless speculation on what could have been. She drove them to Great Falls National Park, where the rumbling of the infamous Potomac River wheedled into the brain and drowned out errant thoughts.

They dumped her car and quickly found the path along the canal that paralleled the river. There was the usual Saturday crowd, especially as the weather was unseasonably warm. Serious bike riders competed with hikers, and baby strollers, and an infinite variety of leashed dogs.

Lori and Brandon dropped into the flow of pedestrian traffic as he slipped his fingers between hers. Lori, was still amazed at the invulnerability created with that one small gesture. When they neared the falls, she steered them off the path and onto steep boulders lining the river. They had to scramble and hop over deep crevices. Not yet seeing the falls, the sound of them grew even louder. It had impressed Lori her first time there, years ago, that in the middle of a populated city, you could stumble upon such wilderness.

She and Brandon didn't try to talk above the rumble. When they finally stood on the precipice, watching the river plunge and froth, skirting the stubborn rocks in its way, Brandon squeezed her hand, and she knew he liked the place.

They stayed like that for a long while, side-by-side, only their fingers touching. Lori felt a penetrating contentedness, despite the roar; being in a place she loved, with a man whom,

149

the realization was slowly rippling to the surface, she had always loved. Still loved deeply.

She turned to watch Brandon following the tumultuous path of the river. He finally met her gaze. She smiled, grateful to have gotten them there. Brandon pulled her to him and kissed her softly, guiding them back a few steps from the edge before his lips opened hers, his tongue pierced, then filled her, seeming to speak about love and longing and the need to get back to where they always should have been. Her mouth and tongue followed in agreement.

Some teenagers scrambled up the rock, interrupting them mid-kiss. She shied away from Brandon, though he kept his arm firmly around her waist as the intruders moved past.

"They're probably up here to do the same thing," Brandon said grinning.

"We're supposed to act like grown-ups."

"Fuck that!"

Lori knew there would be more people coming. Too many people lived in the area these days, with too little green space.

"Let me take you some place nice to eat," Lori said.

"Don't tell me you're afraid of people seeing us make out?"

"I don't care about that."

"Because if I recall, you liked going places we might get caught, even got turned on by the possibility."

"I don't think so."

"We might have to agree to disagree," Brandon said, grabbing, and pulling her close again, "until I can prove you wrong."

He kissed Lori hard as he slipped his hand between her legs and rubbed, from her ass to her crotch, and back again. Lori felt a part of her disappearing into the swoon of desire, thoughts muffled by the roar of the falls. She stopped him.

"We might get distracted and fall off!"

"I'll always keep you safe. Let me just play with you a little."

Then he didn't, really, just tipped her chin up, and slowly, repeatedly, stretched his fingers through her hair. She closed her eyes, blissed out by his stroking and the warmth of the sun on her face.

"You look so beautiful."

"I wish I didn't have those years without you lined on my face."

"You look beautiful, period."

"Let's go somewhere," Lori tugged him back toward the path. "Hopefully, we'll bump into someone I know, and start gossip about the gorgeous hunk I was with."

They opted for a nearby Irish pub, away from traffic and the nightmare of parking in the main part of her town, because, really, Lori just wanted to be with Brandon. Once there, they were swept into a different kind of ease, together, amidst a group of strangers under the influence of alcohol and live music. Everyone seemed nicely buzzed. Lori, especially, simmered in the contentment she felt next to Brandon. He took it all in, nodding to the music, slightly bemused at the scene, with his hand on her thigh, moving teasingly up and under her skirt.

"I've got this nice flat screen TV in my bedroom that I never use," Lori said. "We could watch a movie when you get tired of this."

"What did you have in mind?" He was grinning hungrily and asked for the check.

"Clearly not the same thing as you! I was thinking something light and fun."

"We can start with that, then I'll find us something a little more interesting."

"Okay, as long as I get first pick."

* * *

Lori chose Sleepless in Seattle.

"I should warn you. That might just put me to sleep," Brandon said as they climbed into her bed, stripped down to their shirts and underwear, with glasses of wine and some popcorn.

It was much later, apparently, when a noisy bird woke Lori. She listened, surprised to hear that it's call sounded distinctly like right now, right now. She didn't recall a thing about the movie past Meg Ryan tearing up while she listened on her car radio. Tom Hanks was talking with the dubious psychologist about what had been so special about his dead wife, the million tiny little things that added up to the fact that they were meant to be together, and he knew it from the moment he first touch her hand. Brandon must have taken the wine glass out of Lori's hand, and noticed the blinds, too. He'd shut them against the coming light and had tucked them both under the covers.

Lori was in her new, favorite position, curled tight against Brandon, head under his chin, hand holding his penis. It was hard, of course. Brandon was sound asleep. When she squeezed his cock, it swelled further against her palm. She stroked it with one finger, up and down, enjoying that it seemed to have a life of its own. His cock bounced playfully until she held it down and fingered the hard ridge around its head, willing Brandon awake, now that she was up, and wanted more. The rest of him didn't stir. She remembered what Brandon had said. Should I really just climb on top? Would she be able to slip him inside while he slept?

She felt herself already wet, so she moved over Brandon, nuzzled her knees against his hips. Lori slid back and forth over his erection, moistening him, until she lifted her hips and pressed his hard cock inside her, slowly, feeling each and every point of its contact against the lining of her vagina until it knocked up against her cervix, as if asking, please, take me further.

She sat down, feeling the entirety of him. Paid attention to the sensation of fullness in her pelvis, slightly uncomfortable for a short moment, then deeply satisfying. Slowly she began to move, to roll her hips up and down. Free and cocky like a cowboy. Though the horse beneath her might be powerful and brash, it moved as she directed, as if one being. Brandon's shut eyes suddenly popped open, shifted, disoriented, then almost immediately, half closed again, hooded with the potency of his own desire. He started moving with her, the rolling of their hips matching thrust for thrust.

"Take off your shirt," he said gruffly.

Lori paused, lifted her t-shirt up over her head. Brandon reached for her breasts. His large hands cupped all of her, massaging the flesh, his thumb teasing her nipples at the same time. She put her hand on one of his, rubbing her breast along with him, letting her finger brush against a nipple, still surprised that touching her own body could ignite such a lancing stab of desire.

Lori brought his other hand to her face, letting him stroke her cheek, until she put several of his fingers in her mouth. He moved his hand from her breast to her pussy, and found the spot quickly, fingered her fast and hard. Their hips moved again, in tandem, the rhythm of rider and horse in a full canter. She could feel her own eyes become slits, knew they were darkened now with pleasure, and she sucked his fingers, hard and noisy, salivating unabashed, saying with her eyes, these fingers are your cock, this is what I am doing to you.

"This is the most beautiful I have ever seen you," he rasped.

Lori humped Brandon as fast as his fingers on her clit.

"Your hair is almost wild again."

Lori just smiled, far too gone to speak. She took back her hands, tousled her short, thick mane as best she could, wanting it to look as luxuriant and savage as she felt riding him. She moved her hands behind her, grabbed her ass cheeks to spread them farther, to bring him even deeper inside. She kept her hands there, her back arched, thrusting faster still. They both were noisy now, grunting like animals. A loud, unearthly sound escaped both mouths when they climaxed. Lori collapsed onto Brandon's chest, licking the sweat collected at his clavicle. Their breathing finally slowed.

"Wake me like that every morning!"

"I promise," Lori said, and then she realized it was Sunday. Brandon would fly back to Seattle. She would wake in her bed tomorrow, alone.

Chapter 26

"So how are you doing?" Jeanette asked, giving Lori a look that said don't bullshit me.

They were out for their weekly coffee, though it'd actually been many weeks since their last.

"I can't really tell from your texts," Jeanette said.

"I'm okay," Lori answered. "New things to worry about."

Jeanette gave her a what now frown.

"It's not even spring break, and I'm already worried about the school year ending. We haven't made any camp plans for the kids, and you know around here, if you don't sign up by January, forget it."

Jeanette nodded. "Absurd, and exactly right."

"The whole summer thing just fell through the cracks of the separation. Ben's more than old enough to get a retail job at the mall, and I will have the pleasure of driving him to and from his shifts unless I want to be left without a car. That leaves Catherine, home all day, bored." Lori made a face of excruciating pain.

Jeanette laughed. "We'll take the girls to the pool. A lot!"

Jeanette's daughter, Chloe, was a few years older than Catherine and always gracious about hanging out with her when asked.

"There was no getting Chloe to sign up for camp this summer. She just...," Jeannette did a fantastic imitation of teen age eye rolling, "and said seriously, every time the subject came up."

"Will she get a job?"

"Maybe a little babysitting. I'm spreading her name around to neighbors with small children."

"I had a summer job from the time I was twelve. It was called mother's helper, but I had full responsibility for taking kids to the town beach, for the entire day. By sixteen I was waitressing six shifts a week. What has happened to our kids?"

"We happened."

"What a mess."

"But, you," Jeanette said putting her hand on Lori's, "how are you?"

This was the part Lori hated, the vague feeling of pity that emanated from friends since her separation, even good friends like Jeanette, as if saying, we still love you, but your lesser social standing has been duly noted.

"How's the dating going? Met anyone special?" Jeanette raised her eyebrow.

Before Lori could answer Jeanette said to her,

"Richard knows someone at his firm who recently got divorced. He's a little older, very successful, and his kids are grown. That would make things easier, right? Richard says he really enjoys the finer things. Apparently, he has a beautiful beach house. Richard thought maybe the four of us could go out to dinner."

"Let me guess, he really, really likes to hear the sound of his own voice." Lori tried to say it jokingly, to protect Jeanette's feelings.

"Lori, that's not fair. He could be a very nice man. If you're dating again, would it be so bad for the guy to be successful. He could treat you well. The way you deserve."

Lori gave a noncommittal smile, pondering the assumption that with money, someone would assuredly treat her well. If she thought about it, her sister Emily's life was infinitely better with her second husband, mostly because Thomas was kind and generous. Things her first husband ultimately was not. The daily grind was undeniably sweetened, though, by Emily and Thomas sipping cocktails from Adirondack chairs facing a view of the Long Island Sound, as members of a country club that Lori's family couldn't afford growing up. With their blended children mostly out of the house now, Emily and Thomas had even started to travel. What if I had money?

"Hello there," Jeanette said waving her hand in front of Lori. "You still here?"

"Sorry, Jeanette, my mind wanders these days. How are your kids doing? I remember Jason was struggling with that honors class."

"We're here to talk about you, remember?"

"We are?"

"What about the work front? Are you thinking about giving anything a try?" Jeanette was being tactical, Lori guessed, letting her proposed date with Richard's colleague settle in, or maybe she didn't like discussing Jason's difficulties.

"Honestly Jeanette. Who's going to hire an ex-attorney who hasn't had a real job in fourteen years?"

"You're the smartest, hardest working person I know. Any employer would be lucky to have you."

"You might believe that, I might even believe that. Actual employers, especially around here, Jeannette, where everyone has three advanced degrees and knows someone, who knows someone, who's kids hang out with the President's kids, they're not gonna buy it."

"You're selling yourself short."

"Maybe. I've barely been able to keep it together as the only available parent ninety percent of the time. I'm still dealing with the fall out on the kids. Ben's not doing well. I've still got to find a new house. Then there's all the crappy paperwork I have to pull together to keep the pressure on Peter. He's dragging his feet again."

"Do you think that, maybe, Peter realizes he made a mistake?"

"Peter, admit a mistake? Not likely. Sometimes, though I hate to say it, I think about us trying again."

"Really?"

"I was at Catherine's school helping out with Grandparent's day for the lower grades. Seeing those old married couples pouring in, with their name tags showing how far they'd traveled. I felt so sad. I wanted us to be the ones with the comfort and pride of a long marriage, all that history together, like you promise in your vows, through the good and bad..."

"Maybe Peter's feeling that too. Maybe he wants to try to work things out."

"The problem is, Jeanette, there hasn't been working things out for a long time. It's just been me holding it together, making the life I thought he wanted. Not very well I guess."

"Maybe he sees that now, how much you do for him and the kids."

"You know what my sister told me the other day?"

"No, what?"

"That it was painful to watch me, jumping to attention to keep Peter happy, flying around trying to keep the kids occupied and out of his cross hairs."

"We all saw some of that. How demanding he could be, and short tempered with the kids, that is, when he was even around."

"It wasn't always like that." Lori looked at Jeanette imploringly. Why was it so important to convince others that she hadn't always been weak and misguided?

"I mean, he had those WASP genes programmed to maintain status and influence above all else." Lori gestured as if saluting the captain of a vessel. "And, of course, nothing as messy as relationships were permitted to veer the ship's course."

Jeanette leaned forward and nodded, seeming to want to let Lori get it all out.

"I knew all that going in," Lori paused, sighed. "Peter swore he didn't want to be that person. He promised to mutiny against all his crappy training." Lori gave Jeanette a weak smile.

"I'm drawn to the rebels, I guess. A rebel with a Mayflower pedigree, how could I resist?"

Jeanette patted Lori's hand.

"He really tried those first few years," Lori was wiping at her eyes, "and my god, how he swooned over Ben when he was a baby. Then Peter made Partner." Lori's tone turned angry.

"He wed himself to the law firm, at the mere cost of inhumane and absurd work expectations, forsaking all others."

"That's a little melodramatic, don't you think?" Jeanette shrugged back into her chair.

They each sipped their coffee.

"I remember when Ben was about two," Lori said making circles on the table with her cup. "I made plans for an overnight trip, so we could all ride a steam train. Ben loved anything to do with trains. We loved making Ben happy." Lori sat back too, finally looking up.

"At the last minute, something came up at for Peter at work, blah, blah. It was all planned, and I was already persona non grata at the firm, so I took Ben. I mean, I traveled alone for work all the time. I remember being nervous, though, with such a young kid in a kinda backwards motel in the middle of nowhere." Lori sipped again.

"It was a day long ride and the car was filled with these model train aficionados. They got such a kick out of Ben." Her gaze wandered, reliving it for a moment.

"I'll never forget the sweetness of that day." Lori suddenly frowned. "I remember too, thinking this is so wrong, Peter not being here. I should've heeded that voice in my head."

"Did you tell Peter how you felt?"

"No. Then we went and had Catherine. Things just got worse. There was no competing with what the firm asked of him, what his clients felt it their right to demand in light of Peter's increasingly astronomical hourly rate. The kids and I never had a chance. I see that now." Lori looked hard at Jeanette.

"What makes me really sad is that I lost the courage to ask for what I wanted. After all, some of his partners manage to spend quality time with their family."

"That's my point. If you took him back, you could try again. Get it right and be a family again. It's what's best for the kids."

"It wasn't just work though, Jeanette, or the firm. It was us too. I'm not sure when, or even why it happened. We stopped being equals. There wasn't a place for me to be strong and unafraid." Lori signed deeply." I'm not sure I could go back to that, not even for my kids."

Chapter 27

Later, waiting at Catherine's bus stop, Lori found herself revisiting the conversation with Jeanette. *Had she always been intimidated by Peter? Where was my blind spot?*

A memory surfaced of the night Peter asked her to marry him. It'd had been an elaborate evening in New York City. Peter proposed in a jazz bar. Lori wasn't totally surprised. She knew she would say yes, yet she struggled to find the words to answer him. Peter's face immediately darkened. He grew angry and took back the ring, saying *don't make a fool of me.* Lori had quickly sputtered, *of course, I'll marry you,* and slipped on the lovely, reappearing ring that Peter had designed himself. It fit perfectly, and the moment passed. She knew she had blown it in his eyes. Lori was embarrassed when people asked them their engagement story.

So, why hadn't she told Jeanette about finding Brandon again, after all these years, especially the beautiful thing he said to her. *I've been searching for someone like you my whole life.* Maybe, because there was nothing else to tell. It had been months since she and Brandon had seen each other. Neither could make it work to hop on a plane, what with the holidays, and custody schedules, and the school calendar. They texted constantly, though, just like in their letter writing days. They were at least trying to rebuild their relationship with words, if they couldn't build it with proximity.

Still, she could have told Jeanette about this new man in her life whom, it felt like, she'd known forever, known better than she'd ever known Peter. Tell her that, despite the fact that he lived

159

thousands of miles away, her feelings for Brandon weren't a fling or distraction. She felt alive. Jeanette might accuse her again of being melodramatic, but Lori could see now she'd been riddled with a pain that she'd hidden even from herself. She wanted Jeanette to know the ways Brandon didn't just expose the wound. He tended to it, gratefully. With his whole body, and with what he could do to hers. It was dizzyingly addictive, and important, she realized, oh, so important.

Lori wasn't exactly sure how Jeanette would respond to information about Lori's new sex life. Would she be happy for her? Envious, maybe? She might just think it inappropriate for polite conversation. She'd probably remind Lori that sex, even really great sex, wasn't enough to build a relationship. Oh, and you do you realize that Seattle is about as far away as you can possibly go in this country. You couldn't find anyone closer to fuck? Well, Jeanette wouldn't say that.

She could tell Jeanette about the other things Brandon had given back to her. The simple ease of holding hands and staring at a river, texts to remind her she was missed and cherished, and big things too. Because with Brandon, Lori could daydream a whole new life, still unclear in the details, yet filled with purpose and partnership, and long conversations about all they might become. Part of her wanted to shout it out to the world, to her friends, to her sister at least. I am with somebody wonderful now. I will be somebody wonderful. It's not too late.

Really, though, what was there to say?

Chapter 28

The lawyers were closing in on the terms of a divorce. Maybe it was Peter's worship of rules, that, or his guilt. Lori would likely receive a good financial settlement, for a time. She would be recompensed for what she had given up so that Peter could succeed spectacularly. Money to compensate for all those critical career building years that she'd spent, instead, stirring pot luck contributions and tending sickbeds, shepherding foam pieces into caterpillars and medieval castles, handling teacher conferences, play dates, and mean girls, all the while lugging around a pitching machine in the back of her SUV.

It was only getting harder. The homework battles. Battles lately with Ben about everything, really. Meanwhile unraveling the mysteries of the internet sufficiently to deter the pornographers and predators lying in wait on her children's smart phones. Still the endless carpooling, of her kids, and their friends, and the kids of working moms, so that those women wouldn't have to disappoint their bosses.

It was terminally thankless, undervalued work that, nevertheless, kept the trains running on time, and seemed to require graduate degree skills in psychology, business management, coding, not to mention regular doses of self-doubt. She tackled them with a heavy nod to how Peter would want things done, even when that didn't feel exactly right, because that also mattered to her.

Peter never got that. He never had to say no at the office or put his family's needs ahead of the law firms. She even cleaned up nicely, when summoned, for dinners with partners and clients. Her competition she now realized, even though she'd been handcuffed for the fight. For all this, she would be paid off, in a fashion.

* * *

The problem was, everything Peter was proposing would leave her stuck, as unequal as ever. She would be promising, in black and white, to share their kids nicely, show up at important events together, give Peter the opportunity to play dad when it would have the least impact on his work life.

He would provide her the necessary funds, begrudgingly. She could continue to prioritize their children's needs without the need to restart an already dead career. It was what her lawyer said made sense, what thoughtful books suggested. It would scan as pleasant and respectable to anyone looking to judge them.

Lori was beginning to understand just how much Peter would retain the upper hand. She would be parent in charge the bulk of the days, and still also the backstop, responsible for the kids whenever work got in the way. When hadn't work got in the way!

If, and when, she was done playing the bizarrely conflicting roles of Peter's spurned wife, and uber-helpmate in raising the children, that's when his money cut off. Exactly too late for her to be hired for any real job, too late for anyone to notice her romantically. For the kicker, he was insisting on a clause that if she dared fall in love and remarry the money ended immediately. Nada.

Lori hadn't signed anything yet. She knew he was getting too much from her. Could there every be too much when it came to her children? Anyway, what other choice did she have? What career could she build? It was still all about the money, that Peter earned, that he controlled, that he would continue to control her with.

* * *

I can still hold tight to my delusional daydream, Lori reminded herself when she felt the noose tightening. Where she chucked it all away, ran away with her kids, gave them a fantastic new start, someplace with more manageable expectations. One that did not require pages of dense, pontifical language to establish a simple custody schedule. Where they could still live well, with a whole lot less, less money, less stuff, less grabbing for the brass ring.

With Brandon, of course, Brandon and Fiona. Someplace they could build together. Why not in Montana, or the Scottish Highlands? Places she'd never been, but they seemed beautiful, wide-open, a little wild. We could belong in a place like that. Not exactly live off the land, that seemed a few leaps too far. They could run a business together. Something that mattered to people. At the end of each day, they'd share the prized moments, and the hard struggles, that added up to being a family.

Is it ridiculous to be thinking like this? Lori worried the answer was yes. She couldn't help herself. She and Brandon had spent all of six or seven days on the same coast, in the same room, most of it in bed. His current life, work, and responsibilities resided three thousand miles away. She was not oblivious to these crazy facts. Panicky, though, she could feel life moving away from her. She wanted him now, damn it, and what they'd once had, shared commitment, defying what was ordinary and expected.

Maybe that's why she hadn't yet mentioned Brandon to Jeanette, why it took her so long to tell Emily. She felt burdened by the weight of their expectations. As with the vicarious hopes of her book club friends, and the assumptions that slipped into her parents' seemingly innocuous questions about her plans for the future. None of them were imagining a bold new life for Lori, much less open rebellion.

Collectively, they seemed to have conjured Lori's Life, Version 2.0. It was an update that fixed the bugs; nicer second husband, perhaps a few step kids, definitely more money and privilege if she played her cards right, and if she was smart, she would play them well. No one expected her to scrap a perfectly good application, a comfortable, accomplished suburban life.

Why not with Brandon? He was more than a devoted father

and had made Fiona a lovely home. She suspected he'd made some painful choices so that Fiona would have the things she wished for. He'd built a career despite at times being, genuinely, scarily, a lone wolf, single-parent. The work he did each day was so much more important than helping some company make more money. He protected strangers. He put his life on the line. He would be good to Lori, for her, every single day. Not just because he loved sex with her.

Brandon wasn't a CEO, though, or JD, or VP, or even a regular white-collar guy. He was the first to admit he lived pay check to pay check. Heresies in her world. Maybe that's why she wanted Brandon in a secret box. She would not let his decency and hard work be tarnished by, how else to say it, snobs.

Or was she really just cloaking her own shame? The fact that she was considering an agreement with Peter that would fit like cement, affixing her old life. She hadn't dared speak to Brandon about her settlement with Peter, or her crazy dreams of.... What? Becoming artisanal cheese makers in Montana and home schooling the children. Crazy! All she could promise Brandon was daydreams.

Chapter 29

"You awake? I miss you. It's been too long since we've been to-gether." Lori texted Brandon a little on the early side, Seattle time.

"It's been way too long, baby. I was dreaming about you."

"Go back to sleep. I'll text you a little later." It was enough to be called baby, she could ride that prize for a while.

"No, I'm awake. It was a damn good dream though. We were wandering somewhere, not here. It was tropical. I think we were lost."

"I'm surprised we were dressed."

"I didn't say we were."

"We were wandering naked?"

"No one seemed to mind."

"We weren't alone?"

"Nope. I think it was an island. Clothes seemed optional."

"Have you been watching Fantasy Island reruns?"

"LOL. How are things going with the kids?"

"Trying to be chill with Catherine. If she reads for thirty minutes after her homework, she can watch TV and do whatever else on her phone."

"Actually, you should watch what she's doing on the phone."

"I know. Honestly, it's too hot to argue. We're having an un-bearably warm spring."

"I guess I shouldn't mention that it's 65 and breezy here ☺."

"No fair 😩."

"If you want, next time I see you I can show you some tricks for monitoring what sites your kids are visiting."

"Not sure I want to see what's on Ben's phone these days. I think he has a new girlfriend."

"Have you met her?"

"No, He's been super secretive and constantly checking his phone. He blushed the other day."

"Sounds like hormones."

"I was thinking it was love."

"LOL, not love."

"Where's your sense of romance?"

"Sorry, I can still remember what seventeen feels like."

"Believe me, I know. Most of your texts make me blush!"

"What? I haven't mentioned your pussy once yet this morning☺."

"There you go! My kids have noticed that my phone, the one I used to hand them all the time to read me my messages or the google map, is suddenly off limits. Catherine asked me if I had a boyfriend!"

"What'd you tell her?"

"I said no... then changed the subject. Little does she know it's the x-rated language I'm hiding from her, not the boy. I feel like a modern teenager."

"Is that so bad? You're way hotter than most women half your age."

"I never imagined that when my kids were discovering the opposite sex, I'd be too ☺."

"Hopefully there's a lot less angst this time around!"

"I'm not so sure. You wouldn't believe the things your text tone does to me. When I don't hear from you, my mood collapses, the day's shot, because maybe the boy doesn't like me."

"I can get really busy at work, Lori, but you know how I feel."

"I know. It's just, when I think about us, the sexy things we do, sometimes it's all I can think about, and then it feels like all we have is this stupid phone. It makes me feel close to you, and so far, away."

"Sounds like you need to get out here for some real lovin'."

"I didn't know you did corny."

"I'm serious. I need you."

"I need you too. I'm trying to get Peter to take the kids for a week. Could you stand me for a whole week?"

"You should see what just happened to my cock."

"LOL. I will talk to him today and make him commit."

"Let me know and I'll get time off work. Would you be comfortable if Fiona spends some of the time with us?"

"I'd love that."

Chapter 30

It took weeks of prodding. Peter finally agreed to have the kids for spring break. He was going to take them somewhere in the Caribbean, even pull them out of school for a few days. Lori suspected his secretary would be doing the work to find them some super fancy resort with a sufficient number of organized activities to keep the kids busy while he snuck calls to the office. It still surprised her what could be accomplished if you threw enough money at it. Peter's extravagance was reminding her also, ruefully, of the many things they hadn't done as a family.

The took a fancy trip, once, to the wine country in France. The kids were too young, and it'd mostly been exhausting for Lori. Finding ways to keep them occupied and far away from expensive items. For all their money, it had been years since they'd rented a beach house, or headed off skiing, or gone away for spring break. It made her uncomfortable that she still pondered, maybe even hoped against all evidence to the contrary, whether the four of them could have gotten closer on a relaxing vacation, bonded over a bit of luxury...

* * *

Ben, meanwhile, was moaning about the trip with his dad, claiming he'd have too much school work to catch up on so he should to stay home with Lori. She should just tell Ben, sorry I won't be here, and let Peter deal with it. After all, wasn't that Peter's constant refrain during their recent meetings with the woman their lawyers insisted they hire (at a steep hourly fee) to draft a custody plan. I don't need your help, Lori. I'm just as capable a parent, and I can hire a nanny. You're being at home all these years wasn't healthy for the kids. You coddled them.

Hearing those last things left Lori reeling with anger, even physical pain. Her doctor wanted to put Lori on blood pressure medication. She felt something worse. To have my life's work dismissed as unworthy. So yeah, Lori thought, Peter can worry about the fucking details. If she didn't remind Peter to make arrangements with Ben's teachers, though, it wouldn't happen. She was sure Peter didn't know what classes Ben was taking or how to use the school network. The night before the trip there would be a crisis, Ben would insist that he couldn't possibly go. That would suck for everyone, especially Lori, if it meant Peter's lack of planning threatened her trip to see Brandon. I can't let that happen.

* * *

"I thought I was gonna die from frustration a few times this week." Lori wondered if her texts could ever convey the magnitude of her longing. "Just over a week till I head out to Seattle. I've started packing already."

"You won't need much ☺," Brandon texted back immediately.

"If we're doing stuff with Fiona, I assume you'd like me to wear clothes ☺."

"I suppose ☺. Joking aside, Fiona's really excited that you're coming. She's made all kinds of plans."

"That's so sweet."

"There's an "off limits list" too. She can't have us mingling with mere ordinary tourists."

"Even better! Does she know I was already there?"

"Yeah, since I was acting like a love-sick puppy the moment you left."

"I thought the male of our species is supposed to be good at compartmentalizing feelings."

"I keep what happens at work bottled up tight. I don't want

her worrying about me doing my job. She's had to deal with my previous, not so successful, relationships, though. She can tell this is different."

"Is she worried about it?"

"Worried?"

"I don't know, about sharing you, with me?"

"Maybe, a little. Fiona hasn't always liked the women I've been with. Lately if feels like she's taking a more expansive view of my happiness."

"What a nice thing to say about your own child."

"Do your kids know you're coming out?"

"No. I told them I'm visiting my sister."

"How come?"

"I don't know, I'm not sure they're ready. We haven't even finalized the separation agreement."

"I didn't know that."

"The lawyers are taking their sweet time, and I'm sure billing lots of hours."

"You okay with it really being over?"

"Of course, I am. Shit, Catherine is yelling at me to take her to the mall. Can I text you later?"

"If you want."

"What size is Fiona? I want to bring her a little something."

* * *

She texted Brandon when she got back from a marathon shopping trip with Catherine for new bathing suits and a cover up. "How's your day going?"

"Fine, busy. Spring seems to be an especially busy time for shitheads and scumbags."

"Really?"

"Bad guys are always busy, but yeah, for some reason, busier as the weather improves."

"I hope you'll tell me more about what you do."

"Careful what you wish for."

"Why?"

"It's like that cliché about sausage making. Most people want their communities clean and safe. They don't really want to know what goes into keeping them that way."

"I'm not most people."

"You're not ☺. People are right to suspect it can be ugly, more grisly than dangerous most days. You see things you hope other people never have to see. It can make this job pretty lonely."

"Are you saying I can't appreciate what you do?"

"No. I hope you can. You might not get a lot of company ☺."

"I don't care what other people think."

"If you say so."

"Hey, I snuck into Victoria's Secret while Catherine shopped with her friends."

"Snuck?"

"I didn't want Catherine asking what I bought."

"Not PG-13?"

"LOL, definitely not."

"I hate to break it to you. Victoria's Secret is pretty tame compared to what's out here."

"How do you...? Wait. I don't want to know."

"How about a sneak preview for me?"

"I want it to be a surprise."

"I hate surprises. How about you model it for me on FaceTime?"

"I don't know. You'll probably just want me to take it off."

"That depends on what it looks like ☺."

"Ha ha, let me see if I can get the kids to sleep at a reasonable hour."

"Promise?"

"We'll see."

* * *

Later that evening, Lori put on the teddy and modeled it in front of her mirror. She'd bought it without trying it on. She was going for sexy, but elegant too, kind of what she hoped Brandon saw when he looked at her.

The front was low cut. It plunged, practically to her belly button, then had lots of busy lace to cover her belly. There were sheer lacy strips that went up, cutting in sharply, before rounding her neck and hooking at the back. A heavier-patterned lace covered her breasts, sort of, the straps hit only a bit past her aureoles. She was like one of those woman on the red carpet who you look at and think, how does her dress stay on over her boobs? The bottom cut way up on her thighs. Around the back, it dipped low across, barely covering her backside, leaving the rest of her back fully exposed.

She turned side to side, stretching her neck to try to see how well it covered what she didn't like about her body. The thing worked, covering love handles, and creating breasts that peeked out in a way to seem bigger. Her legs appeared longer, her butt rounder, all of it sexier than she'd expected. Maybe Brandon would be satisfied with a screen shot. She couldn't imagine how they would navigate a video chat.

Her phone buzzed with a text. It was as if Brandon was a fly on the wall, watching her primp and worry.

"So, the kids locked away in their rooms?"

"I better check. Wait, are you making fun of me?"

"Not at all ☺. Are you wearing your new outfit?"

"Yes, I was just going to send you a picture."

"Get your iPad instead, so you can model for me."

"I'm not sure about that, but I'll try find it. Call me in a few."

Lori grabbed a bathrobe from the far back corner of her closet. She knocked first on Ben's door.

"Yeah," he called out. She didn't open it, just talked to the door. He seemed so annoyed with her these days, even if she just peeked her head in to ask a question.

"Go to bed soon, okay. You've got to get up early."

"Yes, Mom," Ben said in the miffed tone she had to assume was the inflection of teenagers since time immemorial.

She next went in search of her iPad, which she found buried

under several catalogues on the kitchen table. She climbed back upstairs, knocking on Catherine's door as she opened it. Catherine was already in bed, typing furiously on her phone.

"Hi Mom." Catherine grudgingly pulled her face from the screen. "You're wearing a bathrobe?" Her voice suggested Lori was wearing an alien spacesuit.

"So?"

"You never wear a bathrobe."

"I was cold."

"Whatever. Hey, can I borrow your iPad." Catherine had spied it tucked under Lori's armpit.

"No. I need it!"

"K, okay."

"Anyway, you should be getting to bed. Who are you texting?"

"It's just a group chat."

"Those are the ones that get you in trouble. Is everyone being nice?"

"Yes, Mom, it's fine."

"Well say goodbye. I want to see you put the phone away on your desk."

Catherine got up slowly, still typing as she walked. Lori met her by the desk and kissed her forehead.

"Go to bed. I'm turning off the light on my way out."

"Love you Mom."

"Love you too."

Chapter 31

Lori walked back to her room, closed the door and engaged the lock. It was a flimsy thing. Nothing she could do about it now. She sat on the edge of her bed and pried open the iPad in the clamshell case that held it. There were several FaceTime notifications from Brandon she hadn't heard. She fumbled to figure out what setting she'd inadvertently messed up, the mute button. She fixed it before she propped it on the bed.

When she clicked on the app she was startled, as always, to see her own face, looming in front of her, distorted, though every pore and wrinkle was clear as a bell. Am I really going to do this? Suddenly Brandon's face was on the screen, almost like he was there in the room. She hit the green button and her image, thankfully, shrank and shifted to a corner.

"Thought you might be hiding from me," he teased.

She glimpsed Brandon's grin, and his eyes crinkled with humor, expressions on his face she often read between the lines of his texts. It was nice to see them for a change.

"You know how it is. Takes a while to shut down the zoo." She smiled back awkwardly, sorting out where to gaze, at him, not herself in the little corner.

"I thought you said you were wearing something sexy," Brandon said, feigning disappointment.

"I am."

"Really? You kinda look like my mother right now."

"That's mean! I just put on my bathrobe to check on the kids."

"So that's a bathrobe?"

"I know, it's kinda grubby. I usually just wear pajamas."

174

"Ach, pajamas. This isn't getting any better." He grimaced.

"I told you," Lori hated the whiny sound of her voice, "I'm too self-conscious for video chats. Can't I just text you a picture?"

"I really want to see you. Take off your, what did you call it... mommy robe." Again, that grin.

He was laughing with her, but she could see hunger in this eyes. He wasn't going to let her off the hook.

"Undress for me like you did when you were here."

Lori humphed, another behavior she'd apparently appropriated from her teenagers. Brandon smiled at her pout. He didn't say anything, just waited. She got up off her bed, fiddled with the iPad so that her whole body was in view. When she caught her own face, it was as if there was another woman in the room, looking both mortified and overly determined to be sexy.

"Hey Lori, just take it slow and easy." Brandon spoke softly through the screen. "You're so beautiful. I just want to see you. Don't try to be anything but yourself. Please."

Hearing that kindness in his voice, Lori calmed a bit.

"Okay. I really hope you like it."

She quickly dropped the robe off one shoulder, then she tried to grasp it back at her waist so that when she slid off the other shoulder the whole mess would slide down slowly, maybe a little bit sexily.

"Ta da," she said when it dropped to the floor. Trying to relax her shoulders, she thrust out her breasts. "I'm terrible at this."

Brandon actually made the whistling sound, the one that says you're hot.

"I didn't know you could whistle."

"Neither did I," he said with his big sexy grin. "Wow! You look great."

"Really? You like it?" Lori glanced down like she was seeing the teddy for the first time.

"Not as much as seeing you naked. Way better than imagining you in pajamas."

"Enough with the pajamas. It's what normal people wear to bed."

"Again, we're gonna have to agree to disagree because I don't want to get side tracked. What else can you show me?"

"Nothing." Lori saw panic on her screen face. "This is the only thing I bought."

"Will you show me your breasts?"

"Oh." Lori said, biting her lip.

She'd guessed things would go there, not quite so fast. She sat down again on the bed, brought her legs up and crossed them under her, reached out and repositioned the iPad at arms-length, took a deep breath. Finally, she unclasped the strap behind her neck, and nudged the lace straps so that they slid down her arms, un-caging her breasts.

She spotted herself in the corner, looking vulnerable with the lacy material falling around her waist, breasts exposed and made fuller by desire, hands resting in her lap, almost like a young girl again. It emboldened her to see that her nipples were already hard.

She shifted her shoulders back, strengthening her posture. She wanted Brandon to know that his watching her, the way he asked her to do things, it felt weird, but the impact of his gaze, his encouraging words, were working their way into her body. That desirous hum in her pussy, nudging at her consciousness since she'd fondled silk and lace in the lingerie store, had morphed into the intense buzzing wetness she experienced whenever Brandon touched her. It was only his voice now, and his eyes.

"Tell me what you're feeling."

"Well, umm, I was nervous. That's kind of been subsumed by…"

"Horniness?"

"Oh my god, yes." Lori's words came out in a rush. "It feels like you're, you know, really here, touching me. God, I wish you were."

"Why don't you touch yourself."

"You mean right now? With you watching?"

"You can do it."

"How?"

"Just rub yourself, through the teddy. Tell me how it feels."

Lori brushed between her legs with two fingers. "It's nice. The lace feels a little rough, it makes it more, you know, feelingful."

"Interesting word. Now tell me how your pussy feels. I want to feel it with you."

"Wow. This is hard. It's difficult to find words." Lori realized she was rubbing harder, her voice getting raspy.

"What do your lips feel like?"

"Lips?" Lori touch her mouth with the fingers of her other hand.

"I like that," Brandon said, his voice depending, "when you touch your mouth. Lick your fingers and rub them around your lips."

Lori did as Brandon asked. Staring intently at his face in the screen, her inhibitions were fading. She could see by the slitting of his eyes he was getting turned on. The sense of power loosened something. She deliberately slowed down her fingers, kept her eyes on Brandon's, like a missile locked on target. Lori rubbed her lips with just her middle finger, forcing them apart slightly, pulling her lower lip into a pout. She puckered them and inserted that finger in her mouth, all the way past the knuckle, curling her lips around it, pushing in and pulling it out again, opening her mouth enough so that he could see her tongue playing with her finger. She moved close enough to the screen that he could see the moisture of her saliva glistening.

Lori had Brandon's hooked attention, and she was aroused by her own finger play. Her lips below were suddenly clamoring to join the fun. Brandon seemed to know just what was happening.

"Tell me how your pussy lips feel." He kind of growled, in a low voice.

Without breaking eye contact she moved her wet fingers to the crotch of her teddy, pushing it aside with her other hand, she touched herself, avoiding that spot, not wanting to push her pleasure beyond where she could articulate it for Brandon.

"They're fleshy and soft, plumped, like ripe fruit. And wet, though that's not the right word, it's more like a velvety moisture. My pussy is a juicy, fat papaya." Lori's voice purred around her attempt at a joke.

"That's the spirit, I can taste it. Take off the teddy, and move the screen down. I want to see you."

Lori unfolded her legs and plucked off the remaining lace. She put the iPad between her knees, fumbled with the device so that her vagina filled the corner of the screen. Yikes, she slid her bottom backwards a bit, remembering that whatever she saw in the corner would fill up the screen on Brandon's end.

"That's good Lori. Your pussy is beautiful."

Lori was sure she smirked.

"None of that, he said, even though he couldn't possibly have seen her face. "Look at me while you play with your clit."

Lori tried to play with herself the way that Brandon touched her. She held open her lips with one hand and with her other fingers rubbed, hard and fast, clit against cartilage. It felt good. She knew she was holding back, too self-conscious with Brandon there, and not really there, to kiss away the embarrassment.

"Don't think, just feel. Show me how wet you are."

Lori reluctantly squirmed a little closer to the screen. She took a good look. It was so different than what she saw in the mirror trying to save a few dollars by waxing her own bikini area. That vagina was grey and pale. What she saw now was pulsing with life, swollen, red, and gleaming. She put her middle finger inside and drew out a silky thread of moisture.

"I want to drink you," Brandon purred.

"You do something to me Brandon. My vagina looks like a rabid sea creature, truth be told, but it's hot."

"You are hot, and still thinking too much. Do you have the toy I gave you?"

"Toy?"

"Your magic wand. Haven't you used it since I left?"

"No. I was afraid once I started, I might not be able to do anything else," Lori said laughing.

"Understandable! Go get it. I want to watch you use it."

"I don't think I..."

"Yes, you can. You'll see."

Lori went to her bedside table where she'd tucked it away. Even though she hadn't used it, she thought about the possibility of it, many times, something she could draw on when missing Brandon felt like more than she could bare. She bent over to plug in the wand behind her bed.

"Stay like that for a sec," Brandon said, "you have a very fine ass."

Lori surprised herself, jutting her hips back, placing a hand on her butt and rocking side to side, turning her head to give him the pout. She felt like she was starring in a porn flick, and kind of liking it.

"Spread your cheeks, I want to see your asshole."

That felt, suddenly, like a step too far. Lori turned and flopped back on the bed, peeking at the wand in her hand as if someone else had put it there.

"Don't sweat it. We'll explore your ass when you're out here next." It sounded like a tease...and an order. "I remember you liked me to play with your ass."

"I did?" Lori sounded unbelieving.

"It's like you gave yourself sexual amnesia."

"I have a really good memory, everyone says so."

"Let's see if you remember how to use your toy. Touch yourself."

It was immediate, sharp, electrifying, just like the first time. Lori pulled the wand away, sucked in her breath.

"It's so intense, like an instant orgasm."

"See if you can slow it down."

Lori tried a lighter touch, in different spots, pulling it away when she got close to spilling over.

"That's good," Brandon said, his eyes changing, his gaze intensifying.

Lori could tell he was playing with himself. It was a little unnerving, so she glanced at the corner screen. She could see the changes in her own face too. Her mouth was open, puckering as if in search of some satisfaction, and her eyes had changed with whatever was rendering her incapable of pulling the wand away. Hunger had taken over. She used her whole palm to grind the head of the device hard against her. It pulsated her hand uncomfortably. The rest of her was locked into the zone beyond feeling and delectation.

She stared hard at Brandon. His curled, hungry lips, read that he was rubbing himself faster and with greater intensity. She closed her eyes and her orgasm burst forth rocking her entire pelvis. An animal groan (was the stranger back?) and fluid released, squirting in tandem with her pussy's contractions and making a surprising slushing sound.

When she opened her eyes, Brandon was there, face relaxed, released from the grip of his own craving.

"That was incredible. Your squirt, I heard it. I think it hit the screen! God, I wish you could have seen yourself." Brandon was grinning wildly.

"I did a little. When I peeked at the corner screen, I could see my own eyes telling me there's no turning back. It helped me let go."

"We need to work with that. I don't want you holding anything back."

"I never," Lori paused and said each word slowly, for emphasis, "never…ever, could have imagined doing what I just did."

"Ha! You're becoming a squirting junky."

"OMG, I think I just might."

"I can't wait for you to get here."

"Me too. Promise me you won't stop touching my hair. Can you tell I'm letting it grow out?" She turned her head, stretched out a strand to show him.

"I'm glad, and I promise. Get some sleep. I'll text you in the morning."

* * *

"Hope you slept well—my dirty, sexy pet ☺." The text from Brandon was waiting for her when she woke up. He must have sent it in the middle of the night West Coast time.

"Morning! I hope you're asleep. Just to let you know, I did."

She threw the phone back on the bed, considered how long it had been since she woke up feeling that relaxed. Another text came quickly despite the early hour.

"What are you gonna wear on the plane?"

"Wait, shifting gears. I guess what I wore last time. I like having a reason to wear a short skirt and some heels ☺."

"No panties. Okay."

"What?"

"Don't wear panties under your skirt."

"That sounds kind of exposed."

"See how it feels."

"Um, okay. I think," Lori said, with a tentative pout, though, as her thoughts were equivocating, her pussy was saying game on.

"That way I can play with you as soon as you arrive."

"In the airport?"

"I'll try to wait until we get into the car."

"Do other people behave like this?"

"You're so cute when you show your naiveté."

"I feel like I missed a decade or something in the universe's sexual awakening."

"I mean it, no panties."

"I heard you."

"On another note, Fiona's planned a great week for us."

Lori smiled at how nice that sounded.

Chapter 32

She was online ordering another sexy camisole to pack. Wondering whether she'd really have the nerve not to wear underwear, when she got a notification of an email from Peter. Even before she opened it, a sudden knot in her stomach tightened. The re line was innocuous. Spring Break. There were sentences of mumbo jumbo, judge's order, client in big trouble, getting on a plane immediately, probably stuck in Houston for a week, can't be helped. Bottom line, he was cancelling his trip with Ben and Catherine. He'd make it up to them with a beach week this summer, blah, blah. He was sorry if he'd inconvenienced her. He was sure she understood, after all, his clients paid her bills too.

That asshole! Inconvenienced her? Peter had totally fucked over her plans. Ben and Catherine would understand. They took bets on how close it would get before Peter cancelled on them. She'd allowed herself to believe that divorce would mean something different for her. No longer beholden to Peter's, or the firm's, or his clients' whims. No more golden leash and collar. Fuck, fuck, fuck. How was she going to wait another, who knew how many weeks, months even, to see Brandon? How was she going to tell him that she wasn't coming? He'd jumped through hoops to get the time off and Fiona had made all those plans. Fuuuuck!

* * *

Lori was dreading the call, put if off for hours, and when she finally dialed, thankful it went straight to Brandon's voicemail. She texted him instead, short and sweet, only hinting at a problem. She knew it was cowardly. Brandon called her back within minutes.

"What's going on?" There was an edge to his voice.

"Peter just cancelled his trip with the kids. I'm stuck here. I can't come out."

"I don't understand. Peter committed to the time, right?"

"Yeah, but he's getting on a plane in a few hours. A big client meeting tomorrow."

"Don't you have a parenting agreement?"

"Sort of..."

"What does it say about one parent being unable to care for the kids when they're scheduled to."

"I know what you're getting at. He's supposed to ask me if I can take them and if I can't, he's supposed to make other arrangements."

"So..."

"I know Peter. Believe me, he doesn't even know how to make his own arrangements."

"Why are you letting him off the hook so easily. Have you even asked?"

"No," Lori said quietly, furious at Peter for pulling his usual stunt, and annoyed with Brandon, because he didn't seem to care about what would happen to her kids.

Brandon let the silence hang for a minute. "Lori, I know you're worried about what plan he'll concoct, and I wouldn't let you leave your kids if they weren't absolutely safe. I'm telling you, though, if you let him dump this on you, he'll do it always. Once a bully, always a bully."

"What should I do?"

"I'm not going to tell you what to do, Lori."

"What would you do?"

"You're an attorney, quote him back the language from your parenting plan. Tell him you've made other plans and he'll need to find someone to stay with the kids."

"Is that what you did when Jocelyn left?"

"That's not fair."

"I'm sorry. I just don't want to push Peter right now."

"Why?"

"We still don't have a final agreement. We're close, but we haven't signed anything. He's still paying the mortgage, all the bills. What if he decides to screw me?"

"He's screwing you already."

"What if I tell him he has to take them another week, and then I'll come out?"

"And he'll be sure not to cancel again? Lori could feel his anger through the receiver, then Brandon's voice softened. "Lori, you do what you have to do, but don't let him treat you like your life is less important."

* * *

They hung up and Lori sat staring at her phone on the table. It looked as innocent as a spent grenade. She didn't know which felt worse. Not flying off to be with Brandon? That left her gutted. She'd been doing all the things that already felt like ritual. Lori had shaved carefully, conditioned her hair, taken the time to scrub and moisturizer down to the tips of her toes. Inside, almost in secret, her body had been preparing. Instead, she felt pain. Worse had been that awful sound of someone else's disappointment in her, not the actual words, but that thud when the disheartened turd landed at her feet.

Confronting Peter? Why is that so difficult? She was reminded of what a therapist had said a few years back, when Lori thought she should deal with her vague and constant melancholy. The woman asked Lori why she didn't get angry and insist that Peter give her what she needed. Why are you so afraid? Lori didn't have an answer. Maybe it was her Catholic background; or that her arrangement with Peter worked, in its own sick, pragmatic way; or, maybe, he was better at being a bully than she was feeling brave. The therapist warned Lori that if she didn't talk to him, her marriage was in jeopardy.

Lori had left the session feeling smug. Peter would never

leave her. He got too much out of the deal. She knew it sounded arrogant, but she was the one that had settled. His friends and colleagues, even his family, preferred her company to his pontificating—all the same people that were sticking with him after the divorce. How had money, and his professional prestige, and this twisted town, reversed their past like a camera obscura?

The therapist's question should have raised the alarm, though. Not that Lori hadn't tried. There was a night Peter missed dinner, as usual. She texted him that she'd wait for him to eat. Lori opened some wine. It was near midnight when he finally came in to find the bottle three-quarters gone, and Lori with her head down on the table. When he nudged her, buzzed and only half-awake, Lori found the strength to describe her longing for them to feel connected again. To be more, just simply, fun, as a couple and as a family.

Peter had zero patience. I'm tired, he told her, don't you understand how hard I work? I do it all, everything, precisely for this family. So, you'll never want for anything. Since we're talking about it (she remembered Peter got really testy then) it would be really nice if, just once, you and the kids pretended you were glad I came home. Lori shut down after that, realizing that love could be worn down into friendship, no, partnership, at least for the benefit of the kids. Until allies turned into enemies. She wouldn't bring up her needs again, not if it jeopardized her children.

She hadn't been wrong either. Peter's leaving had done them real damage, hard as she'd tried to convince herself that the fallout should be minimal. Dad moved out. Dad was never there anyway. Nothing's really changed. How naive she'd been. Ben in particular was struggling. His therapist told them he was having trouble processing the separation because he had a tenacious sense of loyalty. To family. How ironic.

Now, as if on cue, Ben and Catherine were becoming pawns in a struggle between their parents. Something Lori had promised never, ever to do, even if it killed her. She would never be the one to hurt them. But if Peter constantly took advantage, she would be giving up, not on her kids, but on something just as essential. How was that fair? She couldn't build a relationship with Brandon thousands of miles away when she still had so little control over the one right here, the one that supposedly was over. Brandon believed it wasn't too late to change. What if I'm still a coward? Ugggg. She nearly growled aloud.

Chapter 33

She hadn't heard much from Brandon. He responded to her texts, but there was something missing. An absence that caused a grasping fear at her core, enough that she almost got sick a few times. Feeling frantic, she would think of any dumb thing to text him about, and then pick up her phone, again and again, just like her children, devastated when there wasn't an immediate response.

I'm going to miss out again. The words howled around her skull. All the potency and happiness of being treated as someone equally worthy. She was losing Brandon, despite his polite responses, she could feel it in her bones. When she tuned into the background tape scrolling through her restless brain, she actually heard herself whispering, he loves me, he loves me not. Exactly the same child-like passivity she'd clung to with Peter.

* * *

"What's going on?" She texted Brandon.

"Not sure what you mean, Lori."

"I'm Lori, not baby anymore?"

"Just words. It doesn't mean anything."

"I think it does. It's like you've shut down."

"Work's been pretty intense the past few weeks. We're closing in on something awful. It's been around the clock. I haven't slept much."

"That sounds like something Peter would say."

"Lori. I'm not your ex."

"Then why does it feel that way?"

187

"You have to answer that."

"Why are you shutting me out just when I need you?"

"Nothing's changed with me. I'm here, if and when you want me. You've got to figure out what you want."

"I want to be with you. Of course, I do, but now I'm not sure if that's what you want."

"Look Lori, we've gone from zero to sixty pretty fast. I don't mind. In fact, I want it, if we're moving there together. I can't get burned again."

"I would never do that to you!"

When he didn't respond Lori texted again.

"My heart's moving fast too. I've been daydreaming about us constantly, how we could live together somewhere, with our kids. You know, finally get it right."

"It sounds like a very nice fantasy. How's that gonna work if you can't figure out how get here for a week?"

"I've been thinking. What if you travel here instead? Bring Fiona, we can do things with the kids, you know, all together. I'd be fun."

"You haven't even told them about me. Anyway, Fiona's got school."

"Would you really move back east, like you said you would, that Christmas when we kissed?"

"Where the hell did that come from?"

"My stomach's tied in knots, Brandon. I can't see through to how we'll be together, and I can't imagine not being with you again. It's killing me."

"Yes, Lori. I would consider moving, but not living under Peter's thumb."

"That's not fair. You've had a lot more time to work out this divorce stuff."

"I know men like Peter. It's not time you need."

"What does that mean?"

"You've got to stand up to him, Lori, or he'll control you forever, at least until he doesn't need you anymore."

"I'm just worried about the kids. I don't want to leave them alone, unsupervised."

"Do you really think Peter's gonna put them in jeopardy?"

"I don't know, maybe. I'm telling you, he's got nothing in place, no back up."

"If you don't make him fix that situation, you'll never have a life of your own."

"There's the whole divorce agreement too. We're so close. You don't know Peter, he'll screw me if I give him the slightest reason."

"What reason would you be giving him?"

"Jealousy. You. I think he's always suspected that I still cared about you. Cared too much that is."

"Of course, he suspected. He knew from the day you were married, but he left you, Lori. In the cruelest way possible. He traumatized your kids. What grounds does he have to screw you now?"

"It's what he does for a living."

"Lori, he moved out. You have a right to move on."

* * *

"I think I can get to Seattle, like we planned."

Lori had waited to text him until she was sure she could get plane tickets for Ben and Catherine. They were ridiculously expensive this close to the travel date. She would squint hard and press the complete purchase button, if Brandon said yes.

"That's great. What about your kids?"

"That's the thing. I can get there if I can bring them. Would that be okay?"

"It's fine, Lori. Are you sure?"

"We'll only stay four days, I don't want to push it. Can we take it slow? Keep things cool between us?"

"What are you going to tell them?"

"Just that I want to do something since their dad cancelled

their trip, that I have an old friend who lives in Seattle, who has a daughter their age, that it would be fun to visit. It's all true."

"Yea, but kids are smart."

"I've got to see you Brandon. This is the all I can figure out for now."

"Okay, we can try. To keep our relationship under wraps, I mean. I would like to meet them."

"Thank you! I can't wait to get there. God I've missed you."

"I've missed you too."

"It'll be great! The kids will like each other, don't you think?"

"We'll see☺."

* * *

It wasn't as hard as she feared to get Ben and Catherine excited about a visit to the chilly Pacific Northwest—after dreaming about Caribbean sunshine—though Ben did wonder why they weren't going to Aunt Emily's, their usual default destination.

Then things moved fast. Before she had time to think about what she was doing, they were on the plane, to Seattle. Ben on her left. He beat out Catherine in the coin toss for the window seat. Headphones were plugged in. Neither kid would talk to her for the next six hours. Plenty of time to think. What am I doing?

Lori ordered two of those mini bottles of wine on the flight attendants' first go around. Catherine gave her a smirk, then went back her music, singing aloud for a minute until Lori held her finger to her lips with the universal parent language to be quiet.

Chapter 34

Lori had learned her lesson. She didn't even try to imagine what things would be like when they arrived, not in those first few moments. Brandon insisted he and Fiona would park and come inside. They would find them at the baggage carousel. As Lori waited for their bags, one eye cocked toward the entrance doors, she wondered if that was a mistake. If Brandon had picked them up at the arrival zone, the first few moments would be fast and frantic, and she could avoid the issue of how to greet Brandon.

It didn't help that she was buzzed from the wine she had on board and found herself thinking about Brandon's last kiss, when she dropped him at the airport. It had been intense, almost desperate. He'd cradled her head between his hands, kissing her lips and eyes and cheeks, everywhere Lori's tears spilled.

* * *

Ben was grabbing bags and handing them to Lori when Brandon was suddenly at her side. She couldn't help grinning stupidly as she fumbled to stabilize the suitcase tipping over next to her. It was just so good to see him. How she'd missed the feeling of being tightly embraced. She tried to keep things chaste, giving him a tight hug with her head down. She assiduously avoided his lips, but the smell of him, feeling his strong arms on the small of her back, moving ever so slightly toward her ass. It was difficult to leave it at that. Thankfully, Brandon stepped back. He didn't try to kiss her, but looked at her that way that he did. Could her kids possibly miss his meaning? Thankfully Ben was still busy locating their bags and Fiona was fiddling with her phone.

Lori turned and gave Fiona a quick squeeze, trying to regain her composure. She got Ben and Catherine's attention and introduced everyone. The teenagers all mumbled hellos, shifting their feet uncomfortably. Catherine was a hugger and Lori could see her debating what to do. In the end, she grabbed for her suitcase.

"Thanks for coming to get us," Lori said.

"Of course," said Brandon.

"You know, guys," Lori said turning back to her kids, "Brandon and I have known each other for almost thirty years. Isn't that amazing?" Lori looked at them imploringly. They kept their mouths shut.

"We went to high school together, the same high school your cousin Sam attends."

"Cool," Ben said finally.

"Actually, I've met Fiona before, at Christmas, when we stopped to visit Aunt Emily, remember?"

Fiona nodded and smiled. Ben looked at Lori as if say, what are you talking about?

"Fiona, my kids have never been to Seattle. I hear you've got all kinds of great things to show them."

Fiona's smile broadened. She still wasn't speaking. This was going to be harder than Lori expected.

"You've never been to Seattle either, Mom," Ben said, again with that questioning look.

Lori had forgotten to invent an excuse for how she'd been there before. She couldn't just lie. Fiona would remember that Lori had visited Brandon, even if it was months ago.

"You guys must be starving." Brandon shifted them from Lori's awkward pause. "Ben, I remember when I was your age, I was hungry, like, all the time."

Ben gave Brandon a wide, conspiratorial smile.

"Let's get out of here and get some lunch," Brandon said.

There was a debate about who would take which bags. Brandon offered to take Lori's, and Lori said she would take

Catherine's. Ben fell in line behind them as they exited, hoisting his own bag on his shoulder. That left the two girls unencumbered and bringing up the rear. They already seemed to have plenty to talk about. Lori allowed herself a few silent phews.

Until they reached the car and loaded the bags in the back. Then there was a new moment of distress about where everyone would sit. The distance from Brandon was killing her, and he seemed to be indicating that Lori should sit next to him. Lori wasn't sure if she was ready to sit up front, like a couple, or, yikes, the parents, and she wasn't sure about throwing Ben in the back with the now chatty girls. Anyway, it looked like Fiona was eyeing the shotgun seat, probably thinking, it's a no-brainer, I go with my dad.

"Ben, why don't you sit up front with Brandon, us girls will take the back." She smiled at Brandon, hoping he agreed.

They exited the parking garage and Lori saw Ben playing with his phone. She inserted herself between the front seats and said,

"Ben, I don't think I've told you. Brandon is an FBI agent." Ben turned to look at Brandon, as if seeing him for the first time.

"That's cool," Ben said then looked at the road.

"So, like, do you have a gun?" Ben asked after a few more minutes of silence.

"I do, Ben. Although, in most circumstances, I think of it as my least important weapon."

"What do you mean?"

"Usually our best tactics are to be smarter than the bad guys, and to know how to fight really well before knowing how to use a gun."

"For sure," Ben said, "but like, do you have it with you, right now?"

"I do."

How does Brandon handle his gun at home? Lori suddenly wondered. How did he keep it safe from Fiona? Lori realized she and Brandon needed to sneak in that conversation when they were alone. Shit, will we ever be alone?

"Can you teach me to shoot?" Ben was quietly, almost shyly, asking Brandon.

"I can take you to the range, if it's okay with your mom."

Lori was lucky, Ben didn't ask her right then. That was another thing she'd have to figure out and quickly.

Chapter 35

Brandon took them to a fun, Hawaiian themed restaurant where the owner was a former actor. There were pictures lining the wall from movies like the Karate Kid. Score one for Brandon, she thought. Who doesn't like to talk about movies, and the kids seemed to get past their initial awkwardness.

"So, the guy who owns the place, is he, like, a karate expert?" Ben asked Brandon, but Fiona answered.

"He's studied a lot of different martial arts."

"Oh." There was a long pause.

"So, do you, like, do martial arts?" Ben asked Fiona.

"I've studied judo, kendo, and now mostly BJJ."

"BJJ?" Lori asked.

"Brazilian Jiu jitsu."

"Oh, girls do that?" Lori asked.

"There's some girls at my school."

"Martial arts are a requirement for any kid of mine," Brandon said. "The training makes you strong, it's built on good values, and kids have to be able to defend themselves."

"Did you train when you were a kid?" Lori asked.

"I wish. I had to learn to fight the hard way. I didn't start judo until I was in college."

"I don't remember that."

"I kind of snuck off to the classes. It wasn't too popular among our preppy classmates."

"I can believe it," Lori said. "Ben and Catherine took tae kwon do for a while."

"Mom!" Ben sounded mortified.

"What? You did."

"Depending on the school, it doesn't really qualify as a martial arts," Brandon said.

"Really?" Lori asked.

She was going to push it, as she noticed Fiona and Brandon exchange a knowing look. She decided to change the subject, for Ben's sake.

"What else do you like to do, Fiona?"

"I tried out for the play in the fall. We performed Narnia."

"Wow. You got a part?"

"Kinda, I was in charge of the back end of the Aslan puppet." Lori could see Ben suppress a laugh.

"Your mom tells me you're a real bad ass at hip hop," Brandon jumped in, talking to Catherine.

"Brandon!" Lori said.

Catherine gave him a huge grin. Lori tried hard to censor Catherine's rough language, but Brandon somehow guessed Catherine's natural talent for using phrases that would make a sailor proud.

* * *

They decided to hang out at the house since it was already late in the afternoon. They would let the kids relax and work through the jet lag. Lori offered to make a run to the grocery store.

"I think I've got most of the basics. If there's things your kids like..." Brandon said.

"I'll get something to make for dinner, and a few bottles of wine." Lori gave Brandon an anxious smile. "I think I might need some."

Brandon handed her the keys to his car.

"Are you planning on coming back?" He winked.

"Ha ha, maybe not."

"Seriously, you know where you're going?"

"The Safeway, right? The one a few blocks from here?"

"Just watch out for people hanging out in the parking lot, they're sometimes up to no good."

"Really?"

"You may not be able to tell, but, yeah, really."

"It's hard to decide if your job makes you smart, or just paranoid."

* * *

When she pulled the car up to his sidewalk forty-five minutes or so later, Brandon was outside on the small lawn with all three kids, engaged in some sort of sparring. At that point, he was taking on all three at the same time easily, but gently, knocking each to the ground. Everyone was laughing. As she got out, Catherine came running over.

"Mom come here! See what Brandon taught me."

She dragged Lori over and stood facing Brandon with her hands up, dancing on her feet, her face very serious. She went after Brandon. He spun her around.

"I didn't do it right, show me again, pleeeease..."

"Okay, just one more time," Brandon said, and he slowly walked her through it, until Catherine had Brandon's arm twisted behind his back. She grinned wildly.

"Good job, Catherine. You're getting it. We'll try it again later."

Catherine looked disappointed, but she flopped on the ground next to Fiona.

"Fiona," Brandon said, "please get the groceries from the car."

Fiona got up and Lori started to walk with her.

"Ben can help Fiona, right Ben?" Brandon turned in Ben's direction.

Lori noticed a brief note of confusion on Ben's face before he got up and went to help.

* * *

By the time the five of them sat down for dinner, the kids seemed more comfortable. Catherine never got to be center-stage at home, so she'd been thrilled to find herself smack in the middle of Ben and Fiona, holding her phone between them, showing off some of her favorite YouTube videos.

Meanwhile, Ben and Fiona had bonded a bit over a video game. The competition had gotten pretty intense. Ben won, Lori was grateful for that, but she was happy to see that Fiona had given him a run for his money. Sometimes these stupid devices can be useful. Lori smiled, recalling that the same thought occurred to her the night she left Brandon standing outside his mother's house. One kiss had ignited something fierce, and later, at a loss, she'd reached for her phone.

Fiona and Catherine set the table. Lori put out spaghetti and meatballs, salad, garlic bread, nothing fancy but things she figured everyone must love. Platters got passed. Food was gobbled up. Fiona and Catherine traded stories about friends and school. Ben was quiet, just the occasionally jab. Lori wished he'd say more.

She was stealing peeks at Brandon, realizing how good it was to see him in the flesh. She'd almost forgotten his face. It'd been that long. He had a strong, square, almost stern, countenance. She loved how his eyes changed though, sparkling bright and gentle when he smiled. They were all in a room together, around a table, sharing food, even occasional laughs. Lori couldn't quite believe it, or help thinking, this is how it could be.

With some trepidation, she asked her kids to do the dishes. She'd trained them well enough not to gripe. After a few minutes, she got up to help, coaching them not just to load the dishwasher, but scrub the pots and wipe down the counters. They'd managed the job with each asking her only once, are we done yet?

Chapter 36

They still had to deal with one more complication. Where would everyone spend the night? Catherine was a fitful sleeper. She found things to be afraid of, and not infrequently begged to sleep with Lori. With Peter, Lori had hung tough and said no. Since the separation, though, it was easier just to let her in. Lori didn't mind the company, but maybe that hadn't been the best plan.

Fiona offered to share her room with Catherine, and Catherine, thankfully, jumped up and down and said yes! There was a guest bedroom where Ben could sleep. Brandon offered Lori his room and said he would sleep on the couch.

"I can sleep on the couch, Brandon. I don't want to kick you out of your bed."

"I sleep there all the time," he said, "when I have crazy late shifts at work. I insist. Really, I like it."

* * *

Getting beds ready, and everyone settled, took some time. Finally, Brandon and Lori were alone, on the couch, deciding to finish off the opened bottle of wine.

"That went well, don't you think?" Lori lifted her glass so that Brandon could refill it.

"Were you worried it wouldn't?"

"Yes! A little. There was, you know, kind of a lot to pull off today."

"Your kids are great. You shouldn't worry so much."

"That's like me saying you shouldn't try so hard to catch the bad guys."

"Touché." Brandon raised his glass; they clinked and settled back into the couch.

"I think it's gonna be a while before the girls stop talking and go to sleep," Lori said, as she put her head on Brandon's shoulder and snuggled into his neck.

"We could watch a movie while we wait."

"Wait for what?"

"For everyone to be asleep so I can take you to my bedroom and fuck you. Excuse me, make love to you." Brandon gave her a huge grin.

"You don't really think we can do that?"

"Why not?"

"With all the kids in the house? It's not that big a house."

"I'll let that slide." He laughed.

"It's just, I mean, they'll hear us."

"We can be quiet as mice."

"Yeah, right."

"If the circumstances call for it, we do what's necessary," Brandon said, as if planning a secret military campaign.

"What if Catherine wakes up and comes looking for me?"

"I've got a lock on my door."

"She can be very insistent, especially in the middle of the night."

"I'll hide in the closet until you can get her back to bed."

"That sounds ridiculous." Lori was shaking her head.

"How can it be that we've gone from teenage to middle-age, and we still can't find a good place to fuck?" Lori hesitated only the tiniest bit on the last word.

Brandon laughed. He got up and flicked off the light, came back to the couch and lay across it, propped his back up against the sidearm, positioning Lori between his thighs, pulling her back against him, to face the TV.

"Just watch for a while, and relaaaax," he said, drawing out the second syllable, rubbing her shoulders in deep circles with his thumbs.

"Alright, I get it," Lori sighed, "and keep doing that. It feels great."

Brandon grabbed the remote and channel surfed, still massaging her shoulders and neck with his other hand. They passed over the History Channel in favor of Seinfeld reruns.

"That's about all I can handle tonight," Lori said, snuggling in tighter against him.

Brandon tucked his hand through the top of Lori's shirt, slipped it under her bra, resting it lightly on her breast, his other hand resting on the back of the couch. Lori exhaled a long, deep sigh.

To be doing something as ordinary as watching TV, with a man with whom she felt not just at ease, she'd lost even that with Peter, but someone she was mad about, thought about every minute of the day. A man who wanted continual intimacy, to hold her breast casually. Even better, she didn't have to miss her kids in order to enjoy this simple tenderness, because they were with her too, if dangerously close.

Brandon started moving his middle finger languidly around her quickly hardened nipple, stopping to flick the edge of his thumb against it, even as he seemed fully engaged in the TV show. Lori sighed again, maybe this can be enough while the kids are underfoot. It occurred to her that even their couch cuddling would seem unusual to her kids. They rarely saw evidence of affection between her and Peter. A fact that struck her suddenly as so sad. Even more crazy, she now felt compelled to hide from them healthy displays of affection.

It was all a bit maddening, not to mention she could feel Brandon's increasingly hard erection pressed against her tailbone. Still, they watched TV until no noise came from the bedrooms. Lori turned to see if Brandon was still awake. His eyes were open, burning with desire, apparently waiting for her. He lifted his torso off the sidearm. Lori twisted her body to reach Brandon's lips, touching them for the first time since she'd set eyes on him almost twelve hours ago. Wow. She didn't think they had it in them.

There wasn't much satisfaction from that angle, so she turned around fully, up on her knees facing him. Brandon reached for the remote and turned off the TV. It was pitch dark.

"Should we go to the bedroom?" Lori asked.

"We'll trip and wake them up."

Brandon guided her face down to him instead. He kissed it gently, her cheek, and temple, lips fluttering over her eye lashes, finally meeting her lips. He pushed open her mouth and his tongue was as fearless and possessive as always, but careful to be near noiseless. Lori felt the old thrill of sneaky lovemaking. It'd always seemed necessary to hide, from so many people, maybe even from themselves.

When she finally drew back to look at him, her eyes had grown accustomed to the darkness. She believed they could communicate and still keep the silence. Brandon must have agreed. He put his hands under her blouse, unsnapped her bra so it hung loose off her shoulders. He reached under, cupping and stroking the firm swell of her breast, not making a sound as he teasingly working his way to her nipples. His languor only intensified her need for him to reach, please god and soon, the titillated targets. She sucked her breath in sharply when Brandon finally made contact with her screaming hard nipples. He stayed, and played, their eyes locked.

When she could no longer reasonably ignore his erection, Lori lifted herself, bunched up her long, swoopy skirt around her waist, and held it there while Brandon dragged her thong down to her thighs. Before she could sit back down, he had his thumb hard on her clit, the blaze of desire in his eyes. His fingers, smooth and agile, brought her to a state of delight more intense than anything he'd ever done before. It happened so quickly, her orgasm announced silently with her lips open and rounded around what would have been the vocalization of her cumming. It was difficult, but she chocked back all sound.

She took a few breaths, kept her eyes fixed on his, even as she fumbled with his button and zipper, even as she lifted her hips and he pulled down his pants just low enough to release his erection, even as she sat on his cock, taking all of him inside, letting her skirt fall around them like a cloak. They moved together, slipped unconsciously into a rolling, compatible, near noiseless rhythm. She felt the pressure, the fullness, the pleasure between her legs. It was the strangest sensation, as if their eyes alone were doing the fucking. Brandon came silently, his eyes lit with surprise, his lips circled hard to cabin the vehemence of his release.

They stayed that way for a long moment, eyes locked, no movement, bringing their breath back to normal. Lori finally lifted off Brandon. She turned back around, smoothed down her skirt and flattened her loosened bra. She snuggled again between Brandon's legs while he tucked his other hand under her bra, resting it, again, lightly on her breast. A few minutes later, they heard Catherine calling out from Fiona's room.

Chapter 37

Their little group covered a lot of territory in the next few days. Picking up Fiona early from school each day, they explored, skipping, exhilarated, from one view to the next atop the Space Needle. Lori and her kids oohed and aahed like obvious tourists when the fishmongers began yelling and tossing whole fish at Pike Place Market, and they all squished together in a gondola for a few vertiginous turns on the Great Wheel. She and Brandon hung back to watch their teenagers, acting like children again, skipping through Chihuly's glass garden. With the squeeze of his hand she knew they were experiencing the same wistful joy.

The kids paddled on Green Lake, and they made it to one museum, MOPOP, formerly the Experience Music Project and Science Fiction Museum and Hall of Fame, a name that got Ben and Catherine's attention. They even had the best pizza ever, according to Catherine, at Serious Pie, though it was lost on her that a modest pizza place could be run by one of Seattle's most famous chefs. Fiona acquiesced to such conspicuously touristy activities since, she acknowledged, it was Ben and Catherine's first time in the City.

Lori had grabbed a private moment with Fiona to let her know that her kids didn't know about the first visit. Fiona seemed to understand, though Lori sensed a tension there. Fiona's pride in having information about something only the grown-ups knew, and discomfort at her vow to keep the intelligence from her new confederates. Lori wasn't exactly sure where that strain would break. So far, Fiona hadn't said anything to Ben and Catherine.

Lori also worried her kids might have noticed her too

obvious attempts to get close to Brandon. It came back to her in a rush, the years of frustrating friendship with Brandon when she desperately wanted more, and at the same time was compelled to avoid exactly that. When she helplessly telegraphed desire out of a primal need to connect with him, even as she didn't try to hide her longing from the other people in their various triangles. It wasn't very mature of her now, how she hung to Brandon's side, touched him when she was making a point, made asides that required close contact with his face.

There were major improvements this time around. She knew that her desire was reciprocated. She didn't feel the nagging worry that Brandon might be working the odds, playing her against another woman. What a difference that makes, she smiled to think it, but she and Brandon still hadn't touched each other in any serious way since that first night. Part of Lori was relieved. She'd been worried about their next full-on sex since Brandon had mentioned wanting to explore her ass. Nothing like that was likely to happen. The days were long and busy. Catherine had gotten over her initial thrill at the sleep over with Fiona and was insisting on sharing Lori's bed.

* * *

Their game of musical chairs continued around the shotgun seat. It was alternately won by Fiona or Ben, Catherine didn't have a chance. Lori was happy to ride in the back, where she didn't put as much pressure on herself to make sure everyone was happy.

When Fiona was next to her dad, they usually talked about books Fiona was reading. They were grown-up selections, certainly not beyond Ben's intellect. Too bad that was Ben's cue to plug in and tune out. Lori listened to them with half and ear. She was impressed, though she occasionally wondered how well Fiona got along with her peers.

"Hey Ben." Brandon was trying to get Ben's attention, during his turn up front, as they drove through the University District. "See that? Over there?"

"Where?" Ben slipped off his headphones.

"Those four kids."

"Yeah."

"That's a drug deal going down."

"Really! How can you tell?"

"I know this area well. You learn to see the signs."

"Like what?"

"The foot traffic, loitering, the conspiratorial gathering and quickly separating. It's the patterns."

"Huh."

"See that guy on the bike, I'll bet you a hundred bucks he stole it."

"He looks like a college kid."

"There's no books in his backpack, and he's not wearing a helmet. If you look carefully, he's giving little nods to other kids on the street."

Ben seemed engaged, kept his headphones off, staring more attentively out the window.

One afternoon, they'd driven home via Aurora Avenue because Ben wanted to spy on a legal marijuana store. Brandon gave them an entertaining education on the seedier side of Seattle.

"See that woman?" Brandon lifted his head in the direction of a woman on the side walk who had stopped, briefly, and changed directions.

"What does she do Fiona?"

"You mean the prostitute?"

Catherine whipped her head around. "Where?"

"That woman."

"She doesn't look like a hooker."

"Catherine! Where'd you learn that word?"

"Mom," Catherine said with disdain.

"But it's, like, daytime," Catherine said, "and her clothes aren't all slutty."

Lori gasped and laughed simultaneously.

"They have to work day and night. That's what all these crappy motels are for. It's a horrible life." Brandon kept glancing at his rear-view mirror, so he could talk to the girls. "You see how she keeps walking, then changing directions, trying to make eye contact with car drivers?"

"Yeah."

The traffic light turned green, so Brandon turned into the adjacent strip mall parking lot.

"She keeps walking so the cops can't stop her for loitering. If you watch long enough you realize she's not going anywhere. Keep looking, eventually she's gonna sit at the bus stop. Then she can say she's waiting for the bus."

Sure enough, the woman sat down, looking at her watch, like she was expecting the bus soon. A City bus stopped, blocking their view.

"She's still there!" Catherine exclaimed, when the bus had moved on.

"How do the guys know that she's a...," Ben was asking.

"Maybe that's enough education for one day," Lori said.

Brandon gave Lori a wink through the rear view and pulled back on the road.

* * *

After one of their whirlwind afternoons of sightseeing, they came back to the house to find Fiona's mother parked in front. Jocelyn was sitting inside her car, scrolling through her phone when they pulled in behind her and spilled out. Lori hadn't seen Jocelyn since Lori's own wedding twenty years ago and she hadn't expected to see her now. Jocelyn got out and strode forward, already talking to her daughter.

"Fiona, sweetie, you left your history study guide at my house." She turned to Brandon.

"Fiona needs it for a test next week."

"Hey Mom." Jocelyn gave Fiona a quick hug then Jocelyn and Brandon exchanged a kiss on the cheek. She turned toward Lori.

"It's been a long time," Lori said as she recovered from the surprise and gave Jocelyn a quick hug. "These are my kids, obviously, Ben and Catherine."

Lori's children nodded in Jocelyn's direction.

"Guys, this is Fiona's mom. Jocelyn went to college with us too." Lori saw Ben do a quick double take.

"So how have you been, Jocelyn?"

"You want to hear about all twenty years?"

They laughed, and Brandon asked Jocelyn if she wanted to come in.

"Sure."

He offered to make some tea and Lori and Jocelyn caught up in the perfunctory way of old acquaintances, about careers, and raising teenagers, and a few of their mutual friends. Jocelyn even dared ask Lori how she and Brandon reconnected after all these years. It was a fluid enough conversation to anyone listening. Lori felt uncomfortable by what was not being said. Was Jocelyn recalibrating Lori and Brandon's friendship in college and after? Did Jocelyn care how much Lori knew about Jocelyn absenting herself from parenting Fiona? That kiss between Brandon and Jocelyn. It was sort of an air kiss, then again...

The kids came in to graze and everyone stayed at the table to recount for Jocelyn what they had seen and done in just a few days.

"Wow. It seems like you guys hit every one of Seattle's highlights. Let me guess, Fiona organized?" Jocelyn smiled at her daughter, as Lori nodded.

"You definitely want Fiona on your team when the zombies take over," Jocelyn said. They all laughed.

"Well, I guess I should be going. It was nice to see you Lori. You've got great kids."

"Thanks, and it was good to see you too. We've really enjoyed hanging out with Fiona. Thanks for letting us monopolize her."

"No problem. Fiona, I'll pick you up Friday night."

"Okay Mom. Did you remember I have BJJ on Saturday morning?"

"Of course."

* * *

Later, Brandon asked Lori how it was to see Jocelyn.

"Weird."

"How so?"

"I don't know, the last time the three of us were together, she was your girlfriend. You guys seem awfully cozy."

"Really?"

"It just seems like she's put you through so much."

"There was a time..., believe me. You can't stay mad forever, without it eating away at your soul, and I really need her help with Fiona. Bottom line, I want Jocelyn and Fiona to have as loving a relationship as possible."

"Do you think she minded us being here, getting all this time with Fiona."

"No. She's been living with a guy for a while. She does things with his kids."

"Really? I feel like I'm being inducted into a new club."

Brandon laughed. "You mean the society of unraveled and reconstituted families?"

"Something like that."

"Just add water."

"You make it sound so easy."

"That's just time and learning to behave yourself. It takes a lot of practice, and just letting shit go."

"I can't imagine kissing Peter again, not even on the cheek."

"I'm sorry. Did that bother you?"

"No. Well, maybe. It's just that life can be...so circuitous. I have to get used to that."

* * *

Brandon let Fiona miss a day of school and they took a long road trip to Anacortes and back, driving through Deception Pass, and down through Whidbey Island. The kids had done well, despite all the time in the car, and the unusually warm weather, the constant stops and forced hikes, and Lori's frequent (they might say compulsive) urging that they forget their phones and take in the view.

She and Brandon had done well too, with one moment of awkwardness. Lori noticed Brandon looking anxious when the bill arrived at their last food stop of the day. It was yet another de rigueur organic food establishment with a kick ass view and pricey food to match. Lori quickly took the bill even though she'd already paid for their earlier meals. She whispered to Brandon that she was putting the whole trip on Peter's credit card since she was covering his ass by taking the kids. Brandon let her pay, but he didn't seem comfortable about it.

On the positive side, Lori had been in the front seat most of the day and for the first time since they arrived. They'd stopped for a quick breakfast and had an especially fun conversation about comic books. When they got back to the car, all three kids just slipped into the back, still talking, and closed the door. Lori found herself unexpectedly standing at the passenger side front door and Brandon quickly nodded for her to get in. It felt right, though her hand itched to hold his.

On the last leg of the drive, heading south on I 5 back to Seattle, Mt. Rainier was in glorious view, the peak rising, seemingly out of nowhere. A giant coconut cupcake whose sides had begun to collapse. Lori tried, without much success, to impress on Ben and Catherine how rare it was, to see it so clearly, if at all; that it was a sight that should take their breath away. They took it in, declared in cool once they heard it was an active volcano that could erupt anytime, and that was all they needed. Lori found herself drawn to the view, over and over again.

* * *

By the time they got home, everyone was exhausted. The kids were near comatose in the living room, in front of a movie, while Lori and Brandon made dinner. When the chicken was in the oven, they sat down at the small bistro table in Brandon's kitchen. Brandon opened a bottle of wine. They didn't say anything, just took occasional sips. Lori's glance alternated between Brandon's face, his calm eyes, she assumed, pondering an interesting thought, and the view out the kitchen window where the sun was finally setting on a long day.

In the quiet lull, Lori conducted a review of her body. She didn't feel the usual stress between her shoulders, or tightness across her forehead, aches and pains that liked to drop in when she was schlepping the kids, or reading an email from Peter, or getting another call from her attorney, or Catherine's teachers, or Ben's therapist. Nor did she feel the grabbing in her belly, the too-tight feeling that was a physical manifestation of how much she missed Brandon, and her inability to see past the scheduling or, really, the much bigger obstacles, to their being together. Maybe it was the day's highs, or the wine. Her usual feedback loop of doubts and anxiety had momentarily quieted. She leaned over to kiss Brandon, using her tongue to convey her contentment.

He pulled back. "Are you sure?"

She cocked her head toward the living room, held still while she listened. The preternatural silence from the other room was a strong enough indication that the kids were settled in and not moving for a while.

"Yes," she whispered.

Lori and Brandon kissed ravenously, as if to make one kiss everything, since that seemed all they could grab. Lori opened her senses; felt precisely the texture of Brandon's tongue against hers; noticed how their saliva pooled; tasted the way wine changed flavor when she discerned it in his mouth. Brandon's thumb brushed lazily back and forth across her breast, through her shirt, finding her breasts immediately attentive.

That touch sparked the familiar ache in her pelvis and almost without her willing it, Lori shifted closer, wrapped her legs around Brandon's, her hands on his knees, straining her neck to stay in contact with his lips. He adjusted his legs, causing hers to open wider and stretch against the seams of her shortish skirt. Lori was momentarily glad of her penchant for wearing them, instead of pants.

Brandon slipped his hand beneath the cloth, drew his finger playfully along the soft flesh of her inner thigh until he slipped it inside her panties and brought it directly to her clit. He began fingering her discretely, intensely, in a way that was reminiscent of her very first times being touched. She leaned into it, knew he would find her slick and wet. Please, please, touch me deeper, she was silently pleading, pushing her pussy harder against his finger, eyes wide open, one ear still cocked cautiously toward the doorway.

His finger entered her, and they swallowed their moans inside joined mouths. Brandon's eyes held wonder, as if he too was feeling the silky, opulent wetness of a woman for the first time. With his fingers teasing both her clit and her hole, she came quickly. Before, or because, the children might stir? She dripped a little squirt on the chair.

It was still a shock that it could happen like that. That she wouldn't cum at all remained a fear, even with Brandon. Lori had worried, over so many years, that if she took too long, it would get tedious for Peter.

Eventually, she and Brandon sat back in their chairs, mirrored sneaky grins, Lori allowing Brandon's fondling to reverberate inside her.

Chapter 38

It happened the next day, the thing Lori feared, the thing she must have known would happen if she brought her kids to Seattle. She and Brandon were pulling together a quick dinner. They'd gotten so good at the couples' kitchen dance, deftly moving in tandem around the small space, and producing reasonably interesting food for the crowd of five. The kids were at the dining room table, starting in on some snacks. They were talking about their respective adventures that day, their last day in Seattle.

Lori had finally allowed Brandon to take Ben to the shooting range, after repeated, though patient efforts to explain the safety protocol involved. Brandon made a convincing case that given the country was awash in handguns, and wasn't going to change anytime soon, it wasn't a bad idea for Ben to know how to use one safely. When the two returned to the house, their playful exchange of punches and comments indicated they'd passed through some ritual of male bonding and exited with mutual respect.

Meanwhile, Lori had taken the girls to do some shopping at University Village. She hadn't felt much effect from the outing except to lighten her wallet. Still, the girls had fun. There were plans to go to the movies after they ate, if everyone agreed on one. The current picks were being debated by the kids, with occasional lobs thrown in their direction from the grownups in the next room, as to whether or not the choice was appropriate family viewing. So nice...and normal...and Brandon right here with me. She turned a smile in his direction, to acknowledge the happiness she was feeling, and he kissed her. Nothing terribly sexy, but straight on.

Brandon lingered, tugged lightly at her bottom lip, definitely not a kiss of friendship, just as Ben walked in.

"Mom!"

"Ben. It's not..."

"Don't lie to me. I'm not stupid."

"I'm not...," Lori tried to respond, walking after Ben as he backed out of the kitchen doorway.

He turned away from her and practically ran to the guest room.

"Shit," Lori said, her hand to her head, as she followed Ben with her eyes.

The girls lifted questioning faces, first in Ben's direction, then at Lori. Fiona quickly returned her attention to her food.

"What's wrong Mom?"

"Nothing Catherine. Dinner will be ready in a few minutes." Lori backed her way into the kitchen, slumping against the counter in the corner.

"It was gonna happen Lori."

"I should have done something to prepare him."

"In my experience, it doesn't really help."

"Now what do I do?"

"Go talk to him. I'll keep the girls occupied."

* * *

"Ben," Lori knocked gently on the door, "can I come in?"

"I don't care," Ben said.

Never a good answer, thought Lori, as she slowly opened the door, then closed it behind her.

"I'm sorry you saw that Ben."

"Does Dad know?"

"That's not important right now," Lori said, though a warning flag went up. Something in the parenting plan discussed letting the other parent know before you introduced the children to a new partner. That wasn't this, was it?

"Nothing big just happened, Ben."

Oh really? Nothing?" Ben's voice was rising. "I just watched my mother kiss another man."

"Your dad and I have been separated for a while now. We'll be divorced soon. You know that, right?"

"Do you know what it's like to see your mom making out with someone?"

"Ben, it was hardly making out. But I'm sorry, I didn't..."

"So, does this mean, like, you're gonna make us move to Seattle."

"You're going way to fast. Nothing has changed. I've known Brandon a long, long time, since I was your age. I like him very much and I trust him...well...like family. He and I are just starting to consider the rest."

"Yeah, well I like him too. Now, it's just going be so awkward."

Chapter 39

They never made it to a movie. It was already late by the time they ate dinner. The ease and affability of the past few days were missing from the table. Ben only answered direct questions, meaning that he mostly passed food. The girls knew something was up and asked if they could go to Fiona's room. Brandon asked Fiona to do the dishes first.

"You know what girls, it's your last night to hang out. I'll do the dishes," Lori offered.

"May I be excused?" Ben asked.

"Sure, or you can stay with the grown-ups." Lori said the last words with a wink.

"No thanks."

As quickly as the five of them had sat at the table to eat, she and Brandon were, just as suddenly, alone.

"Well," Lori said, "that wasn't much fun."

"It could've been worse," Brandon volunteered. "No formal inquisition about my intentions."

"He was all over the board with his anger," Lori said. "I'm not sure if he's grossed out, offended on his father's behalf, or disappointed that you might be my boyfriend, and not just his new friend."

"Probably all of that, and then some. Kids hold on, for a long time, to their fantasy about parents getting back together."

"First, they hate us for divorcing, then they hate us for trying to move on?"

"It does all kind of suck for them."

Lori nodded.

"Want me to talk to him?"

"I don't know. What will you say?"

"Depends. I'll hear him out. Make sure he knows how much I enjoyed my time with him, and that my designs on his mother are entirely honorable."

"Wow. I thought things were already complicated." Lori made a small, pained sound as she gathered up the dirty plates.

* * *

Brandon was in the guest room for a while, long enough that Lori suggested that Catherine get ready for bed. They would leave early for the airport.

She'd convinced Brandon to let her and the kids take a taxi, since their flight was so early, and he had to get Fiona to school and himself to work.

"I'm gonna sleep with you tonight, right?" There was an anxious edge to Catherine's question.

"You can, but it's your last night with Fiona and I'm not going to bed yet. You'll be in there for a while by yourself."

"Why can't you go to bed now? You have to get up early too."

"I've got things to do. I've got to pack and get us ready."

"Do it in our room."

"Catherine if you push me I'm gonna get really angry."

"But Mom..."

"Catherine..." Lori's voice was rising, and her head was throbbing.

"Fine. You better come soon."

* * *

Lori was nursing her glass of wine at the dining room table when Brandon came out of the guest room, gave Lori a half smile, and knocked on Fiona's door. He was only in her room a few minutes before he joined Lori. She was absentmindedly checking their boarding passes to make sure they had seats together.

"So?" Lori felt desperate to hear about the conversation.

"So."

"Well?"

"He's processing things. He's a good kid, Lori."

"I know. It's just, he's so sensitive these days."

"We talked about other stuff, but he wanted to know how long we'd been, I think he said, going out. He might be feeling a bit left out."

"What'd you tell him?"

"That it was a new relationship. That you've been my friend and I've cared about you for a long time. He wanted to know if we'd gotten together before you separated from his dad."

"He asked that? When in the world...?"

"I asked him whether he thought you would do that to his father, and he said not really."

"Not much of a vote of confidence."

"I think the whole oedipal thing is playing out."

"Again, with the psychology degree." Lori made a face.

"You're his mom, he's supposed to get over his erotic desire for you by identifying with his more powerful father, but now, here I am, sticking my nose where his father was supposed to."

"Brandon!"

"Sexual pun intended."

"Do you really believe this stuff?"

"Honestly, who knows what goes on in the mind of a teenage boy. He's worried."

"About what?"

"He's worried about you. That you'll get hurt again. That he'll lose you."

Lori winced.

"He wasn't really asking me, but I think he's starting to ask questions about what this all means."

"Shit."

"Yeah."

"So, what'd you and Fiona talk about?"

"I let her know what was going on."

"I bet she liked being the one in the know."

"That's not very nice, Lori."

"I'm sorry, it's just, you guys...you've done this dance so much longer, and sometimes it feels like you two have your own private club."

"That's not true. Fiona and I have been through a lot. Peter may be a jerk, but he hasn't abandoned your kids."

"He kinda has," Lori grumbled.

"Fiona was forced to confront things a kid should never have to. Peter's trying, you two are working together for your kids in your own way. For that, you need to be grateful."

"Maybe. I don't feel it yet." Lori signed. "Let's not argue tonight. Want to chill and watch some TV?"

"Okay, but We're gonna have to talk about these feelings sometime."

"I know," Lori said frowning.

She took Brandon's hand and lead them to the couch. She tucked her bottom between Brandon's reclined body, settled back against his chest. She loved to feel her head rise and fall with his breath. She was waiting, hoping for his hand to rest on her breast, when Catherine called.

"Mom, are you coming?"

"Catherine, I'll be there when I'm ready."

"But Mom, I'm..."

"Just go," Brandon said, "she probably guessed something's up."

Lori paused, sighed again deeply, but got up. She quickly brushed Brandon's lips, then went into his room where Catherine was waiting.

Chapter 40

Lori hadn't expected to fall asleep. The rest of the house was pitch dark and eerily quiet, though, when her eyes popped open. Catherine was snoring ever so gently next to her. The day and night came back in a rush. Ben's anger, Catherine's pesky anxiety, Fiona's occasional whiffs of superiority, Brandon's...what? So many things.

He must be out there on the couch. Dare she go to him? Is he waiting for me? If Catherine woke and called for her, it might just be the complication, the need, the interruption, that made her skull explode. If she didn't, her less than kind words after dinner would be their last in who knew how long. Not that Lori really wanted to talk. There was nothing words could sort out before morning.

She'd traveled so far to see him, though. She had to have contact before she left. Despite that it'd been her brilliant idea that they not display their romantic tie this visit. Over the course of these few days, a future with Brandon had gotten both easier and so much harder to imagine. She needed to—I must!—bring enough of him back to survive the coming, indeterminate, drought.

Lori climbed carefully out of the bed and tucked the covers around Catherine. She walked to the half-opened door and paused. Catherine hadn't stirred. Lori tiptoed the few steps down the hall, through the dining area and stood staring at Brandon on the living room couch. He seemed to be asleep, a light blanket pulled up to his bare chest. When she sat down next to him, though, his eyes opened quickly. Lori put her finger to her lips and pointed to the French doors in the dining room that led out to the back of his house. They got up and walked there, quiet as mice, Lori smiled as she thought it. They slipped outside.

She hadn't yet been in his backyard. Maybe it'd been too chilly on her first visit, or they'd just run out of time. The warmth of the past few sunny days lingered in the evening's stillness. The moon hung softly, watching, only a quarter full, and the City lights shed their soft, orange glow.

Lori could see the outlines of shrubs against a short fence separating the neighbor's back yard, and some flower pots that marked off a small patio with two lounge chairs. Brandon led her to one, and then onto the chair when he sat back in it. Lori curled sideways, drew up her knees across his lap and rested her head on his chest. She closed her eyes and listened to the night sounds. They stayed like that for what seemed like hours.

"It's a beautiful night," Lori said, finally, without moving her head. "I'm glad we got outside."

"I've had fantasies about doing things with you, out here, under the stars."

Lori smiled into Brandon's chest. "I didn't see any stars."

"It's true. You probably can never see them with all the ambient light."

"We can still do things."

"You say that."

"I mean it." Lori swallowed a silent prayer that Catherine not wake up. She extended her neck to reach Brandon's lips.

She kissed him to tie a knot, a kiss that would remain long after her flight back east. Lori flattened, darted, then curled her tongue to fill every corner of his mouth, to assure herself there was no doubts lingering there. She wrapped and unwrapped it, like a snake in a mating dance, or a lasso intent of locking down its prey. A kiss that would be enough.

It wasn't. Lori rested her head back on Brandon's chest, chin down sulkily.

"I need you inside me," she said in a mumble of frustration.

"Baby, I can't hear you."

Lori tipped her face up, still trying to keep her voice low. "I need you inside me. I can't leave without that."

"Let's play it safe tonight. You don't want to take home any more complications."

"I don't want to play it safe, not tonight, not any night."

"I know, but my bedroom window, Catherine's room, it's almost right above us."

"I don't care. Why do we have to care?"

"Because they're your kids."

"We're not doing anything wrong. I want to be with you more than I ever wanted to be with their father. I want them to understand that."

"I know you do, Lori, but they never see it the way you want them to, or care the way you wish they would."

"Wow. That's depressing."

"I speak from experience."

"Does that mean it can never work? Our kids aren't going anywhere."

"No. It just makes it harder."

Lori's body grew rigid. She was focused on the bushes, trying to digest the lurking frustration that sat like a rock in her belly. Brandon's hand was moving rhythmically, from the part of her hair over her ear and back, cradling her and muffling sound. It was soothing, and it helped. It just wasn't enough.

Lori sat up and took his hand. She shepherded him off the lounge chair, pulling him to the side fence where there was a patch of grass, and no bushes, and a large tree blocking the side neighbors' window. She faced him standing, glanced around to see that the back neighbors' windows were dark.

"Take off your pants and lie down."

"Lori, let's not do something you're gonna regret."

"Shhhh." She cut him off by kissing him, then stepped back and nodded, looking down at the jeans he'd not taken off before settling onto the couch for the night.

Brandon slipped them off. A commando day. He was

suddenly naked. They met standing, he was already hard and rubbed himself against the cloth of the oversized t-shirt Lori had worn to bed. His cock pushed up the material enough for her naked pussy to peek out and thrill at the warm air, massaging her lower belly like it had the power to break up all her tensions there. She lifted up on her toes to reach his mouth, all in quickly, lips, tongue, teeth. When her feet got tired she pushed him gently down by his chest, her body following, still kissing, till he was on his back, her knees wrapped around his torso.

Finally, she sat up and lifted off her own shirt, seeing the heat rise in Brandon's gaze. Lori loved his watching her, wanted to give him something more to enjoy. With the palms of her hands she began massaging her breasts, around the outside swell, pushing them closer together. She looked down at what she'd created, fleshy, swollen mounds with a deep, dark slit between, an alternate pussy.

Keeping her breasts pushed tight, she bent over Brandon's penis, put it between them and rubbed back and forth, over and over, increasing the pressure, wringing out quiet moans from Brandon until she released him, and working down further, ran her soft, open lips over his shaft, finally settling on his balls. Her mouth watered from touch and provocation. She released her saliva onto them, alternately sucking and licking the puckered seam down their middle with the taut tip of her tongue.

The noise she made, a wet, slurpy sound of greedy contact, filled the night air. Brandon tried to muffle his groans, his erect cock pushing straight to the sky. She circled it with her fingers, stroking up and down while her mouth continued to play with his boys. She could tell he was about to cum, so she stopped, held his cock still, sat straight on top, and brought him inside her. She was slick, and he entered easily. She rode him, her eyes shut tight, so she could remember it all later, by feel alone. When she opened them again, adapting her sight to the shallow darkness as she glimpsed the night sky, she thought she saw someone at the back neighbors' window.

Lori felt a shock to think someone was watching, but

Brandon was too close, and she too committed to his orgasm, to stop. Perhaps she didn't care if they were being watched, because she tightened all her muscles around him, grinding on him fast and firmly. She collapsed to his chest when he came. Then she looked back up and saw a shadow of movement at the same window. When she blinked to clear her eyes, no one was there. Still, Lori hastily rolled off of Brandon, patting the ground for her shirt and slipping it on.

"Is Catherine here?" Brandon asked, sitting up and grabbing for his pants. "I didn't hear anything."

"No. Thank god. I think your neighbor may have been watching."

Brandon turned his head quickly as he pulled on his jeans.

"I don't see anyone."

"I think they moved from the window when I looked up."

"It was probably Tom. He's a bit of an insomniac. I've seen his lights on when I get home from work in the middle of the night."

"You know him?!"

"We've been neighbors a long time. He's a pretty regular guy. Don't worry."

"I won't, I guess, if you're not. I don't have to see him in the daylight." Lori laughed lightly, shaking her head.

"What's so funny?"

"I have worried about so many fucking things today, and, unintentionally giving your neighbor a peep show, well, that just wasn't anywhere on my radar screen. Makes it kinda funny, don't you think?"

"I suppose. What I really want to know is, did you like it?"

"Brandon!"

"It's a real question."

"Like him watching?"

"Yeah?"

"No. It's creepy and weird."

"You didn't stop though?"

"I couldn't, you were so close, and I needed you to cum inside me. Wait, are you mad I didn't stop?"

"Not at all."

"You're not upset at him for watching?"

"It's a free country. We were doing it outside."

"He could have been polite and walked away."

"Lori, I wouldn't mind the whole world seeing how sexy you are."

"Really?"

"Really."

Chapter 41

After the long, indifferent hours spent in the beige world of air travel, Lori was surprised to be hit so strongly by juxtaposition. She felt it the minute they started driving from the airport. Even her house felt unfamiliar.

She'd expected less of a disconnect, this time around, since her kids had traveled with her, and they too brought back memories of a new city; of a new man and his daughter, kinda, sorta, in their lives. In reality, her kids barely mentioned the trip. They'd slipped back into their routine like nothing had changed.

Peter was still away in Houston. He was hinting that his weeklong trip had turned into several, maybe even a month, in order to stem whatever, the client crisis was. He wouldn't be able to meet with his attorney to review and sign the final agreement until he got back. That sucked. It also meant no break from being full-time parent. Just when the pile on of winding down the school year projects began. Damn. Maybe she could entice Emily to visit.

* * *

Jeanette wanted to get together. Her family hadn't had much of a spring break since Jason had a travel soccer tournament scheduled, but she was curious about Lori's. Lori suggested lunch to avoid the implicit rush of a coffee date. If she was going to tell Jeanette about the trip, Lori was going to have to fess up about Brandon.

It was starting to feel weird not telling her. Too many awkward pull backs from conversations because it would have moved them into forbidden territory.

They met at the local salad place. Ordered at the counter, and before even settling into a table, Jeanette began to probe.

"So, you went to Seattle?"

"Yup. Took in all the sights."

"Did it rain the whole time?" Lori winced at what felt like criticism, however slight, in Jeanette's question.

"Actually, we had beautiful, sunny weather. It was almost hot some days."

"I froze my tushie off at a couple of Jason's games."

"See, you never know."

"Where did you stay? I've heard the Palladian is fantastic, though probably wasted on the kids."

"We actually stayed with a friend and his daughter."

"His daughter?"

"An old friend. His name is Brandon."

"You've never mentioned him before."

"We've known each other a long time. He dated my best friend in high school, and then he transferred to my college sophomore year." Lori gave Jeanette a noncommittal smile.

"That's when we became close friends," Lori continued, "but we kinda lost touch over the years. You know how it is."

"Is he an old boyfriend?" Jeanette was suddenly sitting forward in her chair her fork frozen in mid-air.

"Not really."

"What does that mean?"

"We never really dated, but, well, we have some history."

"Lori, are you dating him?"

"We've been texting and I..."

"Wait, you brought your kids to meet him?"

"I thought I'd be fun to go someplace for spring break, especially after Peter cancelled their big trip."

"Do they know?"

"Know what?"

"That you're dating this guy."

"We're not really dating, Jeanette, he lives in Seattle."

"So, your kids think he's just an old friend?"

"Yeah, well we..."

"Thank god." Jeanette finally lowered her fork. "Can you imagine the field day Peter would have with that?"

"Peter and I have been separated for over a year and a half. We're this close," Lori made a small gesture with her thumb and pointer finger, "to being divorced."

"This close is not the same thing as being divorced. Technically, I think it's adultery in Maryland if you have sex with someone who's not your spouse, even if you're separated."

"My lawyer told me no judge ever enforces that."

"Wait. You're sleeping with him?" Jeanette's voice was both hushed and screeching.

"I've gone to Seattle, and he's been here once."

"OMG, Lori are you serious?"

"We met up right after the separation. Remember I visited my sister on my way home from my in-laws?"

"That debacle, yes, I remember. Wait, you've been dating him for over a year?"

"No. We had a quick meeting, and it rekindled some strong feelings. We texted a bit. It was very nice, but I worried it might be too difficult. I let it drop."

"That was smart," Jeanette said, shaking her head and sitting back in her chair.

"A few months ago, I reached out to him again." Lori had shifted forward, looking directly at Jeanette. "He'd told me right from the start... He's been searching for someone like me his whole life. I just kept thinking about that."

"That's very sweet. Is he planning to move east?" Jeanette sat up again, raised her hands as if dumbfounded.

"Because I don't see how you're going to date someone in Seattle. Do you?"

"We haven't gotten that far, Jeanette. He has a job, and his daughter and ex are there."

"Oh Lori," Jeanette slumped back, "this has heartbreak written all over it."

"No! It's been wonderful." Lori's voice rose in emphasis.

"He's everything Peter wasn't. He's interested in me," Lori said as her hand flew to her heart, "and what I want to do with my life. You should see the way he looks at me, like I'm the only person in the room." Lori stared at Jeanette imploringly.

"He's kind...and so affectionate..."

"Is this about sex?" Jeanette asked interrupting. "I always guessed Peter wasn't much in that department. I mean he barely hugs his own kids, or lets them touch him."

"It's not just that. I mean the sex is amazing, I never knew it could be so good..."

"Please, please take my advice and don't say anything to Peter. You'll just give him ammunition to screw you out of what you deserve. Can this guy take care of you?"

"He's not rich."

"What does he do?"

"He's an FBI agent." Lori caught Jeanette half rolling her eyes.

"Jeanette, he's trying to stop the illegal human trafficking trade on the West Coast. Do you really want to sniff at that?"

"I'm sorry," Jeanette said softening her tone. "I'm sure the work he does is very important. He's probably in amazing shape, right? I know those guys have to stay fit."

Lori detected a reluctant smile that Jeanette quickly squashed and scrunched into the face of an interrogator.

"Tell me you're not serious about this, Lori."

"Jeanette, I can't..."

"You've got a whole, new life ahead of you Lori," Jeanette said seemingly oblivious to interrupting again. "This just... I'm sorry. It just seems like a dead end."

"You have to understand, Jeanette." Lori slowed down her words, to get it right, to help Jeanette grasp Lori's own, newfound insight.

"Peter and I thought we had that down pat. We carefully, methodically planned out our perfect life, and it crumbled, to shit, in an instant."

Jeanette just shook her head.

"Just maybe," Lori said, "we don't always require a neat and sensible plan."

"Promise me you won't tell your kids." Jeanette's words rushed at Lori. "This may all blow over and you don't need to make the situation more difficult."

Lori made an excuse to leave. She could feel her hands shaking as she drove away. Jeanette had managed to trash, pretty much, everything. Honestly, though…, all she did was say aloud every problem Lori already lost sleep over.

Damn it, Lori thought, as her hand struck the steering wheel. Would this relationship ever seem more than a checklist of problems? How could she ever convey how each waking dream, every activity and emotion, drifted, swirled, and settled around her feelings for Brandon? Like the stray leaves that blew all around her yard, yet managed to end up exactly in one spot at the top of her driveway.

Maybe it was unrealistic to think that her friends, even her kids, could understand. This was hers and Brandon's to sort out. They could do whatever they wanted. Except—their tempestuous Achilles heel—so many other people, and all their needs, seemed desperately tied to Lori and Brandon's future.

Chapter 42

Emily got herself down for a long weekend a few weeks later. It was so nice to have her around. Emily hadn't been in the house more than a few hours and they'd already slipped into their pajamas and opened some wine. Emily would be dictating plans for arranging the furniture in Lori's future home before they finished the bottle.

Both Lori's kids hovered near the kitchen, drawn to Emily's irresistible combination of bossiness and humor. They served up dinner as soon as it was ready, the four of them pulling up stools to the kitchen island. Lori and Emily were being discreet not to talk about Brandon.

"So, how'd you like Seattle, Catherine?"

"We had the best pizza, Aunt Emmy." Catherine was digging into dinner, apparently food on her mind.

"Tell Aunt Emmy who cooked it."

"I don't know, some famous chef or something."

Lori traded a smile with her sister. "Tom Douglas, and it was amazing."

"Everyone had tattoos," Catherine said, eyes lighting up, "like everyone, and the girls all had their hair dyed."

"You working on your own tattoo design? I'm sure your mom will be fine if you get one."

"Emmy!"

"I don't want a tattoo, everyone says they hurt. But, Mommmmm, please can I dye my hair for the summer, pleeeeeease?"

"We'll see."

"Everyone looked so cool. The styles around here are so boring."

"I guess Catherine liked Seattle. What about you Ben?"

"It was okay. Catherine had Fiona to hang out with."

"Was Fiona nice?"

"She was great," Catherine answered immediately.

"Did you like her Ben?"

"She was okay, maybe a little stuck up."

"You're just mad, because she was almost as good as you at Minecraft."

"I don't play Minecraft anymore, Catherine. I only did it to be nice."

"Enough," Lori said pouring Emily some more wine.

"What about Brandon, did you like him?"

"He was pretty cool."

Did you two do anything special, just the guys?" Emily winked at Ben.

"He taught me how to shoot a gun."

"Oh my, that's not what I was expecting." Emily shot a quick glance at Lori. "Soooo...was it fun?"

"Yeah. He said I was a really good shot."

"Where'd you do this?"

"At the range."

"Okay, so someplace safe."

"Hey guys, tell Aunt Emmy about some of the other sights."

"We went to the top of the Space Needle, and we saw some whales!" Lori was glad to see that Catherine had retained some wonder about the trip.

"Right in downtown Seattle? Very cool."

"No," Lori said, "we saw them in Deception Pass, when we were driving to Whidbey Island. Everyone said it was early for the Orcas." Lori grinned remembering it.

"Emmy, it was just incredible to see the whole pod splashing and playing."

"I'm not sure I've ever seen a whale that wasn't hanging from the ceiling of a natural history museum."

They all laughed.

"So, Ben, was anything particularly interesting for you?"

"Just what everyone else said."

"Nothing stuck out?"

"I don't know. Why don't you ask my mom what she did?"

Lori turned quickly in Ben's direction. "What are you talking about?"

"You know, what you did with Brandon."

"Ben," Lori sighed.

"Can I be excused, please?" Ben left the table without waiting for an answer.

Both Catherine and Emily gave Lori questioning looks.

"It's nothing important. How about some dessert? I got us ice cream."

* * *

"What was that all about?" Emily asked.

They'd sent Catherine off to bed with a promise not to crash the big girls sleepover, and had taken their wine to the porch for some privacy. With Aunt Emmy around, Catherine wouldn't dare interrupt.

"Ben saw Brandon kiss me."

"I guessed it might be that."

"It was just a kiss, standing in the kitchen. Ben hasn't said a word about it since we got back. I didn't know it was still bothering him."

"I told you. It's all complications."

"I tried to explain that I care for Brandon; that nothing about that is going to impact Ben's life. If you could believe it Emmy, he was already worried about us moving to Seattle!"

"Of course, he was. That's where kids go. They don't do subtlety."

"I want them to understand that Brandon's important to me. I wouldn't have taken them out there if he wasn't. I don't want them to overthink it."

"There's the rub. You're talking about a long-distance relationship. That makes it kind of hard to introduce the concept gradually."

"Still, I'm glad I took them. It was just so...normal. I think Ben really liked Brandon. He's great with the kids." Lori smiled to recall the sparing on the front lawn.

"Oh, Emmy, it made me want so much more."

"Honestly, Lori," Emily said, her mouth puckered into serious frown, "I'm not sure taking the kids was a good idea. You and Brandon aren't having a normal relationship anytime soon, not unless you plan on leaving your kids behind."

"Good god Emmy, I could never do that."

"Peter's never going to let you move to Seattle with Ben and Catherine, not in a million years."

"He never even sees them. He's barely a father."

"He's their father." Emily put her glass down and leaned closer.

"Peter has his principles, and you know how much he cares what other people think. If you take the kids, it would conflict with his image of a competent, involved dad. What was that stupid expression he used at your mediation sessions...," Emily seemed to be searching for a word, "full-time, part-time parent?"

"I'd forgotten that."

"Would Brandon move back east?"

"He says he would consider it. Honestly, I don't know." Lori shook her head despairingly.

"Fiona's lived her whole life in Seattle, and her mother's out there... Brandon and Fiona are really tight. What she wants is going to matter... A lot."

"Complications," Emily said sitting back, with a smirk and eyebrows raised as if to say, what'd I tell you.

"Shit, Emmy." Lori took a large gulp of wine. "What've I gotten myself into."

"Love, I'm guessing, or at least infatuation, and that's a good thing, but you've got to remember Lori in all this." Emily looked at Lori, as if wanting to convey her next words carefully.

"You've been catering to others your whole life. You don't want to pick up another set of people to take care of."

"That sounds awful, Emmy. That's not what this is. I'm in love with Brandon."

"That may be, but have you stopped to ask what Lori needs? What Lori deserves, after all you've put up with?"

"He helps me remember who I am."

"Oh Lori." Emily's voice changed, her shoulders lifted and collapsed into a shrug. "Can't you fall in love with anyone closer?"

"Are you seriously asking me that? I don't want to fall in love because it's convenient." Lori spat out the last word, then lowered her voice.

"Emmy, I swear, with Brandon, it feels... Don't laugh, I know it's cliché'd. It's like we're soulmates."

She saw Emily hold back a smile.

"It's true! What we have feels ancient, and essential, and thrilling and new. How do you say no to that, even if it's fucking complicated?"

"What happens next?" Emily asked.

"I don't know. We haven't even planned another visit."

Chapter 43

Lori drowned her worries, not with booze or binge-watching TV, but by getting busy, buried, overcommitted. She said yes to everything, including being in charge of the last day of middle school blow out for Catherine's class. It was a parent sponsored tradition to provide the kids lunch, keep them appropriately entertained half the day, and create a roster of serious and not-so-serious awards. Lori was even expected to give a graduation speech. All of this without offending any parents or embarrassing her daughter. She'd already had a few run-ins with Catherine.

"Please, please don't ask Lauren's father to do his juggling routine," Catherine had pleaded over breakfast one morning.

"He's done it at all your end of year parties. It's a tradition."

"Exactly, and it's stupid every time."

"Does Lauren think so?"

"I'm sure she does."

"Well, I don't want to hurt Mr. Pratt's feelings."

"Mom, pleeeease."

"I would rather talk about your progress on the essay for English class."

"I'm already finished."

"It's not due for two more weeks. Have you really put thought into it?"

"Yes, Mom."

"Do you want me to take a look?"

"No. The teacher goes over it with us."

"You know that parents are invited to hear students read their essays, right? Why don't you try it out on me?"

"Nah."

"You sound just like your brother. Are you sure?"

"I'm sure."

* * *

The next few weeks, Lori was in constant motion. She needed a glass of wine to wind down, not her usual habit. She didn't want to think about complications. Brandon seemed a little worried about her during a recent phone call.

"You've taken on an awful lot, Lori."

"I know. It's the stay-at-home moms that secretly run the world."

"You could say no sometimes."

"Do you say no to work projects?"

"Yeah, I do, if they're going to keep me away from home and Fiona too much."

"It's Catherine's last year. I want it to be special. You don't have to worry," Lori chuckled, "when she and Ben are both in high school I won't be allowed to run any school projects."

"If you say so. By the way, I'm trying to figure out when I can come for a long weekend."

"Really? That'd be great. I miss you so much."

"I miss you too. It's just extra hard with the school year ending. Jocelyn and I always have conflicts over the summer schedule. She doesn't like child care responsibilities interrupting her life."

"That sucks."

"It does, because I'm getting desperate. I miss your body something awful."

"I can't believe it's me saying this. We didn't get nearly enough sex my last trip out there."

"Just enough to get in trouble."

Lori could hear his wink.

"Ben was a little snarky with Emily, about our stolen kiss," she told him. "It seems to have blown over. Life goes on, right? If it's not about them, they forget all about it."

"Very true, young Padawan."

"Funny."

"I try."

"Hey, did you ever see your neighbor? The one that watched?"

"A couple of weeks ago. We both happened to be in our backyards."

"Did he say anything?!"

"No, but he did give me an interesting look."

"OMG!"

"No worries. I think he was jealous."

* * *

In the middle of running around for the Good-Bye Sycamore Hills party, Lori's attorney suddenly needed to see her. Lori tried to do it by phone. The paralegal insisted that she come in for a face-to-face meeting. Lori was hopeful this meant it was time to sign the dotted line on the divorce settlement. It seemed like they had an agreement. Still, the lack of finality, and Lori's continued reliance on Peter to pay the bills, kept Lori in a near constant state of anxiety.

She managed to get in to the lawyer's office mid-afternoon, later that week.

"So, is Peter finally ready to sign off on the finances? He's been traveling so much. He kept telling me he had to put it off."

"Peter's attorney contacted me, not just about the agreement. Peter has raised some concerns about the children."

"What? He hasn't even seen the children in almost a month."

"Yes, well, I guess Ben told him about your trip to Seattle."

"I told Peter. I gave him our travel dates and flights, just like it says in our parenting plan."

"Apparently he didn't realize that you were staying with a man. Your boyfriend?"

"Are you kidding me?"

"Don't misunderstand me, Lori. You are allowed to move on

and have relationships, though waiting till the divorce was final might have been better."

"You told me..."

"I know what I told you. This is more about you not informing Peter of the nature of the relationship since you were introducing the children."

"Geez, I didn't say anything because I was trying to not make it a big deal. We were just going to visit an old friend and his daughter."

"Why, then, do you think Ben talked to his dad?"

"I don't know, probably because he saw us kiss. It was just once, in the kitchen, nothing serious."

"I see."

"You have to know this isn't some random hook up," Lori said exasperated.

"I met Brandon in high school. We've been good friends for a long time. I explained to Ben that it was my relationship, he didn't need to worry about me, or worry that things were going to change. Brandon lives in Seattle. We live here."

"You can see how it might cause concern for the children, you are dating a man that lives across the country?"

"I suppose," Lori said, slumping back into the chair like a child being punished.

"Peter's attorney also said something about Ben being allowed to shoot a gun."

"Ohmygod, Brandon's an FBI agent." Lori rose up, feeling her blood pressure spike.

"He's a trained firearms instructor. He took Ben to a shooting range after explaining, in detail, all the safety protocols required. Ben was not in danger."

"Can you see how Peter might have been concerned?"

"Actually, no. I can't," Lori said, sounding disgruntled again.

"Peter gave Ben one of those Airsoft guns for his birthday. One of Peter's guilt presents for never seeing them. Ben, supposedly, accidentally, shot his sister in the shoulder. She was terrified, not to mention he could have really hurt her." Lori shook her head.

"I didn't say a thing. You know Peter's got his rigid, my house, my rules.

"Lori you can raise legitimate safety concerns at the other parent's house. That does give me some information, though, that Peter's attorney may not be aware of."

"Will Peter sign the agreement?"

"He tried to argue for a reduction in the proposed alimony. I shut that down and I think his attorney will be able to school him away from it."

"What does alimony have to do with whether or not I'm dating someone?"

"Please don't get angry Lori, I'm not the enemy."

"I'm sorry. It's just…"

"People often mistake alimony as the ex-husband taking care of his still dependent ex-wife until she becomes someone else's responsibility."

"You've got to be…!"

"That is not how I see your alimony situation. For you, it is equalizing the wealth that accrued in the marriage. Because, in large part, you gave up a potentially lucrative career to raise the children, and you will have difficulty restarting an equivalent career."

"Thank you," Lori said. It sounded like a vigorous Amen sister.

"Peter is also insisting on a clause that neither one of you can move out of the state with the children without the other's permission."

Lori sighed deeply.

"That's pretty standard. Of course, now he's quite insistent."

"Can we fight it?"

"We can try. As a practical matter, Lori, if he's spending his time with the kids pursuant to your custody schedule…"

"He's not with them. There's a babysitter most of the time."

"Be that as it may, if he is keeping up with the access schedule, a judge will be not be inclined to let you move with the children, particularly as far away as Seattle."

Lori was trying hard to listen politely, not keep letting her emotions get the best of her.

"Now, if Catherine was a little older," her lawyer continued, "and if they wanted to move, it might be a different story. You have to consider how that feels to children, going before a judge and being asked to choose one parent."

"But if..." Lori stammered, trying to catch hold of what she wanted to say.

"Go home and consider what we've talked about. Nothing needs to be decided immediately. I think if you're willing to add the language about not leaving Maryland, the agreement can be finalized fairly quickly."

"We're only stuck in this state because it was good for Peter's career," Lori said petulantly. "My family all live in New York. Peter knew I always wanted to live near them."

"You live here, though."

Lori hurried from the office, desperate to reach the elevator before she burst into tears. She got to her car, turned it on and just sat there, looking down at her trebling hands. It was all so humiliating, like she was a child that had to vet her life decisions with her lawyer, maybe even a judge, and still Peter. Fuck, fuck, fuck!

Peter was the one that chose to leave, blow apart their marriage, and harm their kids. Lori didn't recall anyone requiring Peter to consult her first. Where's the fairness?! She felt like screaming. She called Emily instead.

When she got Emily's voicemail, Lori hung up and drove out of the parking lot, even though her hands were still shaking. She was a few miles from home, but for a moment she couldn't remember how to get there. She pulled over and put the car in park again. A bubble of pressure was building in Lori's abdomen and forcing its way up her gut. The car suddenly filled with a high-pitched, scary-ass sound that bounced back at her from the shut windows. Her own voice. She suspected if someone saw her face, they might have tried to commit her.

She needed to keep moving. To get home. Lori went slowly, weirdly disconnected from the stranger that decided, instead, to turn the car into the parking lot of a tiny strip mall. Maybe I need something to eat. She'd forgotten to, so far that day. There was a Starbucks. Isn't there always? She picked out something sweet. Ordered a large enough coffee so she could hog a spot at a table. Then she sat. Thinking about...nothing. Her brain seemed to have imploded sufficiently not to ask itself questions about her melt down. Luckily, she noticed the time before she needed to be at Catherine's bus.

* * *

"Mommy, you missed it!"

"Missed what?"

"My essay. It was the Eighth Grade Sharing Day."

"That was today?" Even as she asked, Lori knew, of course it was today. How could she have forgotten? After spacing out in Starbucks, focus and feeling came back with a kick to her gut. She never was the one to let her family down.

"Yes, and everyone had a parent there except me."

"Catherine, I'm so, so, so sorry." Lori was struggling to find her voice. "It's just...I've been so busy with the good-bye party, and, then, at the last minute, I had to meet with my lawyer, and..."

"That's what my essay was about."

"Becoming a lawyer?"

"No! You and Dad getting divorced. I worked really hard on it. All the other parents came up after and told me how thoughtful it was, and mature." Catherine said that last word with a snarl.

"But the two people who I wrote it for weren't even there." Catherine started to cry. She looked at Lori sideways, her mouth a grimace of pain and disbelief. "You're always there, Mom."

"Catherine, I'm so sorry. Read it to me now. Please. We won't drive home till I've heard the whole thing."

"It'll sound stupid now."

"Of course, it won't. I really, really want to hear it."

"Maybe later. I just want to go home."

* * *

"I think I'm losing my mind." Lori called Brandon from the car.

Catherine had gotten out almost before Lori put it in park. Then Catherine had slammed the car door, presumably went straight to her room and slammed that door too.

"What's going on?"

"I missed Catherine's Share Day at school."

"Lori, these things happen."

"It was a big deal. They read an essay they've worked on for months. All the parents attend."

"Did Peter?"

"Of course not. I never miss these things. It was on my calendar. I knew about it. I just spaced. It's so unlike me and... Brandon, I feel so shitty about it."

"Can you cut yourself a little slack?" He asked gently. "You've got a lot going on, and an awful lot of what you're doing are things for Catherine."

"I know." Lori sighed. "I've already gotten five texts from other parents saying how sorry they were that I wasn't there since Catherine had written such a lovely essay about coping with her parents' separation."

"Ouch."

"Yeah," Lori said, then paused.

"I had to meet with my attorney today. Peter's pulling all kinds of shit."

"About what?"

"He's bitching about the trip to Seattle, and that I introduced the kids to my boyfriend without telling him. Now he wants to put in our agreement that I can't move without his permission."

"He can't do that."

243

"He can if I want to take the kids."

"Just take some deep breaths, baby, and try to relax. I really want to talk, but I can't here at work. I promise, I'll call you as soon I get home. Okay?"

"I sat in my parked car today," Lori continued, "screaming at the top of my lungs. Brandon, am I having a nervous breakdown?"

"No. You're dealing with a lot of stress. It's got to come out somewhere."

"I'm scared."

"It will be okay. I promise."

"I need you."

"I know. I need you too."

Chapter 44

Catherine seemed to recover from her devastation. More quickly than Lori, who alternated between pangs of guilt, and anger with herself for allowing the bar to get set so high. Had she really never missed a school event; and should that answer leave her feeling proud—or ashamed? It never bothered Peter to miss, even the most important things.

She didn't have time to wallow, though. She still had to pull off the Big Day at Sycamore Hills. It was more critical now. For Catherine. The party was Friday, only one more day of craziness. If something didn't get done, it wouldn't get done. Thank god Peter was supposed to take the kids for the weekend.

Lori pulled on some yoga pants, tied up her sneakers, and grabbed her to do list. The traffic, and aggressive focus required to collar an available parking spot at each stop, was almost enough to keep her from revisiting her guilt, her anger, even her anxiety over a future with Brandon.

Every time she grasped for a solution, another problem reared its head. She felt like someone was playing whack-a-mole with her brain. Brandon could move east. Not really. She could move to Seattle. Definitely not. How could they build a relationship on random weekends chosen to accommodate everyone else?

Half way through her list, Lori dashed into Starbucks for a pick-me-up latte. The line was so long she almost gave up, but her brain had committed to the caffeine. She stowed her drink in the cup holder as she made her way on some back streets to find a short cut to her next errand. She reached for the cup, greedily anticipating that first sip and, somehow, she knocked the whole thing over. Shit!

Hot coffee ran down her leg and into the footwell. She reached down for the cup, looked down just for a second to see if she could contain the mess. Bam! A sudden, sharp pain in her nose, a black wall in front of her eyes. She lifted her face, shook away the fog. When the blur cleared, she saw that she'd crashed her minivan into an electrical pole. Fuck, fuck fuck! Her head fell back against the headrest.

She remained there, stunned, hugely pissed at herself, until a woman knocked on her window to ask if Lori was okay.

"Your nose is bleeding."

Lori lifted her hand to feel just a trickle. "I think I'm fine. I'm just not sure what to do."

"Well now. Do you have Triple A?"

Lori nodded.

"Great. If you're willing to give me your card, I'll call them to tow the minivan. Then you can call your insurance company and find out where you should take it."

"Thank you so much for your help. I'm feeling...I don't know, discombobulated."

"Of course, you are. It's the least I can do. Are you sure you're okay? Your face is getting kind of puffy."

"I'm sure. Really, I don't know how I can thank you enough."

"Just pass on the favor to the next person that needs it."

The woman stayed and talked with Lori until the tow truck arrived. She walked away when Lori was talking to the driver. Lori never even got her name.

* * *

Lori called Jeanette from the auto shop. Her head was starting to pound, and she couldn't cope with the thought of renting a car. If Jeanette could just get her home, Lori could close her eyes for a few minutes, then figure out how to get Catherine home from school, and shit...the Good-Bye Party is tomorrow.

She was cradling her throbbing head and didn't see Jeanette come in.

"Lori?"

She looked up.

"Oh my god, your bleeding," Jeanette said looking stricken, "and your face, it's so swollen."

"I must have hit it against the steering wheel."

"We should go to the ER."

"No, no, I'll be stuck there for hours. I've still got so much to do, and..."

"I'm taking you, no buts about it."

* * *

Just as Lori feared, it was well over an hour before she was taken to an examining room. She was going to miss Catherine's bus.

"Tell Peter to pick her up," Jeanette said. "That's what parents do in emergencies."

"I don't know if he's at the office, if he's even in town."

"You won't know till you call."

"I'll have to tell him what happened. I don't want to."

"Why?"

"I'm afraid it will give him ammunition."

"People have accidents all the time."

"People don't usually crash their own car into a pole. He'll say I wasn't paying attention. Or that I'm losing it."

"Are you losing it?"

"Honestly, I don't know. I can't bear to have him start in with the whole, what if the kids were in the car, bullshit."

"But they weren't."

"You don't understand Jeanette." Lori felt her swollen face tighten up some more.

"This divorce nonsense, with lawyers involved, and judges. It's like you're under a microscope. Everything can get twisted into something it's not." She was ready to burst into tears.

"I hate it all so much."

"It's gonna be alright," Jeanette said, giving Lori a careful hug.

"I'll get Catherine and bring her to your house. I'll grab Chloe first, to stay with Catherine, then I'll come back for you."

"Thank you, Jeanette. I don't know what I would do without you."

"That's what friends are for."

They eventually took a CAT scan. By the time the doctor came back with the results, Jeanette had been to the bus stop, and her house, and then to Lori's house, and back to the ER. There were no broken bones. Lori was going to be bruised and swollen for a few days, and she had a slight concussion. The doctor instructed Lori to stay home, put ice on her face, and take it easy. She should call her primary physician if her headache got any worse, or she started feeling nausea.

Lori had been in the ER for almost four hours. The minute she was tucked into Jeanette's plush SUV, panic kicked in.

"I can't take it easy Jeannette, not tomorrow. It's the eighth-grade party. I'm in charge. I've got to run around and make everything happen."

"Lori, that would go against all the doctor's instructions."

"They just say stuff. To cover their asses."

"I don't think so. Concussions are serious."

"It's just a little one."

"It's a brain injury, I don't care how little. Can't someone else run things? Who was helping you?"

"I had some help. The big picture, it's all in here." Lori tapped her head and winced at the touch.

"Lori, you're in pain. Have you seen your face? You'll scare the kids."

"Really? Lori pulled down the visor mirror. "Shit."

"Call someone. Explain what happened. They'll just have to manage."

"It's Catherine's last year, her big day. I wanted it to be special."

"If this is the worst thing that happens to Catherine, she'll be very lucky."

* * *

When Lori explained the situation to Barbara, one of the moms who had helped her the most, Barbara's response was a white knight take over. Lori was not permitted to do another thing. Barbara would find someone to help. They would swing by Lori's that night, grab all the supplies and the notes for Lori's graduation speech, report back to her the next day.

Jeanette, meanwhile, sent Lori up to bed with some tea, brought Lori's kids back to her own house, fed them dinner before depositing them home with their homework all finished.

Lori sat in her bed, binge watching old episodes of Modern Family and icing the sore places in twenty-minute increments. She actually permitted herself to enjoy her sudden state of superfluous. The world had not come to an end.

She was still worried what Peter would say, or do, about the accident, but other people were willing to help, really take on stuff, not just a small gesture. Maybe it was a return favor for the millions of times she'd taken on thankless tasks and raced to others' rescue. Still, she only had to ask. Huh. It was a revelation. Lori's sense of gratitude was a bit overwhelming.

* * *

If Catherine was to be believed when she came home the next afternoon, things had gone off just fine. She was abuzz with news about the party. Lori got a whiff that Catherine enjoyed the whole thing more for Lori's absence, chronicling the day with an intimation of license that Lori doubted Catherine would have experienced if Lori had been there, ubiquitous. It was a lot of new awareness to digest, and Lori still hadn't told Brandon about the accident.

"Hey there." She texted him, snuggled back under her covers, listening to the clanging of pots and pans. Lori asked Catherine to make some spaghetti for dinner. She wasn't sure what to expect.

"Sorry I haven't texted," Brandon wrote, responding quickly. "I figured you were busy being Master of Ceremonies ☺ and I was out all night on a case☹.

"You must be tired."

"Yeah, kinda wiped. You too, I bet. How'd it go?"

"I didn't actually make it to the party."

"What😐. Did you get in a fight with Catherine?"

"Nothing like that. I had a little car accident." Lori was cringing, waiting for his reply when her phone rang.

"Lori, what happened? Are you okay?" He sounded so worried.

"I'm fine. A little bruised, and I have a slight concussion."

"Shit! Did someone hit you?"

"Not exactly. I hit a utility pole."

"What? That doesn't sound like you. You've always been a neurotically careful driver."

"Thanks, I think?"

"I mean it. What happened?"

"I don't know. I spilled my coffee, and looked down to stop the mess. Bam, I was seeing stars. It was weird. One minute, I'm frantically racing around doing errands then, full stop, blackness."

"Have you been to the doctor?"

"Jeanette took me to the ER."

"Good. Do you need me to come?"

"Don't be ridiculous."

"It's not ridiculous."

"I'm fine. It's just a slight concussion."

"Any concussion is serious."

"You sound like Jeanette." Lori laughed lightly. "Anyway, you can't just drop everything and fly out here.

"I would if you need me."

"It's nice to hear you say that. Really, I'm okay."

"You're taking it easy, right?"

"Catherine's making dinner as we speak. They go to Peter's tonight until Monday."

"That's good, but who's gonna check on you? Concussions can be tricky."

"I can ask Jeanette to stop by. She's been great."

"Good. Let her do that. You're sure you're okay?"

"Yeah. I mean...I'm upset with myself."

"Why?"

"It's not like me to be so careless. I'm a little scared."

"About Peter?"

"How'd you guess? I'm sure he's going to tell his lawyer, and then I'll hear from my lawyer. It's so humiliating," Lori hated that she sounded whiny and weak, "and what if he pulls the, she's not competent card."

"If he's smart, which he is, he'll realize it could just have easily happened to him. He doesn't want to set a precedent of tattling on the other parent."

"He's already done that. Uggg...what an ass."

"Remember, he needs your help with the kids. You don't need his."

"I hope you're right." Lori paused a few moments then her voice grew weary.

"Can I ask you something?"

"Of course."

"Does it worry you that I crashed my car?"

"Should it?"

"I don't know, maybe. The car accident, sitting in my car screaming. It's not normal."

"With everything I see, what's normal? Is something upsetting you?"

"I feel like I'm being pulled in too many directions," Lori said, her voice becoming more animated. "I keep picturing kids fighting over a stuffed animal, and," Lori made a ripping sound, "all the stuffing tumbles out. You can't even tell what the thing was. Maybe the accident was a warning."

"What kind of warning?"

"That something's out of kilter. There're too many competing needs, too many moving parts. It's..."

"So, I'm one need too many?"

"I didn't say that! You're the best thing in my life, but this relationship, it makes everything so complicated."

"Too complicated? Are you saying our relationship is too much right now?" There was a long, weighty pause.

"Do you want out, Lori?"

"No!" She sounded frantic and stopped speaking.

"I don't think so," she said after a long moment, her voice faint.

"It's just...my life feels in pieces with people fighting over the scraps." Lori sighed.

"I hate conflict, and I keep wondering, how can I be some-one who doesn't just take care of others."

"Is that what I am? Just another person to take care of?"

She could hear the anger Brandon was trying to mask.

"No! Stop that. It's just.... We live so far apart. How can we bring our lives closer, so we can handle this stuff together?"

"Maybe we can't, I don't know." There was another long pause. Brandon's voice softened.

"Listen, nothing needs to be decided right now. We'll take a page from the Navy SEAL manual. We'll break things down into manageable tasks."

"Ugg. How utterly...male," Lori said, anguish and anger gripping at the words.

"I'm not sure I can live with that answer, Brandon! It's killing me."

"I certainly don't want to cause you more pain," Brandon said, a little too collectedly, then waited. She could hear his breathing.

"If you need me to," he continued, finally, "I'll let you go."

"Don't say that! Please. I don't want that."

"What you're saying..."

"You want to know something?" In her panic, her voice sounded reedy and accelerated. "I really hate that even bringing this up has you running and saying adios. Can't we just talk?"

"I'm not saying good bye," Brandon's words seemed to crawl slowly through the phone, like they had to travel the actual distance from where he was, "I'm just.."

"You're so calm. It wouldn't kill you if we broke it off? After finding each other again after all these years? It scares me that it doesn't seem like it would hurt."

"It…" Brandon's voice became even thicker, leaden, "It would be the fucking hardest thing I've ever done, Lori. It will be much worse if we try to stay committed to something that's impossible for you."

"It's not impossible for you?" Her words raced at him. "Can you see how we make this work?"

"Lori, I…"

"I hate having this conversation 3000 miles apart," she nearly shouted, cutting him off. Her voice changed again, the next words coming out with a whimper.

"I want you holding me."

"I told you, I'll come."

"That's crazy, and you know it," Lori said with resignation.

"You've got work. You've got Fiona. You'd spend thousands of dollars, that you don't have, to get a plane ticket this last minute." She took a breath.

"I'm just so frustrated. I sometimes feel, literally, like pulling my hair out."

"Please, baby. Just. Rest." He nearly cooed, the words falling like soothing drops into Lori's ears.

"We'll talk more in the morning. Call me, or call Jeanette, if you start feeling any worse, physically. Promise?"

"I promise," Lori told him. Her voice drained of conviction.

Chapter 45

Lori hadn't left her bed since choking down some of Catherine's poor attempt at spaghetti. She didn't go downstairs, to see the kids off, because she didn't want to see Peter, or have to answer his condescending questions. She was sure the kids would rat her out as soon as they got in his car. An accident, her bruised face, all of it too extraordinary not to blab about, and she hadn't asked them not to. What was the point? He couldn't use it to hurt her any more than she was going to blame herself.

Lori had taken some sleeping pills left over from a prescription a doctor gave her in the months after Peter left. They'd make her feel comatose, and she probably wasn't supposed to take any with a concussion. Fuck it. The kids weren't there, if she didn't wake up. All Lori wanted was to sleep.

She couldn't bear to follow where her waking thoughts led. That her affair with Brandon—it hurt even to call it that—would never work in the real world. She couldn't hold the pieces together, not if Brandon couldn't be with her, physically be there, when she needed him. Tonight, of all nights. The relationship would destroy her if she tried. Brandon knew it already. He was seeing things clearly. That's why he was saying all those things. Saying… good bye.

Lori knew just how shitty that was going to feel in the morning, but the pills were already working to numb her emotions. She vowed, as she wiggled deeper under her covers, that no matter what happened with Brandon, she would stop being afraid of Peter and his high-handed tactics. It's all thunder, just noise. She was once a person with brains, and convictions, even some balls, and she would be that person again. She deserved her own ambitions and happiness. Just as much as Peter. Brandon had helped her see that. If Brandon left her too, maybe it would be enough… She couldn't process anything more at the moment. The comforter felt warm and heavy, and the pills were thankfully delivering her to insensibility.

* * *

Too soon, way too soon, someone was shaking Lori hard, calling to her.

"Lori, Lori, please wake up."

She was trying her best to crawl out from under the weight of a trance, to be polite and answer.

"Jeanette…" Lori was struggling to pull herself up to sitting, still unable to open her eyes against the morning light.

"No, Lori, it's me."

"Brandon?" She must be dreaming. Lori forced her eyes open.

"You scared me." Brandon glowered as if insanely concerned.

"What? Why?" She cleared her throat, trying to jump start her comprehension.

"You wouldn't wake up."

"I'm awake now. I think. How are you here?"

"I took the red eye. It's early still, you can go back to sleep, now that I know you're okay."

Lori was flailing, trying to sort out how it could be that Brandon was there. Her mind was in a fog.

"I'll just close my eyes for a few more minutes…"

* * *

When Lori woke again, she was wrapped in Brandon's arms. She paused to let that seep in, the comfort of his warm body, the safety in his clutched arms. She could tell by his breathing that he was sleeping, and she tried to recall what he'd said. A red eye. He probably didn't get much rest on the plane. She traced her finger on his chest, drew a circle around his heart.

Brandon stirred. She glanced up and met his anxious blue eyes.

"How are you feeling?"

"Better, less groggy. Sorry I was so out of it."

"Please, don't be. You just gave me a scare."

"Why are you here?"

"Don't you want me?"

"Oh my god, yes..."

"I was really worried about you. I remembered that Joanne's been begging me and Fiona to use her frequent flyer miles for a visit to New York. When she heard that you had a car accident, she called up the airlines and got me a ticket."

"Wow. I'm going to have to do something really nice for Joanne."

Brandon laughed. "What about me? She just got the ticket. I had to sit cramped in the middle seat for five hours next to a guy that snored."

"Oh, don't worry. I'll make it worth your while."

Lori lifted her head to meet Brandon's mouth, a long, soft-lipped kiss, tongues in slow-motion, entwined. Her head hurt a little. That seemed trivial compared to the immensity of her relief not to be alone. To have a someone in her life who would come running (well flying) to her side. Not to have the entire middle of the country between them.

Brandon drew back to eyeball Lori. She remembered her bruises and swelling and tipped her face down.

"Let me see." Brandon touched her gently, traced around the bruising and swelling.

"Do I look awful?"

"You look like you got in a bar room brawl. You sure you're telling me the truth about a car accident?"

Lori laughed, and it made her wince.

"Does it hurt?"

"A little. Less than yesterday."

"Let me make you something to eat." Brandon rolled away from her and off the bed, pulling on a shirt.

Lori took in his naked body, still delighted at the beauty of his powerful torso, his tight ass, and well-proportioned legs, all so strong and sexy.

"Just stay and relax," he told her.

"You won't get an argument from me, not this morning. Though I'm warning you, I'm a terrible patient."

Brandon came back in a few minutes with tea, toast, and an over-easy egg. He'd found a breakfast tray, god knows where. Lori recalled it was a wedding present, and probably hadn't been used in fifteen years. He laid it on the bed and sat down on the edge.

"Aren't you going to eat?" Lori asked, suddenly hungry but nibbling carefully as it still hurt when she moved the muscles in her face.

"I don't usually eat this early."

"Right, it's still practically dawn for you." Lori sipped her tea and handed the mug to Brandon. "At least have some tea." Lori watched him take a gulp.

"I can't fuckin' believe you're here," she said.

That made Brandon laugh. Lori grinned, remembering when he had used the same expression, until pain made her wince again. Brandon's expression shifted.

"You sure you're okay?"

"Yeah, they CAT scanned my face. Nothing broken."

"You must've really hit that pole."

"I wasn't going fast. It was just a little side road, but you should see my car."

"You scared me when you called yesterday," he said.

"I scared you?" Loris asked, surprised. "I thought you were breaking up with me. It sounded like you'd up and decided, all on your own, that it couldn't...that we weren't going to make it." Tears were coming, and she wiped them clumsily.

"Last night," she sniffled, "I tried out your good bye. To see if I could survive the..."

"Lori, I love you."

She froze, studying him for a long moment. "That's the first time you've ever said that."

"I'm sure I said it before. At least, I wanted to, so often... I was stupid."

"We both were stupid."

Brandon moved the tray to the floor and climbed into the bed, half propped up against the pillows. He tucked Lori under his arm, and she put her arm across his belly and snuggled into his chest. It felt so good to have these simple emotions. To graciously accept Brandon's care, even his mostly needless worry, and not feel it as weakness, or she a burden. Not to feel shame. To want Brandon, without finding an excuse to turn away, even if her sore body surely gave her one.

She began to trace her finger with slow deliberate tension, down from his belly to his halo of kinky brown hair. She watched, keeping her head tucked into his body, while his penis, already firm, bobbed like a puppy bounding toward the source of its devotion. Lori's face was still achy, but she wanted to give him her undivided attention, to thank him for coming. She wondered, if with just her hand and his cock, she could convey her gratitude and desire.

She outlined the soft, round head with added strain, and the shaft bounced to follow her finger's edge as if chasing communion. She traced up and down the center vein until she grabbed him firmly, then paused to listen to his intake of breath. With the palm of her hand, she began to rub, up toward the glans then down to his balls, adding pressure in response to his hardening. Brandon was moaning, and Lori could feel her mouth begin to salivate with an urge to suck him. She didn't want to detract from his pleasure with movements that would likely exacerbate her lingering pain. Instead, she interrupted her rhythm to moisten the flat part of her hand. She wetted and played with his balls, before returning to the hardening pressure on his cock.

She brought her hand to her mouth again, glancing up to spy Brandon watching her slobber it with a thick swipe of her tongue. She palmed him wetly, a steady movement up and down his shaft, increasing pace and compression to mimic her own rising fervor. She could feel Brandon close in on his climax, so she encircled him tightly, her whole hand stroking faster, keeping stride with his clenching ass and thrusting hips. She watched as his ejaculation came in waves, splattering his chest and her face.

"Fuuuuuuuuuuuck," he sputtered.

Lori licked what had fallen near her mouth, imagining she appeared as a contented lioness, happy to have fed her pride.

"Shit, Lori. I wasn't expecting that."

"I've got tricks too."

"I never doubted that, but I'm here to take care of you."

"Don't worry, we've got plenty of time for that, don't we?"

"I'll stay as long as I can."

Lori suddenly felt like a little girl again. She crossed her heart and made a wish. Please don't ever leave.

Chapter 46

They dragged themselves downstairs later, taking up their snuggled position on the couch in the TV room, wearing only t-shirts and laying in enough snacks to be lazy for a while. It didn't take long for Lori's worries to slink back like the neighbors' cat. Why did she say they had plenty of time? It was the one thing they didn't have.

It caused Lori to despair, a misery she knew how to wallow in, even with Brandon lying next to her. If she wasn't careful, she would dump all over the incredible fact that he came, and jump instead to the inevitable good bye.

She lost track of what they were watching. That seemed enough reason to click off the TV. Lori pulled herself up to a prim sort of sitting, hands resting in her lap, legs criss-cross apple sauce (funny the things that return, unbidden).

"Brandon..."

"Sounds like we're getting serious." Brandon sat up with her.

"First, I want to thank you for coming. Thanks, aren't nearly enough. I didn't want to guilt you into it, but, I really needed you."

"Of course, Lori."

"It's not an of course," she said emphatically.

"It was a crazy, impulsive thing to do. I can't imagine how you were able to get time off from work, make arrangements for Fiona, ..."

"It was an emergency. You make things happen."

"I didn't know that we could rate an emergency."

"What do you mean?" He looked at her quizzically.

"I thought our emergencies had to be kept local and

handled alone." She looked at him as if her statement was really a question—the question.

"If my crises are yours, then there really is an us," Lori continued in the same tone. "We're not just chasing after weekends for fucking."

"Of course, there's an us."

"You can't say that. Not so fast," Lori said, almost angry. "I've told you, I might not be able to take my kids and move to Seattle, as much as I fantasize about it a million times a day, and I can't leave here without them."

"I would never ask you to do that." It was Brandon's turn to sound shocked, maybe angry, it was hard to tell.

Lori paused to let his words sink in. A huge weight seemed to lift from her.

"If I want to move my kids, we'll have a battle on our hands, against a guy that fights in court for a living."

"I say, bring it on. The judge will see who's the real parent."

"Wow. Really? Okay." Lori felt her face flip through a thousand emotions.

"Lori, you're a fighter. You've always been. You never let people get away with shit."

"I know." Lori frowned. She suddenly felt bereft, longing for her old self. "What happened to me?"

"Must have been some powerful WASP voodoo. We'll exorcise it with black magic."

"Yeah right...," Lori laughed.

"If we could take on Peter. Together… Let's put a pin in that, but I like how it sounds." She was already feeling stronger.

"What about you? Could you and Fiona move here?"

"Maybe. Jocelyn's disappearing acts have cost her clout in the shared custody department. I could probably transfer to a field office somewhere on the East Coast. Or apply for a job at Quantico." Brandon grinned. "I've developed a bit of a reputation, since I started a defensive tactics training course that I lead a couple of times a year."

"Okay," Lori said slowly.

"Joanne's been praying for me to move back east since the day I moved to Seattle."

"I can't believe we're having this conversation," Lori said, still with more skepticism than belief. "An actual discussion about how to be together. All of us." Lori looked down at her hands.

"There's another thing you should know."

"That sound ominous," Brandon said, although he was smiling. "You're not going to tell me we have secret love child that you've been hiding all these years?"

"I'm serious."

"Sorry, tell me."

"Peter wants a stipulation that if I get remarried, he gets to cut off my alimony."

"What the fuck. That's entirely unfair. Any money from him should be for what you've sacrificed for his success, and your family."

"I know. Even my lawyer agrees. Now that Peter knows about us, about me being with you, of all people." Lori pursed her lips at the frustrating truth.

"It's gonna make a fight that much harder."

"Did I ever tell you what Peter said to me at your wedding?"

"I don't think so. I didn't think he even talked to you."

"I was on the receiving line, he couldn't avoid it." Brandon made a face. "You were talking with Jocelyn and he said to me, sotto voce, like he was getting pleasure screwing me out of a business deal, I finally beat you, I won."

"You can't be serious?"

"Yeah. I remember thinking that I hadn't seen Peter be smug before. It left me worried."

I don't know what to say."

"Look. We'll figure things out. Together. It'll take time, but we will. I promise. Meanwhile...," Brandon gave her one of his sexy grins, "I hope we can we still have weekends for fucking. I like how you put that."

Lori slapped his arm playfully.

"Some people might say it's the perfect relationship,"

Brandon said, raising his shoulders in a shrug, "a weekend each month, kids with the other parent, responsibilities left behind on the other side of the country. Freedom to have sex, lots and lots of it. All kinds of screwing around. Everyone will be jealous."

"Funny." Lori smirked, but he was right.

What an extravagant luxury. Then she shook her head, knowing herself, her need to grab up the ones she loved, and keep them all close.

"I know I'll want more..." Then, Lori grabbed both Brandon's hands, like she was sealing a deal.

"Can we promise that for now? One weekend, every month, no exceptions."

"We can do that. It will be a stretch for me financially, but if we alternate months..."

"I'm sorry. I wasn't thinking about the practicalities."

"I can swing it. I already get to Virginia to train recruits, once or twice a year, on the Bureau's expense."

"Thank you, Brandon. I don't even care about the sex, but this not seeing each other for months, not even knowing when I'll see you again. It's making me crazy."

"Clearly." Brandon touched her bruised cheek. "No more crashing your car." He kissed the same spot gently as Lori leaned in, eyes closed. "I can't live without you, Lori."

Lori needed to feel him, more than to see. She kept her head tucked, let him kiss her eyelids, her other cheek, all her bruises, finally, her parted lips, moist from anticipation. Brandon pushed her back gently onto the couch. She kept her eyes shut, a goofy smile on her face. She was as light as a feather. We'll figure it out together. Five perfect words. She and Brandon weren't really any closer to knowing how, still... It's not just my silly daydream.

"Do you really not care about the sex?" Brandon suddenly asked, playfully.

Lori opened her eyes for the enjoyment of seeing his sexy, smug grin.

"Maybe I care, you know, a little," she smirked back, and lifted her arms so he could pull off her t-shirt.

He pinned her arms where they lay over hear head, regarding her body so hungrily it gave her goosebumps. Her nipples hardened before he'd even touched her. Brandon took a mouthful of her breast. She arched her back to offer him more, her breath coming faster. How did she survive months, how would she still make it through weeks, without her body awakening like at this moment?

"I can't say this enough times, Brandon, thank you, thank you, thank you for coming."

He answered with a long, wet kiss. Her body was on fire. To feel so desired, it turned out, was to be fearless. Could she give him more? Something to convey her indebtedness. To let him know she was his, forever this time.

"I want you to take me right now, anyway you want."

Brandon held himself above her with a searching leer. "Really?"

"Yes. What do you want?"

"I'd love to take you from behind, caress your beautiful ass while I'm inside you."

"Do you remember that time in my parents' bedroom?"

"How could I forget. Are you sure, though? You're a little beat up right now."

"It's my ass you want, not my face."

Brandon laughed so hard it made her laugh too, and it took a few minutes before they could speak.

"I'll meet you in your bedroom so your toy's nearby," he said. "I'm going to grab a few things."

Lori shot him a quizzical look, then hustled upstairs.

* * *

Waiting for him, naked on her bed, hearing Brandon riffle through the house, Lori became acutely aware that anticipation, even a little fear, was half the fun of sex. Maybe not half... She closed her eyes, noticing how each part of her body readied for his touch. Her breasts plumped, awaiting the brush of Brandon's lips and the hard edge of his tongue on her nipples. The folds of her pussy pulsed, throbbed, moistened. Even the roots of her hair tingled.

Brandon entered the room cradling a long mirror he must have taken from Catherine's closet. Something else was tucked under his arm.

"Ohmygod, you really do remember."

Brandon just smiled as he propped the mirror on the wall, dropped something on the bed, and pulled off his shirt. That was so much fun to watch. Lori had a brief moment to enjoy it, before he was on her. His mouth was hungry, teeth and tongue, sharp and wet, owing her mouth. Lori had to catch her breath. She shimmied out from under him, and he collapsed, face down, on the bed. She shifted on to her knees and huddled over him, playfully planting kisses down his back. When she reached his ass, she feathered it lightly with her fingers, drew one slowly through his crack. Then she crawled away to the other side of the bed.

"Where are you going?" He asked, eyes following her with a hint of raw anguish.

"Don't worry," she answered, looking back over her shoulders. On all fours like a cat, Lori slowly backed her way toward Brandon. The position felt sexy and flirtatious, naturally spreading her ass cheeks, despite a vague, deep-seated shame. He was viewing immodest parts of her body that she'd never bothered to examine.

Brandon's gaze was loving, though, and incredibly hot, as he budged, lifted his head with his torso so his lips could meet her body. He moved with concentrated energy, his fingers tickling and brushing her ass cheeks over and over and over. Brandon stroked down the crack of her ass this time, then circled her asshole with increasing compulsion, until finally entering her pussy with his finger.

Lori arched and purred. She had longed for just this. Eyes closed, time seemed to stop. When Brandon pulled out, she shot him a look of surprise. He was on his knees, reaching for a bottle. Her best olive oil.

"What...?"

"I'm going to lubricate you more. I don't want anything else to hurt right now."

"I knew there was a reason I spent so much for that brand." She couldn't help making a joke.

"Where's your toy?"

"In the bedside table."

Brandon grabbed for it, plugged it in, and laid it on the bed before he poured some oil onto his thumb. A wholesome fragrance filled the bedroom. Brandon kneeled at her side and massaged her with oil from her ass to her pussy. It felt warm and luscious. There was a throbbing now in both her holes and Brandon took advantage, fingering her, while his thumb pressed against her asshole, making small incursions, breaching slight resistance. Brandon had been right about her being oral. Lori felt the need to be filled there too, so she dropped her head to reach his cock, took him in her mouth.

"You sure you're okay? Nothing hurts too much?"

Lori's answer was to take him deeper, soaking him with her saliva and letting it drip onto his balls. It wasn't long before he was hard as a rock and pulled his erection out of her mouth. Brandon crawled around and positioned himself behind her, turned them both toward the mirror. Lori could see Brandon through the glass pour oil on his cock and work it over with his hand, a desperate need filling his eyes.

"Keep watching," he said, as he poured again from the bottle and smooth it over her ass.

He filled his cupped hand once more with the golden fluid and rubbed down her entire pussy leaving it wet and warmed and tingling. Finally, he grabbed her hips with his hands, opening her further. The head of Brandon's cock bobbed and weaved. He pushed inside her with gentle pressure.

"Tell me if it's too much."

"Okay," she barely murmured, allowing her reflected image to speak for her as she looked back at him in the mirror—eyes slitted, her wet tongue slowly circling open lips.

"God, you look sexy. Use your toy while I'm in you."

"Really?"

Brandon had turned it on and was handing it to her. The moment Lori touched herself with the vibrator everything changed. On her knees, the beautiful torment from her favorite gift was even more intense, fastening her clit into rocking, cresting waves of shimmery palpation that locked onto Brandon's rhythm, and immediately outpaced any lingering pain from her injuries. Her head fell toward her knees.

"If feels so good, Brandon. You can go deeper."

"You sure?"

Lori responded with a feral groan that acknowledged both strain and titillation. She pulled the toy away each time she approached her climax so that Brandon would cum first. Not realizing that the repeated, circled-back return of the wand to her clit, would build her own stimulation to a near unbearable pitch.

"Faster, Brandon." Lori lifted her head with urgency, to see it all. Her breasts free and bounding, the power she had in her own hands, Brandon's look of pleasure, praise, and gratitude.

Brandon's final, deafening groan vibrated the walls, as Lori let herself spill over, rocking back and forth over the still buzzing head of the vibrator until she collapsed on the bed.

"Fuck, Lori that was unbelievable."

She turned with a smile like the cat that did a lot more than eat the canary.

Chapter 47

Brandon's departure still loomed in the background. Lori hated that her default mode slipped past the present, tipped away from Brandon actually being there, to when he would leave. She was going to have work on that, especially since their new-found resolution still included way too many good byes.

Brandon was able to stay until Tuesday morning, so he got to spend some time with her children. She realized, in the moments before they arrived home from school, she didn't care what Peter thought. It was her home, her life, her relationship with them. It gave her a thrill she hadn't felt in a long time.

Her kids were more than a bit surprised to find Brandon in their kitchen, but Ben spoke to Brandon over dinner with interest and respect. He was polite enough to ask after Fiona. Lori suspected that Ben appreciated Brandon's decision to come all the way from Seattle and take on the role of Lori's protector. Ben had been anxious to leave Lori alone so soon after her accident.

Catherine, meanwhile, quickly adjusted, behaving like it was the most normal thing in the world for Brandon to be standing in their family room, walking her through the self-defense moves he'd shown her in Seattle. Kids...

* * *

Lori had remembered to put Brandon's duffle bag in the guest room before Ben and Catherine returned. She messed up the bedcovers for good measure, not sure what she and Brandon would do when it came time to go to bed. In the end, it didn't matter.

They cuddled on the couch after opening a second bottle of wine and talked late into the night about what they might do their next weekend together. The following month. It would be her turn to go to Seattle. Lori would hold Peter to his weekend with the kids, no matter what.

On a lark, she googled the best whiskey bars in Seattle, remembering how much she liked the Manhattans they had on her first visit.

"I can't remember the last time I went out drinking. Do you think we're too old for that?" She asked.

"Fuck, no. You just have to embrace the Seattle vibe."

"What's that?"

"For me, it means sporting a bushy beard and a man bun. Unfortunately, that ain't gonna happen—ever."

"And for me?"

"We need to get you some sexier clothes."

"DC conservative chic won't cut it?"

"Definitely not."

"What do I need?"

"Some leather, maybe a mini skirt or a corset."

"That's an article of clothing I've never owned. Will you take me shopping?"

"Sure. Then I'll take you out and show the world your sexy side."

Lori was thinking that the last time a man took her shopping was when her father took her and Emily to buy Easter dresses. Not the same thing! Maybe regularly scheduled romantic adventures would be enough, for a while. That's what we're talking about, right, nothing more...kinky?

"I've seen a couple of TV shows recently," Lori said, "with basically normal couples, you know, married with kids, but they have a secret, wild, sex life."

"Glad to hear your expanding your horizons."

"Has kinky become the new normal? Is that another thing I've missed in my sexual hiatus?"

Brandon laughed. "There's a lot of divergent stuff out there, in my experience much it exploitative. It can be fine, though, even fun, among consenting adults."

"The couple on one show, they're into S & M. She's the, what do you call it? The bossy one."

Brandon laughed even harder, "I think you mean the Dominatrix."

"Exactly, and he lets himself get tied up. They even go to this club, where everyone dresses for the part. Which is crazy, because if it ever got exposed to the press..., but that's kind of the point. The husband has this very public, high-powered job, and a brow beating father, so it's, like, the one place where he's not in control."

"Sounds like an interesting show."

"My point is she gets to wear some kick ass leather clothes when she's doing her thing."

"Dressing up can be fun, and role play too."

"Wait! Is that why you have those ropes on your bed?"

"Sometimes they're just useful, if you recall." Brandon gave her a long, wet kiss.

"There are places like that," he said after a pause.

"Like what?"

"Social clubs where people can experiment with other people."

"With actual sex?"

"Yes."

"Wow. I don't think I could do that, but I like the idea of wearing some sexy leather."

"It's a start."

Lori gave Brandon a questioning look. He just tucked her head to his chest. Eventually, Brandon's deep, steady breaths lulled Lori to sleep.

* * *

She didn't wake until she heard Ben's alarm go off upstairs, and then it was a scramble. It was always hard when the kids came back from Peter's. Everyone was off a few beats. She had to check

Catherine's backpack for teacher's notes and things to sign, all the tidying up of the loose ends of the school year. She was losing the race against the clock until she discovered Brandon had made the kids' lunches.

"I could kiss you," Lori said, grabbing Catherine and shooing her down to the garage so they would make the bus.

"I'll be waiting."

Lori paused at the top of the steps. As late as she was, she wanted to catch hold of Brandon's frisky grin.

When she got back, there wasn't time for much more than to enjoy the steamy cups of latte Brandon made. Then there were showers and getting dressed, packing up, and Lori was back in the car driving Brandon to the airport.

Lori tried not to feel despondent. She would still have everything Brandon gave her—even in his absence—loyalty and possibilities, self-assurance and hope. Incredible gifts, all. But the time apart would exact its toll. Lori suspected there would be many steps backward, for all their efforts to skip into the future.

I can would worry about that tomorrow, Lori reminded herself, or the next day, maybe not at all. Today, she would rest, like the doctor ordered. She might even enjoy her body's lingering soreness, not from the car accident. From her boundless intimacy with Brandon. Those tender pains were a reminder that everything had changed, in the place that really mattered. Her heart.

* * *

ABOUT THE AUTHOR

ANNA BATTLE is an attorney and mediator. Awake is her first novel in the erotic romance genre. She lives in Maryland with her daughter and their cat. Visit her webpage at annabattle.com

CPSIA information can be obtained
at www.ICGtesting.com
Printed in the USA
FFHW020030231119
56123837-62227FF